The Looking Glass and Other Stories

Anton Chekhov

Translated by Stephen Pimenoff

ALMA CLASSICS

ALMA CLASSICS
an imprint of

ALMA BOOKS LTD
Thornton House
Thornton Road
Wimbledon Village
London SW19 4NG
United Kingdom
www.almaclassics.com

This edition first published by Alma Classics in 2023
Translation © Stephen Pimenoff, 2023

Cover: Nathan Burton

Extra Material and Notes © Alma Books Ltd

Printed in Great Britain by CPI Group (UK) Ltd, Croydon CR0 4YY

MIX
Paper | Supporting
responsible forestry
FSC FSC® C171272
www.fsc.org

ISBN: 978-1-84749-901-1

Contents

The Looking Glass and Other Stories

Introduction

The stories in this collection cover almost the full period of Anton Chekhov's short-story writing career. The initial story is one of the first he ever wrote and published, aged twenty, in 1880; the final one dates from 1898, and is one of the last he wrote before largely abandoning story writing to devote his remaining years to drama. A comparison of the first and last stories gives an intriguing insight into the vast distance he travelled, artistically, over that eighteen-year period. The last story, entitled 'A Doctor's Visit', shows the strength of the social awareness he developed towards the end of his life. Along with some other late stories not included in this collection, it may be the reason why, after the Revolution, he was revered by the Communist authorities, who claimed him as one of their own.

In that period spanning almost two decades, Chekhov wrote literally hundreds of stories (the exact number will probably never be known, as many have been lost). The earliest ones appeared in popular humorous magazines with titles such as 'Dragonfly', 'Alarm Clock' and 'Fragments'; the later ones in more weighty publications like the *St Petersburg Gazette*, *New Time* and the *Northern Messenger*. During his lifetime, several collections of his stories were also published in book form.

Like most writers, Chekhov found it hard to get established. Many of his early stories were rejected by the magazines to which he submitted them, often with scornful comments designed to discourage him. As Irène Némirovsky says in her biography of the author: "From time to time a story appeared, but there was many a setback, many a manuscript rejected with brutal disdain. No one thought of sparing the feelings of a humble and poorly dressed student, himself convinced of his ignorance and lack of talent. Often the manuscript he had brought would not even be read."

Nevertheless, Chekhov developed very rapidly as a writer, and while still in his early twenties was recognized as a formidable talent. Tolstoy was an enthusiastic admirer, and on several occasions wept openly when reading the stories to friends and family. "Chekhov is Pushkin in prose," he once said.

One observant young woman who came to know Chekhov early in his life wrote: "He is amazingly talented and has a refined understanding of people. Although he is still so young and has only just finished medical school, he possesses an enormous fund of humour, an extraordinary poetic sadness and a profound comprehension of the human soul."

Chekhov found the process of writing very easy – indeed, the facility with which he wrote is awe-inspiring. Nine stories appeared in 1880, thirteen in 1881; after that the number increased until 1885, when he reached his maximum output of 129 stories, sketches and articles. Some were extremely short, no more than a page in a book, while others were longer; together, they present the full range of human experience. Some are frivolous and amusing, others more serious – still others almost unbearably sad.

Despite having written so many stories, Chekhov never repeated himself. Although his style is instantly recognizable, every story is different, with its own setting and characters (an exception is a trilogy he wrote towards the end of his life). One's first reaction on discovering this might be sheer wonder at his extraordinary imagination. Yet his imagination was not greater than that of most writers. In any case, one has only to read any biography of him to realize that very little came from his imagination: he knew or had met every character he wrote about, and experienced every incident he described. On the other hand he once said: "I have never written directly from Nature. I have let my memory sift the subject, so that only what is important or typical is left in it, as in a filter."

Nor did he ever give the impression of having exhausted his resources. By the time he died in 1904, at the early age of forty-four, he had led an extremely full and varied life, and had managed to pack more into it than many who die in their eighties.

He was the middle boy in a family of five boys and a girl. Growing up in the provincial backwater of Taganrog on the Sea of Azov, in the south of the country, he came into contact with a wide variety of people from all walks of life. His father, a deeply religious man, introduced him at an early age into the practices and personalities of the Church; in addition he often had to serve long hours in his father's grocery shop, where he met a great assortment of people. Being highly observant, he stored away descriptions of all these people and their behaviour, which he subsequently mined for his stories. As Henri Troyat put it in his biography: "By some mysterious alchemy the people he met and the incidents he experienced turned into words strung together on a page."

Later, in medical school and general practice, he further widened his experience of life. He saw people of all social ranks and occupations: peasants, priests, teachers, students, shopkeepers, civil servants, landowners – and saw them in their joy and in their misery and suffering, and stored it all away for his art. "Reading Chekhov's stories is like taking a whirlwind tour through late nineteenth-century Russia with a cool, lucid guide who shows all but avoids commentary..." wrote Troyat. "Together the stories form an unsurpassed panorama of Russian life."

With his stories, Chekhov broke new ground in the field of Russian literature. Although all the major writers – Gogol, Tolstoy, Turgenev, Pushkin – had written short stories, none had honed the genre to such a fine art. After Chekhov the floodgates opened, and the Russian short story developed to formidable heights. "It is fine for you writers nowadays," Chekhov told the young Ivan Bunin. "They praise you for the little tale, but they used to criticize me for it... If you wished to be a writer then, you wrote novels... For the sake of the miniature story I broke my head against a wall on your behalf."

When Chekhov grew wealthy from his writing and lived in large houses, ending in a villa in Yalta, he was constantly surrounded – in a typically Russian way – by guests and visitors: family, friends, beggars, spongers, indigent relatives, aspiring writers, itinerant actors, journalists seeking interviews and other miscellaneous hangers-on. In 1897 he wrote to a friend: "Imagine, we've had more than ten visitors from Moscow these past few days. I might as well be keeping an inn. They all have to be wined, dined and bedded down." These visitors often slept anywhere they could: on sofas, under tables, in the hall… Chekhov had the opportunity to observe literally hundreds of people.

Nevertheless, there were times when he became exasperated by the number of visitors who imposed on his hospitality: "My bed is occupied by a relative who conducts a conversation with me about medicine…" he once wrote. "Everybody thinks it necessary to 'have a chat' with me about medicine. And when they are bored talking about medicine, they take up the subject of literature… For a writing man it would be hard to imagine a more wretched situation."

Although he complained bitterly from time to time about the number of people who intruded into his life, there is also clear evidence that he thrived on company, and not just because of the ideas it gave him for his stories. "I positively cannot live without guests," he told his long-standing editor Suvorin in 1889. "When I'm alone, for some reason I become terrified, just as though I were alone in a frail little boat on a great ocean."

Despite early on becoming a master of the short-story form, he was uncomfortable with longer works. He did write several short novels, but they were mostly among his less successful creations. As Troyat says: "However secure he felt in works of short and medium length, he could not seem to guide his characters through the long-range trek required by the novel. A horror of digressions, pomposity, of all kinds of excess made him come quickly to the point, and much as he admired certain 'weighty' works, he himself was a partisan of lightness in art."

"Concision is the sister of talent," Chekhov declared to his brother Alexander at the end of his first decade of writing, and he never forgot it.

Indeed, he had a horror of verbosity, and believed the reader to be put off by long-winded, extraneous descriptions. Late in life he gave Maxim Gorky the following advice: "If I write 'A man sat down on the grass', it is understandable because it is clear and doesn't require a second reading. But it would be hard to follow and brain-taxing were I to write 'A tall, narrow-chested, red-bearded man of medium height sat down noiselessly, looking around timidly and in fright, on a patch of green grass that had been trampled by pedestrians.' The brain can't grasp all that at once, and the art of fiction ought to be immediately, instantaneously graspable."

His economy of expression led Tolstoy to say, "His stories give the impression of a stereoscope. He throws words about in apparent disorder, and, like an impressionist painter, he achieves wonderful results by his touches."

The story entitled 'The Looking Glass', which lends its title to this collection, concerns the practice, very popular in Chekhov's day, of young girls gazing dreamily into a mirror in order to foresee their future. (The best day to engage in practices of this sort was 18th January, the eve of Christ's baptism.) Girls would sometimes set up a sort of shrine, darkened with curtains and lit with candles, in order to enhance the experience. They could fall asleep during such sessions, or even faint if the visions they saw were too frightening, and so sometimes asked a friend to be nearby in case they needed help. Russians have always been more superstitious than Westerners: with their fatalism and resignation they tend to be more Eastern in outlook (even their Orthodox faith is more heavily weighted with superstition than other forms of Christianity). It is because 'The Looking Glass' seems symbolic of so much in the Russian temperament that the collection has been given this title.

There are a few Russian words and expressions I did not translate, partly in order to maintain the flavour of Russianness and partly because they have no exact English equivalents. Some words, like tsar, rouble, copeck, boyar and kvass are well known to

English readers and are in any case found in English dictionaries. Others, not found in English dictionaries, have been italicized in the text and annotated at the back. A few explanations of words and customs that may be puzzling to English readers have also been annotated, though I have tried to keep these to a minimum.

Some expressions that are usually translated freely I have kept in their literal form. For example, I have not translated "the devil take it" as "to hell with it" (as it is often rendered) because I feel that sounds rather too "English". Examples can be multiplied.

There are many references in the stories to the ranks of civil servants, military officers and court functionaries; these can be confusing, so a list of them has been provided at the beginning of the book. Readers may find it helpful to know that civil servants in the first four ranks were considered to have the rank of general and were entitled to be addressed as "Your Excellency".

Some readers may be confused by the variety of diminutive nicknames Russians can have. For example, Lida might be called Lidka as a term of endearment, or even Lidochka or Lidushka. This last may sometimes be translated as "dear Lida", but I have left diminutives in their Russian form, unless it is unclear who is referred to.

Once again, I wish to express my thanks to Mrs Masha Lees, a Russian scholar of enviable accomplishment, for checking my translations for accuracy.

– Stephen Pimenoff, 2023

*The Looking Glass
and Other Stories*

Table of Ranks

Civil Service	Military	Court
1) Chancellor	Field Marshal/ Admiral	
2) Active Privy Councillor	General	Chief Chamberlain
3) Privy Councillor	Lieutenant General	Marshal of the House
4) Active State Councillor	Major General	Chamberlain
5) State Councillor	Brigadier	Master of Ceremonies
6) Collegiate Councillor	Colonel	Chamber Fourrier
7) Court Councillor	Lieutenant Colonel	
8) Collegiate Assessor	Major	House Fourrier
9) Titular Councillor	Staff Captain	
10) Collegiate Secretary	Lieutenant	
11) Ship Secretary*	*Kammerjunker*	
12) Government Secretary	Sub-Lieutenant	
13) Provincial Secretary*		
14) Collegiate Registrar	Senior Ensign	

* *(abolished in 1834)*

Before the Wedding

O N THURSDAY OF LAST WEEK, in the home of her worthy
parents, young Miss Podzatylkina was presented as the
fiancée of Collegiate Registrar Nazaryev. The betrothal could not
have gone better. Two bottles of Lanin champagne and eighteen
litres of vodka were consumed. The young ladies drank a bottle of
Lafite. The fathers and mothers of the young couple appropriately
cried; the young couple eagerly kissed; a student in his final year
delivered a toast with the words "*O tempora, o mores!*"* and
"*Salvete, boni futuri conjuges!*",* pronounced with style; red-
haired Vanka Smyslomalov, who was at loose ends as he waited
to be called up for military service, at just the right moment, with
"perfect timing", assumed an intensely tragic pose, rumpled the
hair on his big head, slapped his knee with his fist and exclaimed:
"Damn it, I loved her and I love her still!", thus giving inexpressible delight to the young ladies.

The Podzatylkin girl is remarkable only in being completely
unremarkable. No one has seen or knows anything of her intelligence, and that is why not a word is said about it. Her appearance
is very ordinary: her father's nose, her mother's chin, cat's eyes,
her little bust unexceptional. She knows how to play the piano, but
only by ear; she helps her mother in the kitchen, does not go out
without a corset, observes the Lenten fast, sees in the subtleties
of orthography the beginning and end of all wisdom, and most
of all in the world loves dignified men and the name "Roland".

Mr Nazaryev is a man of middle height, with a blank face that
expresses nothing, curly hair and a head that is flat at the back.
He works somewhere, receives a modest salary that is barely
enough for tobacco; he always smells of egg soap and carbolic
acid, considers himself a terrific ladies' man, talks loudly, day and
night is constantly amazed, and when he talks he sprays saliva. He

plays the dandy, regards his parents condescendingly, and never fails to say to any young lady he meets: "How naïve you are! You should read literature!" More than anything in the world, he loves his handwriting, the magazine *Entertainment* and cleated boots – but what he loves most of all is himself, especially when he is sitting in the company of a young girl, drinking tea with sugar and vehemently denying the existence of the Devil.

So that is what Miss Podzatylkina and Mr Nazaryev are like!

The day after the betrothal, in the morning, Miss Podzatylkina, after waking up, was summoned by the cook to go to her mother. Mama, lying in her bed, delivered to her the following lecture:

"Why did you put on a woollen dress today? You could have worn one of light cotton. How my head aches – it's terrible! Yesterday the bald ugly-mug – that is, your father – was pleased to play a trick on me. As if I need his foolish tricks! He brings me something in a wine glass… 'Drink,' he says. I thought there was wine in the glass, so I drank… but there was vinegar and herring oil in the glass. That's how he played a trick on me, the drunken scum! He only knows how to shame people, the dribbler! I was astounded and surprised that you were happy yesterday and didn't cry. Why were you glad? Did you find money, or what? I'm amazed! Anyone would have thought you were glad to leave your parents' home. Of course, if you have to leave, then leave. But why? For love? What love is there? You are not at all going for love, but only to acquire his rank. Isn't that really the truth? That's exactly the truth. But I, my dear, am not pleased with your fiancé. He is very proud and arrogant. You think you'll reform him… Wh-a-a-t? Don't even contemplate that!… After just a month you'll fight: that's the way he is, and that's the way you are. Only girls like to get married, but there's nothing good in it. I've experienced it myself. I know. You live and you learn. Don't fidget like that – my head is spinning as it is. Men are all fools; it's not easy to live with them. And yours is also a fool, though he holds his head high. Don't always obey him, don't indulge him in everything and don't respect him too much: there's no need. Ask your mother about

4

everything. If anything happens, come to me. Don't do anything on your own, without your mother, God help you! Your husband will not give you good advice, will not set a good example, but always aim for his own advantage. You should know this! Don't listen too much to your father, either. Don't invite him to live with you – perhaps, who knows, you'll foolishly... do that. He'll just try and steal things from you. He'll stay with you for days at a time, but why does he need you? He'll ask for vodka and smoke your husband's tobacco. He's a useless man and a pest, even though he is your father. The scoundrel has a kind face, but a terribly spiteful soul! If he tries to borrow money, don't give him any, because even though he is a titular councillor, he is a cheat. There he is, shouting, calling for you! Go to him, but don't tell him what I just said to you about him. Otherwise he'll take it out on me, that monster with a Christian face, the Devil take him! Go, while I'm still feeling well!... You are both acting against me! If I die, remember my words! You are my tormentors!"

Miss Podzatylkina left her mother and went to see her papa, who was sitting just then on his bed, putting bedbug powder on his pillow.

"My child!" her father said to her. "I'm very glad that you intend to marry such a clever gentleman as Mr Nazaryev. I'm very glad, and approve wholeheartedly of this marriage. Marry, my child, and don't be afraid! Marriage is such a solemn occasion that... well, what can be said about it? Be fruitful, multiply and replenish the earth.* God bless you! I... I... am crying. However, tears are of no use. What are people's tears? Only a psychiatric symptom of cowardice and nothing more! But listen, my daughter, to my advice! Don't forget your parents! A husband will not be better for you than your parents. It's true, he won't be! A husband likes you only for your possessions, but we like you as a daughter. What will your husband love you for? For your character? For your goodness? For your display of sensitivity? No, my dear! He will love you for your dowry. You see, my dear, we shall not be giving just a few copecks for you, but exactly a thousand roubles! You must understand this! Mr Nazaryev is a very fine gentleman, but don't give him more respect than you give your father. He will stick to you, but will not be your true friend. There will be moments when he... No, I had better say nothing, my daughter! Obey your mother, my dear, but warily. She is a good woman, but a hypocrite and a freethinker, frivolous and affected. She is a noble, honest person, but... to hell with her! She can't advise you the way your father – the cause of your being – advises you. Don't take her into your house. Husbands are not fond of mothers-in-law. I myself disliked my mother-in-law, and disliked her so much that I repeatedly took the liberty of adding burnt cork to her coffee, though it tasted all right. Second Lieutenant Zyumbumbunchikov was court-marshalled because of his mother-in-law. Do you remember that? But maybe you hadn't yet been born. The most important person everywhere and in everything is your father. You should know this and obey only him. Then, my daughter... European civilization will encourage the antagonism of women by the belief that the more children a person has, the worse. It's a lie! A fantasy! The more children parents have, the better. However, no! Not so! Quite the opposite! I was mistaken, my dear. The fewer children, the better. I read this yesterday in a magazine or newspaper. A certain Malthus* wrote about it. There we are... Someone has arrived... Bah! It's your fiancé! A real show-off, the rascal. What a scoundrel! What a man! A real Walter Scott!* Go, my dear, and greet him while I dress."

Mr Nazaryev arrived. His fiancée met him and said:

"Please feel free to sit down."

He tapped twice on the floor with his right heel and sat down near his fiancée.

"How are you?" he began with his usual familiarity. "How did you sleep? I, you know, didn't sleep all night. I read Zola* and dreamt about you. Have you read Zola? Haven't you really? Shame on you! It's a crime! A clerk lent it to me. He writes wonderfully! I'll give it to you to read. Ah! If only you could understand! I experience such feelings as you've never had. Let me give you a smacker!"

Mr Nazaryev half-rose and kissed Miss Podzatylkina's lower lip.

"But where are your parents?" he continued yet more familiarly. "I have to see them. I confess I'm a little angry with them. They deceived me badly. You know... Your father told me he's a court councillor, but now it turns out he's only a titular. Hm!... Can it really be so? Then, my dear... They promised to give me your dowry of one and a half thousand roubles, but yesterday your mother told me I would not get more than a thousand. Is this not really a swinish trick? Circassians are bloodthirsty people, but even they don't do things like that. I shall not allow myself to be duped! They can do anything except touch my pride and self-respect! It's uncivilized! It's unreasonable! I'm an honest man, and that's why I don't like dishonesty! I can put up with anything, but they shouldn't trick me, shouldn't make a fool of me, but act in accordance with human conscience! That's all! Their faces are sort of ignorant! What kind of faces are those? They're not faces! You will forgive me, but I have no kindred feelings for them. As soon as we are married, we shall take them in hand. I do not like impudence and barbarity! Though I'm not a sceptic or a cynic, I still see the use of education. We shall take them in hand! My parents haven't said a word to contradict me in a long time. Well, have you already had coffee? No? Well then, I'll join you. Go and get me some tobacco, because I forgot mine at home."

His fiancée left the room.

This was before the wedding. What it will be like after the wedding, I suggest that not a single prophet or fortune-teller can know.

Which of Three?

An old but eternally new story

O N THE TERRACE of the elegant old dacha belonging to Marya Ivanovna Langer, the wife of a state councillor, were standing Marya Ivanovna's daughter, Nadya, and Ivan Gavrilovich, the son of a well-known Moscow businessman.

It was a wonderful evening. Were I an expert at describing nature, I would describe the moon, which was looking tenderly from behind a little cloud and flooding with its soft light the forest, the dacha, Nadya's dear face... I would describe also the quiet rustling of the trees, and the song of the nightingale and the barely audible splash of the little fountain... Nadya was standing with her knees pressed to the edge of an armchair, holding the railing with one hand. Her eyes – languorous, velvety, deep – were staring fixedly at the dark green undergrowth. Dark shadows, like spots, were playing on her pale, moonlit face: these were blushes... Ivan Gavrilovich was standing behind her, and with a trembling hand was nervously pulling at his straggly · beard. When he was tired of pulling his beard, he began with his other hand to stroke and pat his high, unattractive jabot. Ivan Gavrilovich was not handsome. He looked like his mother, who resembled the village cook. His forehead was low, narrow, as if flattened; his nose was snub, blunt, with a noticeable upward curve, his hair bristly. His eyes, small and narrow like a kitten's, were looking enquiringly at Nadya.

"Excuse me," he said, stammering, sighing nervously and repeating himself, "excuse me for telling you... about my feelings... But I have so fallen in love with you that I don't even know if I'm in my right mind... I have feelings for you in my heart that it is impossible to convey! I, Nadezhda Petrovna, as soon as I saw you, straight away fell for you – that is, I fell in love. You will excuse me, of course, but... after all..." He paused. "Nature is lovely just now!"

"Yes... The weather is lovely..."

"And amid such lovely nature, how pleasant it is, don't you know, to love such a pleasant person as you... But I am unhappy!"

Ivan Gavrilovich sighed and tugged at his thin beard.

"Very unhappy! I love you, I suffer, but... you? Can you really have any feelings for me? You are educated, cultivated like the nobility... But I? I am of the merchant class and... nothing more! Nothing at all! There may be money, but what good is money if there is no real happiness? Money without happiness only leads to sinfulness and... a barren existence. You eat well, and... you don't go on foot... an empty life... Nadezhda Petrovna!"

"Well?"

"It's... nothing! I wanted, strictly speaking, to unsettle you..."

"What do you mean?"

"Can you love me?" He paused. "I suggested to your mum... that is, your mother, that I offer my heart and hand concerning you, and she said that it all depends on you... You may, she said, accept me even without parental permission... How do you answer me?"

Nadya was silent. She looked at the dark green undergrowth, where the trunks of trees and patterns of leaves were faintly visible... Her attention was drawn to the moving black shadows of the trees, whose tops were swaying slightly in the breeze. Ivan Gavrilovich found her silence oppressive. Tears appeared in his eyes. He was suffering. "But what," he thought, "if she refuses?" And this unhappy thought cut like a hard frost along his broad back...

"Have pity, Nadezhda Petrovna," he said. "Don't torture my soul... After all, if I approach you, it's from love... Therefore..." He paused. "If..." He paused again. "If you don't answer me, the only thing will be for me to die."

Nadya turned her face to Ivan Gavrilovich and smiled... She extended her hand to him and began to speak in a voice that sounded to the ears of the Moscow businessman like the song of the siren:

"I am very grateful to you, Ivan Gavrilovich. I have known already for a long time that you love me, and I know how much you love me... And I... I... I love you too, *Jean*...* It's impossible not to love you for your kind heart, for your devotion..."

Ivan Gavrilovich opened his mouth wide, began to laugh and, feeling happy, passed a hand over his face. "Is this a dream?" he thought.

"I know that if I marry you," continued Nadya, "I shall be very happy. But you know what, Ivan Gavrilovich? Wait a while for an answer... I can't reply just now... I must consider this step very carefully... I have to think... Be patient for a while."

"But will I have long to wait?"

"No, not long... A day, two at most..."

"That will be possible."

"Go away now, and I shall send you my answer in a letter... Go home now, and I shall go and think... Goodbye... In a day..."

Nadya extended her hand. Ivan Gavrilovich grabbed and kissed it. Nadya nodded, blew a kiss in the air, scampered from the porch and disappeared. Ivan Gavrilovich stood for two or three minutes thinking, and then set off across a little flower bed and through a grove to a clearing where his horses were waiting. He was feeling limp and weak with happiness, as if he had spent the whole day in a steam bath... He was walking and laughing with happiness.

"Trofim!" He roused the sleeping coachman. "Get up! Let's go! A five-rouble tip! Understand? Ha-ha!"

Meanwhile, Nadya scurried through all the rooms to the other terrace, descended from the terrace and, making her way through the trees, bushes and shrubs, ran to another clearing. In this clearing was waiting a friend of her childhood, a young man of about twenty-six, Baron Vladimir Schtral. Schtral was an attractively stout, chubby German with an already noticeable bald patch. He had that year finished a course at university, was leaving for his Kharkov estate and had come to say goodbye for the last time... He was slightly drunk and, reclining on a bench, was whistling 'Strelochka'.*

Nadya ran up to him and, breathing heavily and feeling weary from running, threw herself on his neck. She gave a ringing laugh and, tugging at his hair, neck and collar, smothered his plump, sweaty face with kisses.

"I have already been waiting a whole hour for you," said the Baron, putting his arm around her waist...

"So then – are you well?"

"I'm well..."

"Are you going tomorrow?"

"Yes..."

"You're horrible... Will you return soon?"

"I don't know..."

The Baron kissed Nadya on the cheek and, taking her off his knees, sat her on the bench.

"Well, enough kissing," said Nadya. "Later... There will be more time in the future. Now we have to talk business." She paused. "Have you thought, Volya?"

"I have..."

"Well, what then? When... are we going to get married?"

The baron made a wry face.

"You are on about that again!" he said. "You know I already gave you yesterday... a definite answer... It's not possible even to talk about marriage! I already told you yesterday... Why start to talk about what has already been rehashed a thousand times?..."

"But, Volya, our relationship has to end in something! How can you not understand that? Shouldn't it?"

"It should, but not in marriage... You, *Nadine*, I repeat for the hundredth time, are naive, like a three-year-old child... Naivety befits pretty women, but not in this case, my dear..."

"It means you don't want to marry me! You don't want to? Tell me straight, you shameless soul – tell me straight: you don't want to?"

"I don't want to... Why should I ruin my career? I love you, but you will surely ruin me if I marry you... You will give me neither position nor name... Marriage, my dear, must be half a career,

but you... It's no good crying... We have to reason sensibly...
Marriages for love tend never to be happy, and end usually in a
trice..."

"You are lying... You are lying! That's the thing!"

"Marry, and then die of hunger... Give birth to beggars... We
have to discuss it..."

"But why did you not discuss it then... remember? Then, you
gave me your solemn word that you would marry me... Didn't
you give it?"

"I did... But now my plans have changed... Surely you wouldn't
want to marry a poor man? So why would you force me to marry
a poor woman? I don't want to act like a swine. I have a future,
for which I must answer before my conscience."

Nadya wiped her eyes with her handkerchief, and suddenly,
unexpectedly, threw herself on the neck of the Orthodox German.
She pressed herself to him and began to smother his face with
kisses.

"Marry me!" she said. "Marry me, my darling! I do so love you!
I really can't live without you, my precious one! I shall die if you
leave me! You will marry me? Won't you?"

The German thought for a moment and said in a resolute tone:

"I cannot! Love is a good thing, but it doesn't come before
everything in this world..."

"So you don't want to?"

"No... I cannot."

"You don't want to? Is it really that you don't want to?"

"I can't, *Nadine*!"

"You scoundrel, you rogue... That's what you are! Deceiver!
Damn foreigner! I can't stand you, I hate you, I despise you! You
are vile! I never even loved you! If I yielded to you that night it
was only because I considered you an honourable man – I thought
you would marry me... Even then I couldn't stand you! I wanted
to marry you because you were a baron and rich!"

Nadya began to wave her hands, and, having stepped several
paces away from Schtral, delivered a few more caustic comments

and set off home… "I was wrong to go to him now," she thought as she walked home. "Shouldn't I have known that he wouldn't want to marry me? What a swine! I was a fool that evening! Had I not yielded to him then, I wouldn't have had to demean myself before that… damn foreigner."

Entering the yard of the dacha, Nadya did not go indoors. She strolled through the yard and stopped by a dimly lit window. This window looked out from a room which was occupied by a young first violinist, Mitya Gusev, who had just graduated from the conservatory and had been engaged for the summer. Nadya began to peer through the window. Mitya, a broad-shouldered, not bad-looking young man with curly, fair hair, was in the room. He was lying on the bed without a frock coat or vest, reading a novel. Nadya stood awhile in thought, and then knocked on the window. The first violinist raised his head:

"Who's there?"

"It's me, Dmitri Ivanych… Please open the window a moment!…"

Mitya quickly put on his frock coat and opened the window.

"Come here… Climb down to me…" said Nadya. Mitya appeared at the window, and a moment later was next to Nadya:

"What do you want?"

"This is what, Dmitri Ivanych," she said. "Don't write me love letters, my dear! Please, don't write! Don't love me, and don't tell me that you love me!"

Tears glistened in Nadya's eyes, flowing in a stream along her cheeks and down her arms…

Her tears were genuine, bitter, copious…

"Don't love me, Dmitri! Don't play the violin for me! I am vile, nasty, bad… I am a person who should be despised, hated, beaten…"

Nadya began to sob, and pressed her head to Mitya's chest.

"I am the vilest person, and my thoughts are vile, and my heart…"

Mitya was puzzled. He started to mutter some nonsense and kissed Nadya on the head…

"You are kind, good..." she went on. "To tell you the truth, I love you... Well, but don't love me! I love more than anything else in the world money, clothes, carriages... I die when I think I have no money... I am a disgusting egotist... Don't love me, dear Dmitri Ivanych! Don't write me letters! I am going to marry... Gavrilych... You see... what a person I am! But you still... love me! Goodbye! I shall love you even when I'm married... Goodbye, Mitya!

Nadya quickly embraced Gusev, quickly kissed his cheek and ran to the gate.

Arriving in her room, Nadya sat at the table and, crying bitterly, wrote the following letter: "Dear Ivan Gavrilych! I am yours. I love you and want to be your wife... Your N."

The letter was sealed and given to the maid for posting.

"Tomorrow... he will bring something..." thought Nadya with a deep sigh.

This sigh marked the end of her crying. After sitting for a while by the window and becoming composed, Nadya quickly undressed, and precisely at midnight an expensive downy blanket with embroidery and monogram was already warming the sleeping, periodically twitching body of the young, pretty, devious schemer.

At midnight Ivan Gavrilovich was pacing back and forth in his study and speaking to himself as if in a daydream.

His parents were sitting in the study and listening to his reveries... They were rejoicing, and happy for their happy son...

"The girl is good, well bred," said his father. "A state councillor's daughter and also beautiful. Just one thing is unfortunate: her surname is German. People will think you married a German..."

A Transgression

AT THE END OF HIS EVENING STROLL, Collegiate Assessor Miguev stopped by a telegraph pole and sighed deeply. A week before, at that very spot, when he arrived home from his walk in the evening, his former housemaid Agnia had overtaken him and said angrily:

"Just you wait! I shall deal with you, so that you learn what it is to destroy innocent girls! I shall leave the baby with you, and take you to court, and tell your wife…"

And she demanded that he deposit five thousand roubles in the bank in her name. Miguev recalled this, sighed, and once again, repenting sincerely, reproached himself for the momentary passion that had given him such a mass of trouble and suffering.

Arriving at his dacha, Miguev sat on the porch to rest. It was exactly ten o'clock, and from behind the clouds peeped a sliver of moon. Not a soul was on the street, even near the dacha settlement: the old residents were already going to bed, while the young ones were strolling in the grove. Looking in both pockets for a match in order to light a cigarette, Miguev pushed his elbow against something soft. Having nothing better to do, he looked under his right elbow; suddenly his face was distorted with horror, as if he had seen a snake next to him. On the porch by the door lay a bundle. Something oblong was wrapped in something that felt like a quilt. One end of the bundle was slightly open, and the collegiate assessor, pushing his hand inside, felt something warm and moist. He leapt to his feet in horror and looked around, like a lawbreaker preparing to escape arrest…

"She left it here!" he said angrily through his teeth, clenching his fists. "Here it lies… my transgression! Oh, Lord!"

He stood rooted to the spot with fear, anger and shame… What should he do now? What would his wife say if she were to find out?

What would his colleagues say? His Excellency now would prob-ably slap him on the belly, chuckle and say: "I congratulate you… He-he-he… Grey hair in the beard, but a demon in the belly*… naughty boy, Semyon Erastovich!" All the dacha settlement would know his secret now, and perhaps the respectable mothers of fam-ilies would refuse him entry to their houses. Reports of foundlings get into all the newspapers, and thus the humble name of Miguev will spread through all of Russia…

The middle window of the dacha was open, and through it could be heard the sound of Anna Filippovna, Miguev's wife, setting the table for supper; in the yard, just behind the gate, the caretaker Yermolai was plaintively strumming a balalaika… The infant had only to wake up and start to whine, and the secret would be revealed. Miguev felt a pressing need to hasten.

"Quickly, quickly…" he muttered. "This minute, before anyone sees. I shall take it somewhere, put it on someone else's porch…"

Miguev took the bundle in one hand and quietly, with measured step so as not to seem suspicious, went along the street…

"Appalling, abominable situation!" he thought, trying to assume a look of indifference. "A collegiate assessor is walking along the street with an infant! Oh Lord, if someone sees and learns what this is all about, I'm finished… Why don't I put it on this porch… No, wait, the windows are open here, and someone may see. Where could it go? Aha, I know, I think I'll leave it at the merchant Melkin's dacha… Merchants are rich people, and soft-hearted; perhaps they will even be grateful and see to its upbringing themselves."

And Miguev was resolved to leave the infant at Melkin's, even though the merchant's dacha was situated on the last street of the settlement, near the river.

"Let's just hope it doesn't start howling and fall out of the bundle," thought the collegiate assessor. "No, seriously – a really pleasant surprise! I am carrying a living being under my arm like a briefcase. A living being, with a soul, with feelings, like every-one else… If, who knows, the Melkins undertake his upbringing, perhaps he will turn out to be some... Perhaps, he will turn out to be some professor, military leader, writer... Really, anything in the world may happen! Now I am carrying him under my arm like some rubbish, but in thirty or forty years perhaps I shall have to stand up in his presence..."

As Miguev walked along a narrow, deserted side street, past long fences beneath the thick black shadow of lime trees, it suddenly struck him that he was doing something very cruel and criminal.

"I must say, how despicable this is, really!" he thought. "So despicable that it's impossible to think of anything worse... Why are we moving this unfortunate infant from porch to porch? Is it really his fault that he was born? What harm has he done us? We are scoundrels... We love to go sledging, but innocent children have to carry the sledge...* Really, one should think about all these things! I've led a dissipated life, and because of it this child can expect to have a cruel fate... If I leave him with the Melkins, the Melkins will send him to a foundling hospital, and there everything will be strange, formal... with neither kindness, nor love, nor pampering... Then he'll be apprenticed to a cobbler... he'll take to drink, learn foul language, will die of hunger... He will be a cobbler, but really he is the son of a collegiate assessor, of noble blood... He is my flesh and blood..."

Miguev came out from the shadow of the lime trees onto the road, which was flooded with moonlight, and, unwrapping the bundle, looked at the infant.

"He's sleeping," he whispered. "Just look – the villain has an aquiline nose, like his father... He's sleeping and doesn't know that his own father is looking at him... It's a tragedy, brother... So then, excuse me... Forgive me, brother... You were really pre-ordained to this from birth..."

The collegiate assessor blinked, and felt things like small insects crawling down his cheeks... He wrapped up the infant, put it under his arm and walked on. All along the road to Melkin's dacha social questions crowded into his head, and his conscience gnawed at his heart.

"If I were a decent, honest man," he thought, "I wouldn't care about anything, I would go with this infant to Anna Filippovna, would get down on my knees before her and say: 'Forgive me! I have sinned! Tear me to pieces, but we shall not destroy a blameless infant. We have no children; let's bring him up ourselves!' She is a kind woman, and would consent... And then my child would be with me... Ah!"

He approached Melkin's dacha and stopped, undecided... He imagined himself sitting at home in his drawing room, reading the newspaper, while next to him a boy with an aquiline nose chatters and plays with the tassels of his dressing gown; at the same time in his imagination there crept a vision of the winking of his colleagues and of His Excellency, chuckling and slapping him on the belly... In his soul, next to his gnawing conscience, sat something tender, warm, wistful...

The collegiate assessor placed the infant on a step of the terrace and waved his hand. Insects again crawled down his face...

"Forgive me, brother – I'm a scoundrel!" he muttered. "Don't think badly of me!"

He stepped back, but at once grunted resolutely and said:

"Oh, to hell with it! I'm going to ignore everyone! I shall take him in, and let people say what they want!"

Miguev picked up the infant and began to stride quickly back.

"Let them say what they want," he thought. "I shall go now, kneel and say: 'Anna Filippovna!' She is a kind woman, will understand... And we shall bring him up... If it's a boy, we shall name him Vladimir, and if a girl, Anna... If nothing else, the child will be a comfort to us in old age..."

And he did as he resolved. Crying, frozen with fear and shame, full of hope and vague delight, he entered his dacha, went up to his wife and knelt before her...

"Anna Filippovna!" he said, sobbing and placing the infant on the floor. "Don't punish me, let me say a word... I have sinned! This is my child... You remember Agnyushka? Well, this... is the work of the Devil..."

And, beside himself with shame and fear, not waiting for a response, he leapt up and ran outside as if beaten...

"I'll stay here, in the yard, until she calls me," he thought. "I'll give her time to recover from the shock and reflect..."

The caretaker Yermolai, who was going past with his balalaika, looked at him and shrugged... A minute later he again went past, and again shrugged.

"Here's a to-do, for Heaven's sake," he muttered, grinning. "That woman, the laundress Aksinya, was just here, Semyon Erastych. The fool put her child on the porch outside, and while she was with me someone took the child and carried it off... How strange!"

"What? What are you saying?" shouted Miguev at the top of his voice.

Yermolai, misinterpreting the *barin*'s anger,* scratched his head and sighed.

"Excuse me, Semyon Erastych," he said. "but now it's the summer holidays... one can't manage without... without a woman, that is..."

And, looking at the glaring, angry, astonished eyes of the *barin*, he guiltily grunted and continued:

"Of course it's a sin, but after all, what can one do... You didn't allow other women to come into the yard, it's true, so where are we to get them for our needs. Before, when Agnyushka lived here, no others came in, because... I had my own, but now, please understand... one can't manage without others... In Agnyushka's time, it's true, there was nothing irregular, that is why..."

"Go away, swine!" Miguev shouted at him, stamping his feet and going back into the house.

Anna Filippovna, astonished and angry, was sitting in the same place with her tearful eyes fixed on the infant...

"Well, well..." muttered the pale Miguev, his mouth creasing into a smile. "I was joking... It's not mine, but... but the laundress Aksinya's. I... I was joking... Take it to the caretaker."

The Country Resident

LYOLYA ——, a pretty twenty-year-old blonde, is standing in the small front garden of a dacha and, resting her chin on the fence, is looking into the distance. All the distant fields, the tufted clouds in the sky, the railway station darkening in the distance and the stream running ten steps from the garden, are flooded with the crimson light of the moon that is rising from behind the hill. The breeze, having nothing better to do, is gaily rippling the stream and rustling the grass... All around is peaceful... Lyolya is thinking... Her pretty face is so sad, and her eyes are darkening with such melancholy that, really, it seems cruel and wrong not to share her grief with the moon.

She is comparing the present with the past. The previous year, in this very same fragrant and poetical May, she was sitting final examinations at the Institute. She recalls how her class teacher, Mlle Morceau – a cowed, sick and none-too-clever creature with an eternally frightened face and a big, sweaty nose – took the graduates to have their photograph taken.

"Oh, I implore you," she begged the photographer in the studio, "don't show them pictures of men!"

She begged with tears in her eyes. This poor lizard, who had never known men, felt holy terror at the sight of the male physiognomy. In the whiskers and beard of every "demon" she could read otherworldly lust, inevitably leading to mysterious, terrible disaster, from which there was no escape. The pupils made fun of the stupid Morceau, but, instilled with "ideals", they could not but share her holy terror. They were led to believe that there, on the other side of the Institute's walls, apart from catarrhal fathers and brothers in military service, swarmed hairy poets, pale-faced singers, irritable satirists, intense patriots, vast millionaires – eloquent to the point of tears, terribly interesting defenders... Look at this teeming crowd

23

and choose! In particular, Lyolya was convinced that, on leaving the Institute, she would inevitably encounter Turgenev-like* and other heroes, fighters for truth and progress, about whom authors have always been eager to write, in novels and even historical textbooks – of ancient days, the Middle Ages and modern times…

In this May, Lyolya is already married. Her husband is handsome, rich, young, educated, respected by all. But despite all this (it is shameful to admit in the poetic month of May!), he is coarse, uncouth and as ridiculous as forty thousand ridiculous brothers.*

He wakes up at exactly ten o'clock in the morning, and, having put on a dressing gown, sits to shave. He shaves with an anxious face, painstakingly, with absorption, as if he was inventing the telephone. After shaving, he drinks some water, also with an anxious face. Then, after dressing in immaculately clean, pressed clothes, he kisses his wife's hand and drives in his own carriage to work at the "Insurance Society". What he does at this "Society", Lyolya does not know. Whether he just copies documents, thinks up clever projects or, perhaps, even decides the fate of the "Society" is not known. After three o'clock he returns from work and, complaining of feeling tired and sweaty, changes his underwear. Then he sits down to dinner. At dinner he eats a lot and talks. He speaks mostly of high matters. He settles questions about women and finance, curses England for something, praises Bismarck.* He criticizes the newspapers, medicine, actors, students… "Youth has grown terribly shallow." During one dinner he manages to settle a hundred questions. But what is worst of all, the dinner guests listen to this difficult man and agree with him. He, spouting nonsense and banalities, shows himself to be cleverer than all the guests and serves as an authority.

"We now have no good writers!" he sighs at every dinner – but he did not receive this conviction from books. He never reads anything – neither books nor newspapers. He confuses Turgenev with Dostoevsky, does not understand caricature or jokes, and once, having read Shchedrin* on the advice of Lyolya, said that Shchedrin writes "obscurely".

"Pushkin, *ma chère*,* is better… There are very funny things in Pushkin! I have read… I remember…"

After dinner he goes out on the terrace, sits in a soft armchair and, with eyes half closed, falls to thinking. He thinks for a long time, with concentration, frowning and screwing up his face. Lyolya doesn't know what he is thinking about. She knows only that, after two hours' thought, he has grown no wiser and still talks all the same nonsense. In the evening they play cards. He plays carefully. He thinks for a long time before each play, and if his partner makes a mistake, he states the rules of the game in an even, articulated voice. After cards, on the departure of the guests, he drinks water from a jug and with an anxious face goes to bed. In sleep he lies peacefully, like a log. From time to time he raves, but even his ravings are ridiculous:

"Cabby! Cabby!" Lyolya heard him mutter two nights after they were married.

All night he grunts. The grunts come from his nose, chest, stomach…

Lyolya cannot say anything more about him. She stands now in the garden, thinking about him, comparing him to all her male acquaintances, and realizes that he is the best of all – but this doesn't make her feel any better. The holy terror instilled by Mlle Morceau promised her more.

At the Barber's

MORNING. It is not yet even seven o'clock, but Makar Kuzmich Blyestkin's barber shop is already open. The owner, a man of about twenty-three, unwashed, with a greasy face, but dressed like a dandy, is busy clearing up. There is really nothing to clear up, but he is sweating as he works. Here he wipes with a rag, here he scratches with a fingernail, here he finds a bug and flicks it off the wall.

The barber shop is small, narrow and rather dirty. The wooden walls are covered with wallpaper, reminding one of a coachman's faded shirt. Between two opaque, dripping-wet windows is a thin, creaking, flimsy door, over which is a little bell that has turned green from the damp and quivers and rings weakly by itself for no reason. If you look in the mirror, which hangs on one of the walls, your face will be distorted into a pitiless image. You are cut and shaved in front of this mirror. Everything is on a little table that is just as unwashed and greasy as Makar Kuzmich himself: combs, scissors, razors, hair pomade sold by the copeck, powder by the copeck, strongly diluted eau de Cologne by the copeck. Indeed, the whole barber shop is not worth more than fifteen copecks.

The bell over the door rings weakly, and into the shop comes an elderly man wearing a weather-beaten sheepskin coat and felt boots. His head and neck are wrapped in a woman's shawl.

It is Erast Ivanych Yagodov, Makar Kuzmich's godfather. He once worked as a guard at the department of ecclesiastical administration, but now lives near the Red Pond area, employed as a metalworker.

"Makarushka, hello, dear boy!" he says to Makar Kuzmich, who is absorbed in his work.

They exchange kisses. Yagodov pulls the shawl from his head, crosses himself and sits down.

"How far it is!" he says with a groan. "It's no joke. I walked from the Red Pond to the Kaluga Gate."

"How are you, dear man?"

"In a bad way, brother. I had a fever."

"Really? A fever!"

"A fever. I was in bed for a month, thought I would die. I was given extreme unction. Now my hair's falling out. The doctor told me to have it cut. New hair will grow thicker, he says. So I thought: why not go to Makar? It's better to go to a relative than to someone else. He'll do it better, and won't charge. It's a little further to come, that's true, but so what? It would be an outing."

"I'll do it with pleasure. Please sit down!"

Makar Kuzmich taps his heels on the floor and motions to the chair. Yagodov sits down, looks at himself in the mirror and is evidently satisfied with the sight: in the mirror can be seen a distorted face with Kalmyck lips, a blunt, wide nose and bulging eyes. Makar Kuzmich puts a white sheet with yellow spots over the shoulders of his client and starts to snip with the scissors.

"I'll cut you down to the skin!" he says.

"Of course. So that I resemble a Tatar, or a bomb. The hair will grow thicker."

"How is Auntie, then?"

"Not bad. She gets on all right. The other day she went as midwife to the Major's lady. They gave her a rouble."

"Really. A rouble. Hold your ear back!"

"I'm holding it… Don't cut me, be careful. Ow, it hurts! You're pulling my hair."

"It's all right. Without that I can't do my job. And how is Anna Erastovna?"

"My daughter? She's all right, she's full of life. Last week, on Wednesday, she got engaged to Sheikin. Why didn't you come?"

The scissors stop snipping. Makar Kuzmich drops his arms and asks in a frightened voice:

"Who got engaged?"

"Anna."

"What do you mean? Who was she engaged to?"

"To Sheikin. Prokofy Petrovich. His aunt's a housekeeper in Zlatoustensky Street. She's a good woman. Naturally we're all glad, praise God. The wedding's in a week. Do come, we'll have a good time."

"But how is this, Erast Ivanych?" says Makar Kuzmich, looking pale, astonished, and shrugging his shoulders. "How is this possible? It is... it is utterly impossible! You see, Anna Erastovna... you see, I... you see, I nourished feelings for her... I was intending... How is it possible?"

"Well, that's what happened. She went and got engaged. He's a good man."

A cold sweat appears on Makar Kuzmich's face. He drops the scissors on the table and starts to rub his nose with his fist.

"I had the intention..." he says. "It's impossible, Erast Ivanych! I... I am in love with her and made a heartfelt proposal. And Auntie gave me her word. I always respected you, just like my father... I always cut your hair for free... I've always done you favours, and when Papa died you took the sofa and ten roubles and didn't give them back. Remember?"

"How can I not remember? Of course I remember. But what sort of match would you make, Makar? Are you really a match? You have neither money nor rank, and a piffling occupation..."

"But is Sheikin rich?"

"He belongs to a tradesmen's artel.* He has a deposit of one and a half thousand. That's it, brother... Like it or not, the matter is settled. There's no going back, Makarushka. Find yourself another fiancée. There are plenty of fish in the sea. Well, keep cutting! What are you waiting for?"

Makar Kuzmich stands silently without moving, then takes a handkerchief from his pocket and starts to cry.

"Come, what's all this?" Erast Ivanych consoles him. "Stop it! Good Lord, he's wailing like a woman! Finish cutting my hair, and then you can cry. Pick up the scissors!"

Makar Kuzmich takes up the scissors, looks vacantly at them for a minute and lets them fall on the table. His hands are shaking.

"I can't," he says. "I can't now, I haven't the strength. I'm so unhappy. And she's unhappy! We loved each other, made promises, and unkind people pitilessly separated us. Go away, Erast Ivanych! I can't bear to look at you."

"I'll come tomorrow, Makarushka. You'll finish cutting my hair tomorrow."

"All right."

"Compose yourself, and I'll come back tomorrow, early in the morning."

Half of Erast Ivanych's head is cut bare, and he resembles a convict. It is awkward to be left with a head like that, but nothing can be done. He wraps the shawl around his head and leaves the barber shop. Remaining alone, Makar Kuzmich sits down and continues to cry quietly.

The next day, early in the morning, Erast Ivanych comes again.

"What do you want?" Makar Kuzmich asks him coldly.

"Finish cutting my hair, Makarushka. There's still half to do."

"Kindly pay for it first. I don't cut for free, sir."

Erast Ivanych leaves without saying a word, and to this day his hair remains long on one side and short on the other. He considers it an extravagance to pay for a haircut, and is waiting for the hair on the shorn half to grow back. He even attended the wedding like that.

The Merchant's Estate

SOME TWENTY WOODEN, hastily built dachas are spread around a neglected manorial estate of the ordinary sort. On the tallest and most prominent of them is displayed a blue sign with the word "Inn", along with a picture of a samovar glowing gold in the sunshine. Here and there, alternating with the red roofs of the dachas, despondently peep out the decrepit, rusty and moss-covered roofs of the manorial stables, greenhouses and barns.

It is a May midday. In the air is a smell of *shchi** and smoke from a samovar. The estate manager, Kuzma Fyodorov – a tall, elderly man in pleated boots and a shirt hanging outside his trousers – is walking around the settlement, showing them to prospective tenants. On his face is written dull laziness and indifference: whether or not they become tenants is a matter of complete indifference to him. Behind him plod three people: a red-haired man in the uniform of a railway engineer, a thin pregnant lady and a schoolgirl.

"But how expensive your dachas are," says the engineer, knitting his brow. "All of them are either four hundred or three hundred roubles... terrible! Show us something cheaper."

"There are cheaper ones too... Of the cheaper ones only two are left... This way, please!"

Fyodorov leads the visitors through the manorial garden. Tree stumps and a thin, sparsely growing fir grove can be seen; only one tall tree remains – a shapely old poplar that was spared the axe as if only to mourn the unfortunate fate of its companions. Of the stone wall, arbours and grottoes there remain only traces in the form of scattered bricks, lime and rotting beams.

"How neglected everything is!" says the engineer sadly, viewing the traces of past splendour. "And where does the *barin* live now?"

"He's not a *barin*, but a merchant. He lives in furnished rooms in town... Let's go in!"

The visitors stoop and enter a small stone structure with three windows barred like a prison cell. They are overcome by dampness and a smell of decay. The house is one square room divided in two by a new wooden partition. The engineer screws up his eyes and reads on one of the dark walls the pencilled inscription: "In this abode of the dead, Lieutenant Fildyekosov grew melancholy and attempted suicide."

"You shouldn't wear a hat here, Your Honour," Fyodorov says to the engineer.

"Why?"

"You shouldn't, sir. This was the crypt where the owners were buried. If you were to raise the boards and look under the floor, you would see the coffins."

"What a thing!" The thin lady is horrified. "Apart from the dampness, one could die here from melancholy. I don't wish to live with the dead!"

"The dead, my lady, will not trouble you. Those buried here were not some vagrants, but people like you – gentlefolk. Last summer here, in this very crypt, a military gentleman, Fildyekosov, lived and remained quite contented. He promised to come again this year, but he hasn't yet returned."

"Did he attempt suicide?" asks the engineer, recalling the inscription on the wall.

"How do you know about that? Indeed he did, sir. And because of that, all the problems started. He did not know that here, under the floor, may the kingdom of heaven be theirs, the deceased were lying, and so one night he thought to hide three litres of vodka under a floorboard. He raised this board, and when he saw there were coffins underneath, he went mad. He ran outside howling. He caused a commotion among all the residents. Then he just withered away. He couldn't afford to leave, but it was terrifying for him to live here. In the end, sir, he couldn't stand it, and attempted suicide. Luckily I had taken a hundred roubles from him in advance for the dacha, otherwise perhaps he might have fled in fear. While he was recovering, he got used to it… he was all right... He promised to come back: 'I'm terribly fond of such adventures,' he said. He was a real eccentric!"

"No, you have to show us another dacha."

"As you wish, sir. There is one other – only worse, sir."

Kuzma leads the visitors to the edge of the estate, to a place where stands a decrepit threshing barn. Behind the barn glitters a pond overgrown with grass, while manorial farm buildings loom darkly.

"Can one go fishing here?" asks the engineer.

"You can catch as much as you like, sir... You pay five roubles for the season and catch to your heart's content. That is, if you wish to fish in the river with a rod... but if you wish to catch crucians in the pond, there is an extra charge."

"It doesn't matter about the fish," observes the lady. "We can manage without them. But now, about provisions. Do the peasants deliver milk here?"

"The peasants are not allowed to come here, madam. The residents have to get their provisions at our farm. That's our condition. We don't charge a lot, madam. Milk is twenty-five copecks for two bottles; eggs, as a rule, thirty copecks for ten; butter, fifty copecks... You can also get various greens and vegetables from us."

"Hm... And where can you find mushrooms here?"

"If the summer is wet, there are mushrooms. You can pick them. You pay six roubles per person for the season – and gather not only mushrooms, but berries too. That's possible. The road goes across the river to our forest. If you wish, you can go via the ford, otherwise go across on the temporary bridge. It only costs five copecks to use the bridge. Five copecks there and five copecks back. And if some residents wish to hunt, or go target-shooting, the owner doesn't object. Shoot as much as you like, only keep the receipt that you paid ten roubles. And we have wonderful bathing here. The shore is clean and the bottom sandy up to any depth – up to your knees, up to your neck. We give you complete freedom. It's five copecks for one swim, but four roubles fifty copecks for the season. Spend the whole day in the water, if you like!"

"And do nightingales sing here?" asks the girl.

"One was singing a few days ago on the other side of the river, but my young son caught it and sold it to the innkeeper. Come in, please!"

Kuzma leads the visitors to a dilapidated old barn with new windows. The inside of the barn is divided by partitions into three tiny rooms. In two of the rooms stand empty corn bins.

"No, there is not a chance of living here!" declares the thin lady, looking with disgust at the gloomy walls and corn bins. "This is a barn, not a dacha. It's no use looking at this, George... It's draughty and the roof probably leaks. How could one live here?"

"But people do," sighs Kuzma. "To those without birds, they say, even a saucepan is a nightingale.* When there are no dachas, even one like this is good. If you don't take it, others will take it, and someone will live in it. To me, this dacha is the most suitable for you. It's a mistake for you to... how shall I put it... listen to your wife. You won't find a better one anywhere. But I would let you have it for a little less. It goes for a hundred and fifty, but I would take a hundred and twenty."

"No, my good man, it's not possible. Goodbye, forgive us for troubling you."

"My pleasure, sir. Take care."

And, following the departing visitors with his eyes, Kuzma coughs and adds:

"A tip wouldn't come amiss from you kind people. I spent probably two hours with you. Don't begrudge a fifty-copeck coin!"

At Home with the Marshal's Widow*

E ACH YEAR ON THE FIRST OF FEBRUARY, the day of the martyr St Trifon, a special event takes place on the estate of the widow of the former Marshal of the Nobility Trifon Lvovich Zavzyatov. On this day the marshal's widow, Lyubov Petrovna, celebrates a *panikhida** for the deceased, whose name day it happens to be – and, after the *panikhida*, a thanksgiving service to the Lord God. The whole district comes to the *panikhida*. There you will see the present marshal Khrumov, the chairman of the district council Marfutkin, permanent council representative Potrashkov, both magistrates, police inspector Krinolinov, two local police officers, the district doctor Dvornyagin, who is smelling of iodoform, all the landowners, great and small, and so on. In all, around fifty people gather.

Precisely at twelve o'clock the guests make their way with long faces from all the rooms to the hall. The floor is carpeted, and their steps soundless, but the solemnity of the occasion makes them tread instinctively on tiptoe, balancing with their arms outstretched. Everything is ready in the hall. Father Yevmeny, a little old man in a tall, faded *kamilavka*,* puts on a black chasuble. Deacon Konkordiev, as red as a lobster and already robed, noiselessly leafs through the prayer book and marks a page with some banknotes. By the door leading from the entrance hall, the sacristan Luka, his cheeks puffed up and his eyes bulging, is blowing on the censer. The hall gradually fills with bluish, transparent smoke and the smell of incense. The local teacher Gelikonsky, a young man in a new baggy frock coat, with big blackheads on his frightened face, carries around wax candles on a German silver tray. The hostess Lyubov Petrovna stands at the front near a little table laden with *kutya*,* holding a handkerchief to her face in readiness. All around is silence, interrupted from time to time with sighs. The faces of all are strained, solemn...

The *panikhida* begins. Dark-blue smoke rises from the censer and plays in the slanting rays of the sun; the candles that were lit splutter weakly. The singing, at first harsh and deafening, soon becomes quiet and harmonious as the singers gradually adapt themselves to the acoustical conditions of the room... The tunes are all sad, doleful... Little by little the guests assume melancholy expressions and grow thoughtful. Through their heads pass thoughts about the brevity of human life, about frailty, the vanity of the world... They remember the deceased, Zavzyatov – a thick-set, rosy-cheeked man who could down a bottle of champagne at one draught and break a mirror with his forehead. And when 'Repose with the Saints' is sung and the sobbing of the hostess is heard, the guests begin to shift uneasily from one foot to the other. The more sensitive begin to feel a tickling in the throat and around the eyelids. The chairman of the district council, Marfutkin, wishing to suppress the disagreeable feeling, leans over to the ear of the police inspector and whispers:

"Yesterday I was at Ivan Fyodorych's... Pyotr Petrovich and I took a grand slam without trumps... Really and truly... Olga Andreyevna was so enraged that a false tooth fell out of her mouth."

But now 'Eternal Memory' is sung. Gelikonsky respectfully collects the candles, and the *panikhida* ends. There follows a minute of commotion, the change of vestments and a brief prayer. After the prayer, while Father Yevmeny disrobes, the guests rub their hands and cough, and the hostess talks about the goodness of the deceased, Trifon Lvovich.

"I ask you, gentlemen, to come and have something to eat!" she concludes, sighing.

The guests, trying not to push or tread on each other's feet, hurry to the dining room... There, breakfast awaits them. This breakfast is so sumptuous that every year Deacon Konkordiev, judging by his look, feels it his duty to throw out his hands, shake his head in amazement and say:

"Supernatural! This, Father Yevmeny, is not so much like the food of man as offerings brought to the gods."

The breakfast really is extraordinary. On the table is everything that flora and fauna can offer, but only one thing there is supernatural: on the table is everything except... alcoholic beverages. Lyubov Petrovna has taken a vow not to keep in the house cards or alcoholic drinks – the two things that destroyed her husband. On the table stand only bottles of vinegar and oil, as if to mock and punish the breakfasters, who without exception consist of the greatest drunkards and boozers.

"Eat, gentlemen!" invites the marshal's widow. "Only, forgive me, I have no vodka... I don't keep it..."

The guests go up to the table and hesitantly help themselves to the *pirog*.* But the food does not go down well. In the stabbing with forks, in the cutting, in the chewing is evident some laziness, apathy... Clearly something is lacking.

"I feel as if I've lost something..." whispers one of the magistrates to the other. "It's the same feeling I had when my wife ran off with the engineer... I can't eat!"

Marfutkin, before starting to eat, rummages for a long time in his pockets, looking for a handkerchief.

"My handkerchief must be in my coat! And here I am looking for it," he recalls loudly, and he goes to the vestibule where the coats are hung.

He returns from the vestibule with glistening eyes, and immediately attacks the *pirog* with gusto.

"Isn't it most unpleasant to eat cold food without something to drink?" he whispers to Father Yevmeny. "Go to the vestibule, Father, where you'll find a bottle in my coat... Just be careful not to clink your glass against the bottle!"

Father Yevmeny remembers that he has to tell Luka something, and minces off to the vestibule.

"Father! Two words... in confidence!" says Dvornyagin, following him out.

"What a fur coat I bought for myself, gentlemen, by sheer luck!" boasts Khrumov. "It's worth a thousand, but I gave... you won't believe it... two hundred and fifty! Only!"

At any other time the guests would greet this news with indifference, but now they voice surprise and do not believe it. In the end they all flock in a crowd to the vestibule to look at the coat, and they look until the doctor's assistant, Mikyeshka, surreptitiously carries out of the entrance hall five empty bottles... When the boiled sturgeon is served, Marfutkin remembers that he left his cigar case in the sleigh, and goes to the stables. So as not to feel lonely, he takes with him the deacon, who conveniently feels it necessary to check on his horse...

In the evening of that same day, Lyubov Petrovna is sitting in her boudoir, writing a letter to an old St Petersburg friend:

"Today, as in previous years," she writes among other things, "I had a *panikhida* for my deceased husband. All my neighbours were at the *panikhida*. Crude, simple people, but how kind-hearted! I gave them quite a feast, but of course, as in other years, without a drop of strong drink. Since he died of over-indulgence, I have vowed to promote temperance in our area, and in that way to atone for his sin. To further this temperance, I started in my own home. Father Yevmeny, delighted at my mission, assists me in word and deed. Ah, *ma chère*, if you could only know how those oafs love me! After breakfast, the council chairman Marfutkin squeezed my hand, held it for a long time to his lips and, comically shaking his head, started to cry: there was strong feeling, but no words! Father Yevmeny, that delightful little old man, sat down next to me and, gazing tearfully at me, for a long time blubbered about something, like a child. I couldn't understand what he was saying, but I can understand genuine feeling. The police inspector, that handsome man I wrote to you about, knelt before me and wanted to read some verses of his composition (he is our poet), but... he wasn't able to... he swayed and fell... Even a giant is capable of emotion... You can imagine my delight! It did not end, however, without trouble. The poor chairman of the provincial assembly, Alalykin, a stout, apoplectic man, felt ill and lay unconscious on the sofa for two hours. He had to have water poured over him… I was grateful to Doctor Dvornyagin: he had brought from his pharmacy a bottle of brandy and moistened the patient's brow, after which the man soon regained consciousness and was taken away…"

The Mother-in-Law as Go-Between

THIS OCCURRED ON A BEAUTIFUL MORNING, exactly a month after the wedding of Mishel Puzyryev and Lisa Mamunina. When Mishel had drunk his morning coffee and was looking for his hat in order to leave for work, his mother-in-law came into his study.

"I shall detain you, Mishel, for not more than five minutes," she said. "Don't frown, my friend... I know that a son-in-law doesn't like to talk to his mother-in-law, but it seems that I... get along with you, Mishel. We are not son-in-law and mother-in-law, but intelligent people... We have much in common... Isn't that so?"

The two settled down on the sofa.

"What can I do for you, *Mütterchen*?"*

"You are an intelligent man, Mishel, very intelligent; I also... am not stupid... We understand each other, I hope. I have been meaning already for a long time to have a talk with you, *mon petit*...* Tell me frankly, for the sake of... for the sake of all that's holy, what you want to do with my daughter."

Her son-in-law looked wide-eyed at her.

"You know, I agree with you..." she said. "Very well! But why? Learning is a good thing... it's impossible without literature... Poetry! I understand! It's good if a woman is educated... I myself was educated, I understand... But why go to extremes, *mon ange*?"*

"What do you mean? I don't quite understand you..."

"I don't understand your attitude towards my Lisa! You married her, but is she really a wife to you, a friend? She is your victim! Learning, books, various theories... All these are very good things, but, my dear, don't you forget that she is my daughter! I shall not allow it! She is my flesh and blood! You are destroying her! Not even a month has passed from the day of your wedding, yet she's already as thin as a rake! All day she sits at home with a book, reads these stupid magazines! She copies some papers! Is this really a woman's work? You don't take her out, don't let her live! With you she doesn't mix in society, doesn't dance! It's unbelievable! Not once in all this time has she been at a ball! Not once!"

"She hasn't once been to a ball because she herself hasn't wanted to go. Why don't you talk to her yourself. You'll learn what her opinion is of your balls and dances. No, *ma chère*! She hates your idleness! If she sits whole days at a book, or at work, then believe me, no one will change her behaviour... I love her for that, too... So now I bid you farewell, and ask you not to interfere in our relations in the future. Lisa herself will talk to me if it is necessary to say anything..."

"Do you think so? Do you really not see how meek and silent she is? Love has tied her tongue! Were it not for me, you would be a burden to her, my dear sir! Yes indeed! You are a tyrant, a despot! Be so good as to change your behaviour... today!"

"I don't want to listen to you..."

"You don't want to? Then you don't have to! It doesn't matter! I wouldn't even have started talking to you, were it not for Lisa! I pity her! She prevailed upon me to have a talk with you!"

"Well, you're lying about that... That's really a lie, admit it..."

"A lie? So have a look, heartless soul!"

His mother-in-law leapt up and pulled the door handle. The door swung open, and Mishel saw his Lisa. She was standing on the threshold, wringing her hands and sobbing. Her pretty little face was all in tears. Mishel leapt up to her...

"You heard? So tell her then! Perhaps she'll believe her daughter!"

"Mama... Mama tells the truth," Lisa wailed. "I can't bear this life... I'm suffering..."

"Hm... Well now! It's strange... But why did you yourself not talk to me about it?"

"I... I... you would get angry..."

"But surely you yourself constantly railed against idleness! You said that you loved me only for my beliefs, that you found the life

42

around you repugnant. And I fell in love with you for that! Before the wedding you despised, hated that empty life! So how do you explain such a change?"

"I feared then that you would not marry me... Dear Mishel! Let's go today to Marya Petrovna's *jour fixe*!"* And Lisa fell on Mishel's chest.

"Well, so you see! Are you convinced now?" said his mother-in-law, triumphantly leaving the study...

"Ah, you are a fool," groaned Mishel.

"Who's a fool?" asked Lisa.

"The one who was mistaken!..."

In Rented Rooms

"LISTEN, DEAR SIR!" said Colonel Nashatyrin's wife, who was lodging in room 47. She was red-faced and spraying saliva as she confronted the landlord. "Either give me another room or I shall leave your damned place entirely! It's a den of iniquity! For goodness' sake, I have grown-up daughters, and day and night they only hear disgusting language. Whoever heard of such a thing? Day and night! He sometimes comes out with things that make you sick to hear! Just like a cabman! It's good that my daughters still don't understand anything, otherwise I would have to take them out into the street... Even now he's saying something! You listen!"

"I, my dear fellow, know an even better story," came a hoarse bass voice from the next room. "Do you remember Lieutenant Druzhkov? Well, then, it was the same Druzhkov who once potted the yellow ball in the corner and, as usual, you know, lifted his leg high. Suddenly there was a ripping sound! We thought at first that he had torn the cloth on the billiard table, but when we looked closer, my dear fellow, the whole seam of his United States had come apart. He had lifted his leg so high, the rogue, that not a single stitch remained... Ha-ha-ha. And there were ladies present at the time... Among them the wife of that creep – Second-Lieutenant Okurin. Okurin was enraged. How, he said, could Druzhkov dare to behave so indecently in the presence of his wife? One word led to another... You know what people are like... Okurin sent seconds to Druzhkov, but Druzhkov was not so stupid and said... ha-ha-ha... and said: 'Let him send his seconds not to me, but to the tailor who sewed me these trousers. He's surely the one to blame!' Ha-ha-ha... Ha-ha-ha!"

Lilya and Mila, the colonel's daughters, who were sitting by the window supporting their chubby cheeks with their fists, lowered their astonished eyes and blushed.

"Now, have you heard?" continued Mrs Nashatyrin, turning to the landlord. "And is this, according to you, nothing? I, dear sir, am a colonel's wife! My husband is a military chief! I shall not allow some cabman, almost in my presence, to say such disgusting things!"

"He's not a cabman, madam, but Staff-Captain Kikin... of the nobility, in fact."

"If he has forgotten his nobility to such a degree that he swears like a cabman, then he deserves even more contempt! However, don't try to justify his behaviour, but kindly take action!"

"But what on earth can I do, madam? You are not the only one complaining: everyone's complaining – but what can I do about him? I go to his room and try to reprimand him: 'Hannibal Ivanych! For God's sake! You ought to be ashamed!' – and he immediately raises his fists and says things like: 'Go to hell!' – and so on. It's disgraceful! He wakes up in the morning and goes along the corridor in only, excuse me, his underwear. Or else he picks up a revolver when drunk and fires bullets into the wall. During the day he swills wine, and at night he plays cards... And after cards he fights... I feel ashamed when I think of the other guests!"

"Why don't you throw the scoundrel out?"

"How can I get rid of such a man? He owes for three months, but I no longer ask for money, just beg him to do me a favour and leave... The judge ordered him to vacate his room, but he appealed, and it went to the higher court, and so he keeps delaying... It's a disaster, simple as that! Lord, but what a man! Young, handsome, clever... When he's not drunk, you couldn't wish for a better man. The other day he was not drunk and spent the day writing letters to his parents."

"Poor parents!" sighed the colonel's wife.

"Poor indeed! Is it really pleasant to have such an idler for a son? He is scolded and driven out of rooms, and there isn't a day when he isn't sued for some scandal. What grief!"

"His poor, unfortunate wife!" sighed the colonel's wife.

"He's not married, madam. What chance is there of that? He has enough to do looking after himself – and thank God for that…"

The colonel's wife paced back and forth in the room.

"Not married, you say?" she asked.

"No indeed, madam."

The colonel's wife again began to pace the room, and fell to thinking.

"Hm!… Not married…" she murmured thoughtfully. "Hm!… Lilya and Mila, don't sit by the window – there is a draught! What a pity! A young man, and so undisciplined! And why? A lack of good influence! No mother, who would… Not married? Well… there you are… Please be so good," the colonel's wife went on, still thinking, "as to go to him and ask on my behalf that he refrain from bad language… Say that the wife of Colonel Nashatyrin asked… Say she is staying with her daughters in room 47… has come from her estate…"

"I shall do so, madam."

"Say exactly that: the colonel's wife with her daughters. Let him at least come and apologize… We are always in after dinner. Oh, Mila, close the window!"

"But why, Mother, do you need this… drunkard?" drawled Lilya when the landlord left. "Who on earth have you invited? A drunk, a brawler, a wastrel!"

"Oh, don't talk like that, *ma chère*!… You always talk like that, and, well… sit here! Why? Whoever he may be, you shouldn't pass up the opportunity. All grains are for the use of man.* Who knows?" sighed the Colonel's wife, looking thoughtfully at her daughters. "Perhaps your fate lies here. Put on your best clothes, just in case…"

A Joke

A BRIGHT WINTER MIDDAY... There is a heavy frost, and Nadenka, who is holding me by the arm, has silvery curls of hoar frost on her temples and on the down above her upper lip. We are standing on a high hill. From our feet to the ground at the bottom stretches an even slope on which the sun is reflected as in a mirror. Next to us is a little sledge covered with bright-red cloth.

"Let's go down, Nadezhda Petrovna!" I entreat her. "Just once! I assure you, we'll be all right."

But Nadenka is afraid. The slope from her little galoshes to the bottom of the icy hill seems to her a terrifying, immeasurably deep abyss. She freezes and holds her breath on looking down, when I only suggest that she sit on the sledge. What she would do if she were to venture to fly into the abyss! She would die, go mad.

"I urge you!" I say. "You mustn't be afraid! Try and understand – it's faint-heartedness, cowardice!"

Nadenka finally gives way, and I see from her face that she does so with fear for her life. I seat her, pale and shaking, on the sledge, my arm around her, and together we fly down into the abyss.

The sledge flies like a bullet. The biting air cuts into our faces, howling and whistling in our ears, tears into us, painfully stinging with fury, wanting to rip our heads from our shoulders. The pressure of the wind makes it hard to breathe. It seems as if the Devil himself has caught us in his claws and with a roar is dragging us to hell. Our surroundings merge into one long, swiftly flowing streak... At any moment – even in an instant, it seems – we should perish!

"I love you, Nadya!" I say in a low voice.

The sledge begins to run more and more slowly. The roar of the wind and the whizzing of the sledge runners is no longer so terrifying. Our breathing returns to normal, and finally we are at the bottom. Nadenka is half dead with fright. She is pale, barely breathing... I help her to rise.

"I wouldn't do that again for anything," she says, looking at me with wide, terror-filled eyes. "Not for anything in the world! I almost died!"

A little later, coming to her senses, she looks me questioningly in the eye: did I utter those four words, or was it just the noise of the wind that she heard? I stand next to her, smoking a cigarette, looking attentively at my glove.

She takes my arm, and for a long time we walk around the hill. The uncertainty clearly gives her no peace. Were those words said, or not? Yes or no? Yes or no? It was a question of self-esteem, honour, life, happiness – a very important question, the most important in the world. Impatiently, sadly, Nadenka levels at me a penetrating look, talks irrelevantly, waiting to see whether I speak. Oh, what a play of emotions there is on that dear face – what a play of emotions! I see she is struggling with herself, wants to say something, to ask something, but cannot find the words. She is awkward, frightened, agitated by her joy...

"Do you know what?" she says, not looking at me.

"What?" I ask.

"Let's... slide down again."

We climb the stairs up the hill. Again I put the pale, trembling Nadenka on the sledge, again we fly into the terrifying abyss, again the wind roars and the sledge runners whizz, and again when the sledge is flying at its fastest and noisiest, I say in a low voice:

"I love you, Nadenka!"

When the sledge stops, Nadenka casts a glance at the hill down which we had only just raced, then looks for a long time into my face, listening with detachment and indifference to my voice. Everything, everything – even her muff and hood, all her little figure – conveys the most extreme puzzlement. And on her face is written:

"What's this all about? Who uttered those words? Did he, or did I only imagine them?"

This uncertainty unsettles and exasperates her. The poor girl does not reply to my questions. She frowns, and looks as if about to burst into tears.

"Shouldn't we go home?" I ask.

"Well, I... I like this sledging," she says, blushing. "Couldn't we go down once more?"

She "liked" the sledging, but nevertheless, sitting on the sledge, she was, as before, pale, barely breathing from fear, trembling. We descend a third time, and I see how she looks me in the face, watching my lips. But I press my handkerchief to my lips, cough and when we are halfway down manage to say:

"I love you, Nadya!"

And the mystery remains a mystery! Nadenka is silent, thinking about something. I take her home from the sledging. She tries to walk slowly, slackening her pace, still waiting to see whether I'm going to say those words to her. And I see how her heart is aching, how she is trying hard not to say:

"It cannot be that the wind said those words! And I don't want the wind to have said them!"

The next morning I receive a note: "If you go sledging today, then call for me. N." From this day on, Nadenka and I start to go sledging every day – and, hurtling down on the sledge, each time I utter in a low voice the very same words:

"I love you, Nadya!"

Nadenka soon gets used to these words, as to wine or morphine. She is unable to live without them. True enough, it's still frightening to race down the hill, but now fear and danger add especial fascination to the words of love – words which, as before, form a mystery and torment the soul. The two suspects are still the wind and I. She does not know which of the two makes a confession of love to her, but it seems to be all the same to her: it doesn't matter from what vessel you drink, as long as you get drunk.

Once, at midday, I set off sledging alone. Mingling with the crowd, I see how Nadenka comes to the hill, how she seeks me with her eyes... Then she timidly goes up the steps... It's frightening to go alone, oh, how frightening! She is pale, like the snow, trembling, walking as if to her execution, but she goes, goes without looking back, resolutely. Evidently she has at last decided to experiment: would she hear those amazing, sweet words when I am not there? I see how she, pale, her mouth open with terror, sits on the sledge, closes her eyes and, having bid farewell to the earth for ever, sets off. "Zh...zh...zh..." whiz the runners. I do not know whether Nadenka hears those words... I see only how she rises from the sledge exhausted, weak. And it is evident from her face that she herself does not know whether she heard anything or not. Fear, while she was racing down, robbed her of the ability to hear, to distinguish sounds, to understand...

Now the spring month of March arrives... The sun becomes more welcoming. Our icy hill grows dark, loses its brilliance and finally melts. We stop sledging. There is nowhere any more for poor Nadenka to hear those words, and indeed no one to utter them, as there is no longer a wind to be heard, and I am preparing to leave for St Petersburg – for a long time, probably for ever.

Once, two days before my departure, I am sitting at dusk in the garden that is separated from the house in which Nadenka lives by a high fence topped with nails... It is still quite cold, with snow around the pile of manure and the trees not yet in bud, but already there is the scent of spring and the noisy cawing of rooks as they settle down for the night. I approach the fence, and for a long time peer through a crack. I see how Nadenka comes out on the porch and directs a doleful, melancholy look at the sky... The spring breeze blows straight into her pale, despondent face... It reminds her of the wind that roared at us on the hill when she heard those four words; she grows very sad, and a tear crawls down her cheek... The poor girl stretches out both arms, as if asking the wind to bring her once again those words. And I, who have been waiting for a gust of wind, say in a low voice:

"I love you, Nadya!"

My God, what happens to Nadenka! She cries out, breaks into a wide smile and, joyful, happy, so beautiful, stretches out her arms to greet the wind.

And I go to pack...

That was long ago. Now Nadenka is married. She married, whether by choice or under compulsion – it's all the same – the secretary of the nobility guardianship, and now has three children. That time, when we once went sledging together and the wind brought her the words "I love you, Nadenka", has not been forgotten; for her it is now the happiest, most affecting and wonderful memory in life...

But now that I am older I no longer know why I said those words, why I joked like that...

On the Nail

ALONG NEVSKY PROSPEKT came trudging a group of colleagues from work – collegiate registrars and provincial secretaries. They were led by Struchkov, who was taking them home to celebrate his name day.

"Well, we're really going to have a feast now, my friends!" Struchkov said, as if daydreaming. "How we'll gorge! The little wife has prepared a *pirog*. I myself went to buy the flour last night. There is brandy... Vorontsovsky vodka... The wife is probably tired of waiting!"

Struchkov lived at the world's end. They walked and walked to his place, and finally arrived. They entered the hall. They sensed the smell of the *pirog* and roast goose.

"What do you think of that?" asked Struchkov, giggling with pleasure. "Take off your coats, gentlemen! Put them on the trunk! But where is Katya? Hey, Katya! It's all about to start! Akulina, come and help the guests take off their coats!"

"But what is this?" asked one of the guests, pointing at the wall.

On a big nail which was sticking out of the wall hung a new dress cap with a shining peak and a cockade. The friends looked at each other and went pale.

"It's his cap!" they whispered. "Is... he here?!"

"Yes, he is here," muttered Struchkov. "With Katya... Let's leave, gentlemen. We'll wait a bit somewhere in a tavern, until he goes."

The friends did up their overcoats, went out and strolled to a tavern.

"It smells of goose at your place because the goose* himself is there!" sniggered the assistant archivist. "The Devil brought him! Will he leave soon?"

"Yes. He never stays more than two hours. But I'm hungry! At home, we'll first have some vodka and snack on sprats... Then we'll do it again. After the second vodka we'll immediately have the *pirog*. Otherwise we'll lose our appetite... My wife makes good *pirog*. There will be *shchi*..."

"Have you bought sardines?"

"Two tins. Four kinds of salami... The wife is probably also hungry. He just came uninvited, the devil!"

They stayed in the tavern for an hour and a half, drank a glass of tea each to pass the time and again went to Struchkov's. They entered the hall. The smell was stronger than before. Through the half-open kitchen door the friends saw the goose and a bowl of salted cucumbers. Akulina was taking something out of the oven.

"Bad luck again, brothers!"

"Why is that?"

The guests' stomachs tightened with grief: hunger is no friend,* and on the wretched nail hung a marten-fur hat.

"It's Prokatilov's hat," said Struchkov. "Let's leave, friends! We'll wait somewhere... He won't stay long..."

"And that bastard has such a pretty wife!" A husky bass voice was heard from the sitting room.

"Fools' luck, Your Excellency!" responded a woman's voice.

"Let's leave!" groaned Struchkov.

They went again to the tavern. They ordered beer.

"Prokatilov is a big shot!" The friends began to comfort Struchkov. "He'll stay an hour at your place... but you'll have ten years of bliss. You're fortunate, brother! Why be upset? You don't have to be upset."

"I know I don't have to be, even without your saying it. That's not the point! What's upsetting me is that I'm hungry!"

An hour and a half later they went again to Struchkov's. The marten hat still hung on the nail. Again they had to withdraw.

It was only after seven in the evening that the nail was free and they were able to get down to the *pirog*. The *pirog* was dry, the *shchi* warm, the goose overcooked. Struchkov's day was spoilt! They ate, however, with gusto.

My Nana*

I T HAPPENED when I was not yet an unknown man of letters and my prickly whiskers were not yet even barely noticeable tufts...

It was a fine spring evening. I returned from the dacha settlement's *krug*,* where we had danced like ones possessed. In my youthful organism, to express it figuratively, it was not stone against stone, tongue rising against tongue, kingdom against kingdom.* In my passionate heart the most desperate love was glowing and seething. The love was burning, sharp, gripping my soul – in short, it was first love. I fell in love with a tall, statuesque lady, twenty-three years old, with a foolish but pretty face and with lovely little dimples on her cheeks. I fell in love with those dimples, and with the blond hair that fell in ringlets onto lovely shoulders from under a wide-brimmed straw hat... Ah, in short! Returning from the *krug*, I collapsed on my bed and began to moan like one crushed. An hour later I was sitting at the table, and, trembling all over, having spoilt a whole quire of paper, composed a letter as follows:

"Valerya Andreyevna! I am very little acquainted with you, almost unknown, but this should not serve as an obstacle on the path to the achievement of my desired goal. Omitting fine-sounding phrases, I shall get straight to the point: I love you! Yes, I love you, and love you more than life! It is not hyperbole. I am honest, I work." (There follows a long description of my virtues.) "My life is not dear to me. If not today, then tomorrow; if not tomorrow, then in a year... does it matter? On my table, two feet away from my chest, lies a revolver (six-barrelled). I am in your hands. If the life of a man passionately in love is dear to you, then reply. I await your reply. Your Palasha knows me. You may reply through her." Signed: "The one who was standing opposite you yesterday" (etc., etc...)

"PS: Take pity on me!"

After sealing the letter, I placed the revolver on the table in front of me – more as a "fantasy" than with thoughts of suicide – and went through the settlement to find a post box. The post box was found, and the letter dropped.

This is what happened to my letter, as Palasha later told me. The next morning, at eleven o'clock, Palasha, on the arrival of the postman, put my letter on a silver tray and took it to her mistress's bedroom. Valerya Andreyevna was lying under a light silk blanket, lazily stretching. She had only just awoken and was smoking her first cigarette. Her lovely eyes were capriciously screwed up from the rays of the sun that were importunately shining through the window on her face. Seeing my letter, she assumed a sour expression.

"Who is this from?" she asked. "You read it, Palasha! I don't like to read these letters. They're all silly..."

Palasha opened my letter and began to read it. The more she became absorbed in the reading of my composition, the rounder and wider became the eyes of her mistress. When she got to the part about the revolver, Valerya Andreyevna opened her mouth and looked with horror at Palasha.

"What does this mean?" she asked in perplexity.

Palasha read it once again. Valerya Andreyevna began to blink.

"So who is this? Who is he? And why does he write like this?" she asked tearfully. "Who is he?"

Palasha remembered and described me.

"Ah! But why does he write this? How could he do it? What on earth can I do? I really can't, Palasha! I suppose he's rich?"

Palasha, to whom I had given all my savings as a tip, thought and said that I was, probably, rich.

"I just can't! Today, you see, Alexei Matveich will be with me, tomorrow the baron... On Thursday will be Romb... When can I receive him? Maybe during the day?"

"Grigory Grigorych promised to be with you this afternoon..."

"Well, so you see! How can I? Well, tell him... Let him... Let him at least come for tea today. I can't do more..."

Valerya Andreyevna was on the point of tears. For the first time in her life she learnt what a revolver could do, and learnt it from my letter! I was with her in the evening and had tea. I drank four glasses, though I suffered... To my delight it was raining, and her Alexei Matveich did not come to see her. In the end I was exultant.

Bad Weather

H EAVY DROPS OF RAIN were lashing against the dark windows. It was one of those nasty country rains which usually, once they have started, continue for a long time, for weeks, until the frozen country dweller, having got used to it, is plunged into complete apathy. It was cold; there was a sharp, unpleasant dampness in the air. The mother-in-law of the barrister Kvashin and his wife, Nadezhda Filippovna, dressed in waterproofs and shawls, were sitting at the dinner table in the dining room. On the face of the old lady was written satisfaction that she, praise God, was well fed and well dressed, healthy, had married her only daughter to a good man and could now play patience with a clear conscience; her daughter – a short, plump blonde of about twenty with a mild anaemic face – was sitting with her elbows on the table, reading a book; judging by her eyes, she was not so much reading as thinking her own thoughts, which were not in the book. Both were silent. All that could be heard were the noise of the rain and, from the kitchen, the drawn-out yawns of the cook.

Kvashin himself was not at home. On rainy days he did not come to the dacha, but stayed in town; the damp country weather badly affected his bronchitis and prevented him from working. He was of the opinion that the sight of a grey sky and drops of rain on the windows sapped the energy and promoted depression. In town, however, where there are many comforts, bad weather goes almost unnoticed.

After two games of patience, the old lady shuffled the cards and looked at her daughter.

"I wonder if there will be good weather tomorrow and our Alexei Stepanych will come," she said. "He hasn't been here for four days... This weather is the scourge of God."

Nadezhda Filippovna looked with indifference at her mother, rose and began to pace back and forth.

"The barometer was rising yesterday," she said thoughtfully, "but today they say it's again falling."

The old lady laid out the cards in three long rows and shook her head.

"Do you miss him?" she asked, looking at her daughter.

"Of course!"

"I can see that. How can you not miss him? He hasn't been here for four days. Usually, in May... two days at the most... well, three... but now... is it a joke?... the four days! I'm not married to him, and even I miss him. But yesterday, when I heard that the barometer was rising, I told the cook to slaughter a chicken and prepare a crucian for him, for Alexei Stepanych. He loves them. Your late father couldn't bear to look at fish, but he loves them. He always eats them with gusto."

"My heart aches for him," said her daughter. "We are bored, but surely, Mama, he is even more bored."

"He must be! All day long in court, and at night alone in an empty flat like a recluse."

"And what is terrible, Mama, is that he is alone there, without servants; there is no one to put on the samovar or to bring water. Why didn't he engage a valet for the summer months? And why did he rent this dacha at all, if he dislikes it? I said to him: it's not necessary, so don't rent it. 'It's for your health,' he said. But how is it for my health? I'm suffering because he's suffering such torments on my account."

Looking over her mother's shoulder, the daughter noticed a mistake in the game of patience, leant over the table and began to correct it. Silence set in. Both looked at the cards and imagined how their Alexei Stepanych was sitting all alone in town in his gloomy, empty study and working: hungry, exhausted, yearning for his family...

"But do you know what, Mama?" Nadezhda Filippovna said suddenly, her eyes lighting up. "If the weather is the same tomorrow,

I'll take the morning train to see him in town! At least I could see how he is – have a look at him, give him tea."

And both were astonished at how this idea, so simple and easily effected, had not occurred to them before. It was only a half-hour trip to town, and then about twenty minutes in a cab. They chatted a little longer and, satisfied, went to bed together in the same room.

"Oh… oh… oh… Lord, forgive us sinners!" sighed the old lady when the clock in the hall struck two. "I can't sleep!"

"You are not asleep, Mama?" asked her daughter in a whisper. "And I'm still thinking about Alyosha. If only he won't ruin his health in town! He dines and has breakfast God knows where, in restaurants and in taverns."

"I was thinking about that myself," sighed the old woman. "Save and preserve him, Mother of God. And the rain, the rain!"

In the morning the rain was no longer beating on the windows, but the sky, as before, was grey. The trees had a sad look, and each gust of wind brought water spraying from the leaves. The tracks of people's feet on the muddy paths, the ditches and the ruts, were full of water. Nadezhda Filippovna decided to go.

"Do give him my best regards," said the old lady, wrapping her daughter up. "Tell him not to become too involved in his cases… And he has to rest. He should keep his neck warm when he goes outside: what weather, God save us! And take him the chicken; food from home, even if it's cold, is much better than in a tavern."

Her daughter left, saying she would return on the evening train or the following morning.

But she returned much earlier, before dinner, when the old lady was sitting on the trunk in her bedroom and, dozing, was thinking about what she could cook for her son-in-law that evening.

On entering the room, her daughter, looking pale, upset, not saying a word, not taking off her hat, lowered herself on the bed and pressed her head to the pillow.

"What's the matter with you?" the old lady asked in astonishment. "Why so soon? Where is Alexei Stepanych?"

Nadezhda Filippovna raised her head and looked at her mother with dry, pleading eyes.

"He is deceiving me, Mama!" she said.

"Good Lord, Christ help you!" The old lady was frightened, and her cap slipped from her head. "Who is deceiving you? Lord, have mercy!"

"He is deceiving me, Mama!" repeated her daughter, and her chin began to tremble.

"Whatever makes you think that?" cried the old lady, turning pale.

"Our flat is locked. The porter said that Alyosha has not been home once these last five days. He isn't living at home! He's not at home! Not at home!"

She waved her hands and began to sob loudly, only uttering:

"He's not at home! Not at home!"

She became hysterical.

"What is all this?" muttered the old lady, horrified. "After all, just the day before yesterday he wrote that he never leaves the house! Where does he spend the night? Holy saints above!"

Nadezhda Filippovna felt faint and could not even take off her hat. As if drugged, she dully raised her eyes and convulsively seized her mother's arms.

"You found someone to believe: a porter!" said the old woman, fussing around her daughter and crying. "What a jealous girl! He is not deceiving you – and, anyway, how could he dare to deceive you? Are we really that sort of people? We may be of the merchant class, but he has no right, because you are his lawful wife! We could take him to court! I gave twenty thousand with you! You did have a dowry!"

And the old lady herself burst into tears and waved her arms, and also felt faint, and lay down on her trunk. Neither of them noticed, when blue patches appeared in the sky as the clouds thinned, how the first rays of the sun tentatively crept along the wet grass in the garden, how the sparrows joyfully began to hop around puddles in which the scudding clouds were reflected.

Kvashin arrived towards evening. Before leaving town he had called in at his flat and learnt from the porter that his wife had come in his absence.

"Well, here I am!" he said gaily, entering his mother-in-law's room and appearing not to notice the tearful, stern faces. "So here I am! We haven't seen each other for five days!"

He quickly kissed his wife's and mother-in-law's hands, and, with the look of a man who was glad to have finished hard work, collapsed into an armchair.

"Oof!" he said, expelling air from his lungs. "I really am so worn out! I can barely sit! Nearly five days... Day and night I've been living as if bivouacking! Can you imagine – I haven't been at the flat once! All the time I've been busy with the case of Shipunov and Ivanchikov; I had to work with Galdeyev, in his office annexed to the shop... I didn't eat, didn't drink, slept on a bench, all chilled to the bone... There wasn't a free minute – there wasn't even time to go to the flat. That's why, Nadyusha, I wasn't at home..."

And Kvashin, holding his sides as if his back was aching from overwork, gave a sidelong look at his wife and his mother-in-law in order to discover how they were reacting to his lie – or, as he preferred to call it, his "piece of diplomacy". His mother-in-law and wife looked at each other with joyous amazement, as if they had quite unexpectedly found a treasure they had lost... Both their faces beamed, their eyes shone...

"My dear boy," said his mother-in-law, leaping up. "Why on earth am I sitting here? Tea! Tea, quickly! Would you like something to eat?"

"Of course he would," said his wife, taking from her head a handkerchief moistened with vinegar. "Mama, quickly, bring the wine and *zakuski*!* Natalya, lay the table! Oh, my God, nothing is ready!"

And both of them, startled, happy, bustling about, began to run from room to room. The old lady could no longer look with a straight face at her daughter, who had slandered an innocent man, and her daughter felt ashamed...

Soon the table was laid. Kvashin, who smelt of Madeira and liqueurs and could hardly breathe from overeating, complained of hunger, forced himself to eat and kept talking about the case of Shipunov and Ivanchikov. His wife and mother-in-law could not take their eyes off his face and were thinking:

"How intelligent and kind he is! What an attractive man!"

"Excellent!" thought Kvashin as he lay down after supper on the big downy feather bed. "They may be of the merchant class, but all the same they have a charm of their own, and one can spend a day or two a week here with pleasure…"

He covered himself, got warm and said as he fell asleep:

"Excellent!"

At the Dacha

I LOVE YOU. You are my life, my happiness – everything! Forgive this confession, but I have not the strength to suffer and be silent. I ask not that my love be reciprocated, but that you have pity on me. Come to the old summer house at eight o'clock this evening... I consider it unnecessary to sign my name, but do not be wary of an anonymous writer. I am young, good-looking... what more could you want?

After reading this letter, dacha resident Pavel Ivanych Vykhodtsev, a family man of upright character, shrugged his shoulders and scratched his forehead in puzzlement.

"What the devil is this?" he thought. "I'm a married man, and suddenly such a strange... stupid letter! Who wrote it?"

Pavel Ivanych turned the letter over before his eyes, read it once again and swore.

"I love you..." he mimicked. "So you've found a little boy! I'm supposed to jump up and run to you in the summer house!... I, my dear girl, gave up these romances and *fleurs-d'amour* a long time ago... Hm! She must be some crazy woman, some good-for-nothing. Well, these women are so common! God forgive me, what a floozie a woman must be to write such a letter to a stranger – and a married man at that! Utter depravity!"

After eight years of married life, Pavel Ivanych had abandoned fine feelings and had not received a single letter, apart from greetings, and therefore, however he tried to brush it off, the above-quoted letter strongly perplexed and disturbed him.

An hour after receiving it, he was lying on the sofa and thinking:

"Of course, I am not a silly little boy, and will not run to this stupid rendezvous, but nevertheless it would be interesting to know who wrote it. Hm... It's doubtless a woman's handwriting... The letter is written sincerely, from the heart, and is therefore hardly likely to be a joke... Probably some lunatic or widow... Widows generally tend to be frivolous and eccentric. Hm... Who could it be?"

To answer this question was all the more difficult because in the whole dacha settlement Pavel Ivanych did not know a single woman except his wife.

"It's strange," he thought in perplexity. "'I love you'... When in Heaven's name was she able to fall in love? Amazing woman! To fall in love so impulsively, without even having met me or knowing what kind of man I am... She must be very young and romantic to be capable of falling in love after two or three sightings... But... who is she?"

Suddenly Pavel Ivanych remembered that the day before, and the one before that, when he was enjoying himself at the dacha settlement's dance, his path several times crossed with that of a young blonde girl in a light-blue dress and with a little snub nose. The blonde girl kept looking at him, and, when he sat on a bench, sat down next to him...

"Is she the one?" thought Vykhodtsev. "It can't be! Is it possible that a delicate, sensitive creature can fall in love with a seedy old codger like me? No, it's impossible!"

During dinner, Pavel Ivanych looked dully at his wife and reflected:

"She writes that she's young and good-looking... So she's not an old woman... Hm... Speaking frankly, to be honest, I am not yet so old and worn out that it's impossible to fall in love with me... My wife loves me! Beauty is in the eye of the beholder..."

"What are you thinking about?" asked his wife.

"Well... I have a slight headache," lied Pavel Ivanych.

He decided that it was stupid to pay attention to such a trifle as a love letter, and laughed at it and its writer, but – alas! – human weakness is strong. After dinner Pavel Ivanych lay on his bed and, instead of sleeping, thought:

"But, after all, perhaps she's hoping I'll come! What a silly fool! I can just imagine how she'll fret, and her bustle will be in a twist when she finds I am not in the summer house!... But I shall not go... To hell with her!"

But, I repeat, human weakness is strong.

"On the other hand, maybe I should go, out of curiosity..." he was thinking half an hour later. "Go and see from a distance what sort of joke this is... It would be interesting to see! Just for a laugh! Really, why not have a bit of fun, if a suitable opportunity arises?"

Pavel Ivanych rose from his bed and began to dress.

"Why are you dressing up like that?" asked his wife, noticing that he was putting on a clean shirt and fashionable tie.

"Well... I want to take a stroll... I have a slight headache... Hm..."

Pavel Ivanych prepared himself and, waiting until eight o'clock, left the house. When, before his eyes, he saw, in the flooding light of the setting sun, the brightly attired figures of the male and female dacha residents set against the light-green background, his heart began to pound.

"Which of them is she?" he thought, shyly casting sidelong looks at the faces of the female residents. "I don't see any blondes... Hm... If she wrote that she'll be in the summer house, then she must already be there..."

Vykhodtsev entered the tree-lined path, at the end of which could be seen the "old summer house" peeping out from behind the young leaves of tall lime trees... He quietly padded along to it...

"I'll look from a distance..." he thought, moving forward indecisively. "But what am I afraid of? After all, I'm not really going to a romantic rendezvous! What a... coward! Be bolder! But should I go into the summer house? Well, well... there's no need to!"

Pavel Ivanych's heart beat even more strongly... Involuntarily, against his own wishes, he suddenly visualized the semi-darkness of the summer house... Into his imagination flashed a shapely blonde in a light-blue dress and with a little snub nose... He imagined how she, ashamed of her love and trembling all over, would shyly come up to him, breathing passionately, and suddenly throw her arms around him.

"If I were not married, it wouldn't be a problem at all," he thought, chasing sinful thoughts from his mind. "On the other hand... it would not hurt to have the experience at least once in a lifetime – otherwise I shall die without discovering what sort of joke this is... And my wife... What does it matter to her? Thank God, for eight years I have not strayed a step from her... Eight years of irreproachable service! That's enough of her... it's irritating... I shall go and betray her out of spite!"

Trembling all over and holding his breath, Pavel Ivanych approached the summer house, which was covered in ivy and a wild vine, and peeped into it... It smelt of dampness and mildew...

"It seems there's no one here..." he thought, entering the summer house, and immediately he saw the silhouette of someone in the corner.

The silhouette was that of a man... Looking at him, Pavel Ivanych recognized him as his wife's brother, the student Mitya, who was staying with them at the dacha.

"Ah, it's you," he mumbled in a displeased tone, taking off his hat and sitting down.

"Yes, it's me..." replied Mitya.

A couple of minutes passed in silence...

"Excuse me, Pavel Ivanych," began Mitya, "but I would ask you to leave me alone... I'm thinking about my university thesis and... and the presence of anyone at all disturbs me..."

"You should go somewhere along a dark path," Pavel Ivanych suggested meekly. "It's easier to think in the fresh air, and besides... ah, I would like to have a nap here on the bench... It's not so hot here..."

"You may want to sleep, but I have to think about my thesis," muttered Mitya. "The thesis is more important..."

Another silence set in... Pavel Ivanych, who by now had given free rein to his imagination and kept hearing footsteps, suddenly leapt up and said in a pleading voice:

"Now, I beg you, Mitya! You are younger than I am, and have to indulge me... I am unwell and... and want to sleep... Go away!"

"This is selfish... Why is it essential for you to be here, and not me? I shall not leave, on principle..."

"But I'm begging you! I may be selfish, a despot, a fool... but I'm begging you! For once in my life I'm begging! Indulge me!"

Mitya shook his head...

"What a swine..." thought Pavel Ivanych. "Of course with him here my meeting can't take place! With him it's impossible!"

"Listen, Mitya," he said. "I'm asking you for the last time... Show that you are an intelligent, humane and educated man!"

"I don't understand why you're going on about it," said Mitya, shrugging. "I said I'm not leaving, and I'm not leaving. I'm staying here on principle..."

Just then, a woman's face with a snub nose peeped into the summer house...

Seeing Mitya and Pavel Ivanych, it frowned and disappeared...

"She's gone!" thought Pavel Ivanych, looking angrily at Mitya. "She saw this scoundrel and fled! My hopes are dashed!"

After waiting a little longer, Vykhodtsev rose, put on his hat and said:

"You're a swine, a scoundrel and a rogue! Yes! A swine! It's despicable and... and stupid! It's all over between us."

"Delighted!" muttered Mitya, also rising and putting on his hat. "Know that by your presence here just now you have played such a dirty trick on me that I shall not forgive you as long as I live!"

Pavel Ivanych left the summer house and, beside himself with fury, quickly strode to his dacha... Even the sight of the table laid for supper did not calm him.

"Once in a lifetime an opportunity arises," he thought in agitation, "and then I'm foiled! Now she's offended... broken!"

During supper Pavel Ivanych and Mitya looked at their plates and were gloomily silent... They loathed each other with all their soul.

"Why are you smiling?" Pavel Ivanych turned on his wife. "Only fools laugh for no reason!"

His wife looked at the angry face of her husband and burst out laughing...

"What was that letter you received this morning?" she asked.

"I?... There was no letter..." Pavel Ivanych was embarrassed. "You're imagining things... It's your imagination..."

"Come now, tell me! Confess that you received one! You see, I sent that letter to you! I give you my word – I sent it! Ha-ha!"

Pavel Ivanych turned red and bent down to his plate.

"Stupid trick," he muttered.

"But what else could I do? Judge for yourself... We had to have the floors cleaned this evening, and how could I get you out of the house? That was the only way to get you out... But don't be angry, you silly man... So that you wouldn't be bored in the summer house, I sent the same letter to Mitya! Mitya, were you in the summer house?"

Mitya smirked and stopped looking with hatred at his rival.

Nerves

D MITRI OSIPOVICH VAKSIN, an architect, returned from town deeply impressed by a spiritual seance he had recently attended. Undressing and lying down in his solitary bed (Madame Vaksina had gone to St Sergius),* Vaksin involuntarily began to recall all that he had heard and seen. Strictly speaking, it had not been a seance, but during the evening there had been some frightening conversations. Apropos of nothing, a certain young lady began to talk about reading the mind. From the mind they passed imperceptibly to spirits, from spirits to ghosts, from ghosts to those buried alive... A certain gentleman read a terrifying story about a corpse turning over in the grave. Vaksin himself asked for a saucer and showed the ladies how to communicate with spirits. Among others he summoned his uncle Klavdi Mironovich and asked him: "Is it time to transfer the house to my wife's name?" – to which his uncle replied: "All will be done in due course."

"Much is mysterious and... frightening in nature..." reflected Vaksin, lying under the blanket. "Corpses are not frightening, but the unknown..."

The clock struck one. Vaksin turned over and looked from under the blanket at the blue icon lamp. The light was flickering and barely illuminated the icon frame and big portrait of his uncle Klavdi Mironovich, which was hanging opposite the bed.

"What if in this semi-darkness the shade of Uncle were to appear?" flashed through Vaksin's mind. "No, it's impossible!"

Ghosts are a figment of the imagination, the product of imma-ture minds, but Vaksin nevertheless drew the blanket over his head and shut his eyes more tightly. In his imagination flashed the corpse that had turned over in the grave; images formed of his dead mother-in-law, of a comrade who had hanged himself, of a drowned maiden... Vaksin tried to banish gloomy thoughts from his mind, but however determinedly he drove them out, the clearer the images became, and the more frightening the thoughts. He became terrified.

"The devil knows what's happening... I'm as frightened as a child... It's silly!"

"Tick... tick... tick," went the clock in the next room. The watchman began to ring the bell in the village churchyard. The ringing was slow, mournful, and tugged at his soul... Cold shivers ran along the back of Vaksin's head and down his spine. It seemed as if someone were breathing heavily over his head, as if his uncle had come out of the frame and was bending over him. It became unbearably terrifying to Vaksin. He clenched his teeth out of fear and held his breath. Finally, when a maybug flew in the open window and started to drone over his bed, he could bear it no longer, and desperately pulled the bell.

"Demetri Osipych, *was wollen Sie*?"* the governess was heard saying a minute later behind the door.

"Oh, is it you, Rosalya Karlovna?" said Vaksin with relief. "Why do you trouble yourself? Gavrila could have—"

"You yourself let Hafrila go to town, and Glafira went out somewhere for the evening... There's no one at home... *Was wollen Sie doch*?"*

"Dear woman, I just wanted to say... Ah... Well, come in, don't be embarrassed. I'm in the dark..."

The stout, red-cheeked Rosalya Karlovna entered the bedroom and stopped in an expectant attitude.

"Sit down, my dear... You see, this is what I wanted..." said Vaksin.

"What can I ask her about?" he thought, giving a sidelong look at the portrait of his uncle and feeling that his mind was gradually returning to a state of calmness. "This is actually what I wanted to ask you about. When the man goes to town tomorrow, don't forget to ask him to... ah... call in to buy some cigarette papers... But do sit down!"

"Cigarette papers? Very well! *Was wollen Sie noch*?"*

"*Ich will...** I don't *will* anything, but... But do sit down! I'll think of something else..."

"It's improper for a maiden to stay in a man's room... I see you are a naughty man, Demetri Osipych... a deceiver... I understand... Men do not wake up because of cigarette papers... I understand..."

Rosalya Karlovna turned and left. Vaksin, somewhat reassured by his conversation with her, and ashamed of his cowardice, pulled the blanket over his head and closed his eyes. For about ten minutes he felt better, but then the same nonsense again began to invade his brain... He swore, groped for matches and, without opening his eyes, lit a candle. But even the light did not help. To Vaksin's fevered imagination it seemed that someone was looking at him from the corner of the room, and that his uncle's eyes were blinking.

"I'll call her again, the devil take her..." he decided. "I'll tell her I'm unwell... Ask for some drops."

Vaksin rang. There was no response. He rang again, and, as if in response to his ringing, the bells in the church began to ring. Gripped by fear, cold all over, he ran headlong from the bedroom and, crossing himself, angry with himself for his cowardice, fled barefoot and just in his nightclothes to the governess's room.

"Rosalya Karlovna!" he began in a trembling voice after knocking on the door. "Rosalya Karlovna! Are you... asleep? I... ah... am unwell... Drops!"

There was no response. Silence reigned all around...

"I'm begging you... understand? Begging! Why all this... great modesty, I don't understand, especially if a man is... unwell? Really, how *tsirlimanirli** you are! At your age..."

"I shall talk to your wife... He gives no peace to a virtuous girl... When I lived at Baron Anzig's, and he once came to me asking for matches, I understood... I understood at once what he meant by matches, and told the baroness... I am an honourable girl..."

"Oh, what the devil has this to do with your honour? I'm unwell... I'm asking for drops. Understand? I'm unwell!"

"Your wife is an honourable good woman, and you ought to love her. Yah! She is noble! I do not wish to be her enemy!"

"You're a fool, that's all! Understand? A fool!"

Vaksin leant against the doorpost, crossed his arms and waited for his fear to pass. He did not have the strength to return to his room, where the icon lamp was flickering and his uncle was looking down from the frame, but to stand by the door of the governess in just his nightclothes was embarrassing in every way. What was to be done? The clock struck two, but the fear had not passed and was not abating. It was dark in the corridor, and something dark seemed to be looking at him from every corner. Vaksin turned his face to the doorpost, and at once it seemed to him that someone pulled him gently by his nightshirt from behind and touched his shoulder...

"The devil take it... Rosalya Karlovna!"

There was no response. Vaksin hesitantly opened the door and looked into the room. The virtuous German was sleeping serenely. The little night light illuminated in relief her stout, healthily breathing body. Vaksin entered the room and sat down on the wicker trunk that was standing by the door. In the presence of a living, even if sleeping being, he felt better.

"Let her sleep, the silly foreigner," he thought. "I'll sit next to her, and when dawn breaks I'll leave... It gets light early these days."

Waiting for dawn, Vaksin curled up on the trunk, placed his hand under his head and fell to thinking: "That's what nerves do for you, though! A man may be mature, rational, but nevertheless... the devil knows what it's all about! It's shameful even..."

Soon, having got used to the quiet, measured breathing of Rosalya Karlovna, he completely calmed down...

At six o'clock in the morning, Vaksin's wife, having returned from St Sergius and not finding her husband in their bedroom, went to the governess to ask her for some change in order to pay the cabman. Entering the German woman's room, she saw a strange sight: on the bed, all sprawled out from the heat, Rosalya Karlovna was sleeping, and two yards away from her, on the wicker trunk,

curled up like a *kalatch*,* deep in the sleep of the righteous and
snoring loudly, lay her husband. He was barefoot and in just his
nightclothes. What his wife said, and how stupid the face of her
husband looked when he awoke, I shall leave to others to describe.
I, however, powerless as I am, lay down my pen.

A Good Outcome

A T THE HOME of senior conductor Stychkin, on one of his off-duty days, sat Lyubov Grigoryevna, a staid, rough-complexioned lady of about forty who occupied herself in match-making and many other things which it is pleasant to speak about only in a whisper. Stychkin, somewhat embarrassed but, as always, serious, confident and stern, was walking back and forth in the room, smoking a cigar and saying:

"I am very pleased to meet you. Semyon Ivanovich recom-mended you with the suggestion that you might be able to help me in a delicate, very important matter concerning my happiness. I am already, Lyubov Grigoryevna, fifty-two years old, an age at which many already have grown-up children. My position is secure. Though I do not have a great fortune, I am able to keep a loved one and children. I can tell you, between us, that besides my salary, I also have money in the bank, which I saved because of my way of life. I am a reliable, sober man; I lead a life of regularity and conformity, and can be an example to many. But only one thing I do not have: my own domestic hearth and a companion for life, and I lead the life of some kind of roaming Hungarian, going from place to place without any pleasure and with no one to turn to – and, whenever I'm ill, having no one even to give me water and so on. Besides that, Lyubov Grigoryevna, a married man always has a greater position in society than a bachelor... I am a man of the educated class, with money, but if you look at me from a certain standpoint, who am I? A solitary, lonely man, just like some kind of Catholic priest. And that is why I would very much like to enter into the bonds of Hymen – that is, into lawful marriage with some suitable person."

"An excellent idea!" sighed the matchmaker.

"I am a single man and know no one in this town. Where shall I go and to whom turn to if I don't know any people? So that is why Semyon Ivanovich advised me to turn to someone who is a specialist in this field and whose profession it is to discuss people's happiness. And that is why I most earnestly beg you, Lyubov Grigoryevna, to give your assistance in arranging my future. You know all the marriageable women in town, and for you it would be easy to find me a match."

"It's possible…"

"Please have something to drink…"

With a practised gesture the matchmaker raised a glass of vodka to her mouth and drank without wincing.

"It's possible," she repeated, "but what kind of bride would you like, Nikolai Nikolayich?"

"What, me? Whatever destiny sends my way."

"Of course it's a matter of destiny, but surely everyone has his taste. One loves a brunette, another a blonde."

"Do you see, Lyubov Grigoryevna," said Stychkin, sighing with an air of importance. "I am a positive man, with character. For me, beauty – and outward appearance in general – plays a secondary role, because, as you yourself know, one can't drink water from a face,* and a beautiful wife gives a lot of trouble. So I suggest that the chief attribute in a woman is not what is on the outside, but rather what is found within – that is, that she have a soul, and other qualities. Help yourself, please… Of course it is very pleasant if a wife is a little plump, but for mutual happiness this is not so important: the most important thing is the intellect. Strictly speaking, it is not even necessary for a woman to have intellect, because if she has intellect, she will have big ideas about herself and will entertain various ideals. Certainly it is not possible nowadays to be without education, but there are different kinds of education. It's nice if a wife speaks French and German, and other languages, very nice – but what is the use of this if she doesn't know, for instance, how to sew on a button for you? I am of the educated class, and would mix with Prince Kanityelin, I may say, the same as I do with you now, but I have a simple character. I need a simpler woman. But more important than anything is that she respect me and feel that I make her happy."

"It's a common wish."

"Well, now, concerning essentials... I don't need a rich woman. I shall not allow myself to be so base as to marry money. I do not wish to eat my wife's bread, but that she eat mine, and that she knows it. But I do not need a pauper, either. Though I am a man of means, and though I marry not from self-interest, but for love, it's impossible for me to take a pauper, because, as you know, everything now has gone up in price, and there will be children."

"It's possible to find a woman with a dowry," said the matchmaker.

"Please have some more."

There was a five-minute silence. The matchmaker sighed, gave a sidelong look at the conductor and asked:

"So then, my dear man... As you're a bachelor, maybe you'll need... I have a few girls of good quality. One is French, and another Greek. Very worthy."

The conductor thought and said:

"No, thank you. Seeing that you are so forthcoming, allow me to ask now: how much do you charge for the trouble you go to, finding brides?"

"I only need a little. I usually get twenty-five roubles and material for a dress, and am grateful for that... But for a dowry, there's an extra charge."

Stychkin crossed his arms over his chest and began to think in silence. Having thought, he sighed and said:

"It's expensive..."

"It's not at all expensive, Nikolai Nikolayich! Before, when there were more weddings, I used to charge less, but these days – how much can I earn? If in a good month I earn fifty roubles, I praise God. Otherwise, my dear sir, I don't make anything from weddings."

Stychkin looked at the matchmaker in puzzlement and shrugged.

"Hm!… But is fifty roubles really not enough?" he asked.

"Of course it's not enough! Before, I sometimes earned more than a hundred."

"Hm!… I never expected that this business could bring in such a sum. Fifty roubles! Not every man makes so much! Please help yourself…"

The matchmaker drank without wincing. Stychkin silently examined her from head to foot and said:

"Fifty roubles… That's six hundred roubles a year… Do please have some more… With such an income, you know, Lyubov Grigoryevna, it would not be hard to make a good match for yourself…"

"Do you mean me?" laughed the matchmaker. "I'm old…"

"Not at all… You have a fine figure, and a plump, white face, and so on."

The matchmaker felt embarrassed. Stychkin also felt embarrassed, and sat down next to her.

"You can still be very attractive to a man," he said. "If a suitable husband were to appear – dependable, steady, thrifty – he with his salary and you with your earnings, he may find you very pleasing, and you would live happily together…"

"God knows what you are saying, Nikolai Nikolayich…"

"What do you mean? I meant nothing…"

There was silence. Stychkin started to blow his nose loudly; the matchmaker flushed and, looking at him bashfully, asked:

"How much do you earn, Nikolai Nikolayich?"

"Who, me? Seventy-five roubles, plus bonuses… Besides, I have income from making stearin candles and from hares."

"Are you a hunter?"

"No, we call passengers without tickets 'hares'."

Another minute passed in silence. Stychkin rose and began to pace excitedly around the room.

"I don't need a young wife," he said. "I'm getting on a bit, and what I need is someone… just like you… steady and reliable… and of your constitution…"

"Oh, God knows what you are saying..." giggled the match-maker, covering her crimson face with her shawl.

"Why spend too much time thinking? I like you – for me your qualities are suitable. I am a dependable, sober man, and if you like me, then... what could be better? Allow me to propose to you!"

The matchmaker shed a few tears, began to laugh and, as a sign of acquiescence, clinked glasses with Stychkin.

"Well, then," said the happy senior conductor, "let me explain to you what I wish from your behaviour and way of life... I am an exacting, serious, dependable man, of moral principles, and want my wife also to be exacting and to understand that I am her benefactor and the foremost person in her life."

He sat down and, sighing deeply, began to expound to his fiancée his view of family life and the duties of a wife.

Carelessness

P YOTR PETROVICH STRIZHIN, the nephew of Colonel
Ivanov's wife, the one who had her new galoshes stolen last
year, returned from the christening at exactly two o'clock in the
morning. So as not to make noise, he carefully undressed in the
hall; barely breathing, he stole through to his bedroom on tiptoe
and, without lighting the lamp, prepared to go to bed.

Strizhin leads a sober and regular life; his face presents an edify-
ing expression; he reads only books of a spiritual-moral variety,
but at the christening, out of delight that Lyubov Spiridonovna
had successfully given birth, he allowed himself to drink four
glasses of vodka and a glass of wine, which tasted like a mixture
of vinegar and castor oil. Really strong drinks are like sea water
or glory: the more you have, the more you want. And now, as he
undressed, Strizhin felt an overwhelming desire for a drink.

"I think Dashenka keeps vodka in the right-hand corner of
the cupboard," he thought. "If I have a glass, she'll not notice."

After some hesitation, overcoming his apprehension, Strizhin
made for the cupboard. Carefully opening the door, he felt in the
right-hand corner for a bottle and glass, poured, put the bottle
back in its place, then crossed himself and drank. And at once an
extraordinary thing happened. With terrible force, as if a bomb
had exploded, Strizhin was suddenly thrown from the cupboard
onto the trunk. There were sparks in his eyes – his breath was
taken away, and his whole body felt as if he had fallen into a
swamp full of leeches. It seemed to him that instead of vodka
he had swallowed a stick of dynamite which had blown up his
body, the house and the whole street... Head, hands, feet – all
had been torn off and had flown away to the Devil, into space...
He lay motionlessly on the trunk for some three minutes without
breathing, then rose and asked himself:

"Where am I?"

First, what he clearly sensed on coming round was a strong smell of paraffin.

"Good Lord... instead of vodka I drank paraffin!" he exclaimed in horror. "Holy saints above!"

The thought that he had poisoned himself made him go hot and cold. That he had actually swallowed the poison was testified by – besides the smell in the room – a burning sensation in his mouth, sparks in his eyes, the ringing of bells in his head and a pain in his stomach. Sensing the approach of death, and not deluding himself with vain hopes, he wished to bid farewell to his nearest, and set off to Dashenka's bedroom. (Being a widower, he kept in his house, instead of a housekeeper, his sister-in-law Dashenka, an elderly spinster.)

"Dashenka!" he said in a sobbing voice, entering her bedroom. "Dear Daskenka!"

Something moved in the darkness, and a deep sigh was emitted.

"Dashenka!"

"Well? What?" quickly replied a woman's voice. "Is it you, Pyotr Petrovich? Back already? Well then? What's the girl's name? Who was the godmother?"

"The godmother was Natalya Andreyevna Velikosvetskaya, and the godfather... Pavel Ivanych Bessonnitsyn... I... I, Dashenka, I think I'm dying. And the baby is named Olympiada, in honour of their benefactress... I... I, Dashenka have drunk paraffin..."

"What are you talking about? Did they really serve paraffin there?"

"To confess, I wanted some vodka without asking you, and... and God punished me: in the dark I accidentally drank paraffin... What am I going to do?"

Dashenka, hearing that without her permission he had opened the cupboard, sprang to life. She quickly lit a candle, jumped out of bed and in just a nightdress, with freckled face, bony limbs and hair in curlers, shuffled in bare feet to the cupboard.

"So, who gave you permission for this?" she asked severely, looking in the cupboard. "Was the vodka really put there for you?"

"I… I, Dashenka, drank not vodka, but paraffin…" muttered Strizhin, wiping cold sweat from his brow.

"And why did you need to touch the paraffin? Is it anything to do with you? Was it put there for you? Or do you think paraffin doesn't cost anything? Well? And do you know how much paraffin is now? Do you know?"

"Dear Dashenka!" groaned Strizhin. "It's a question of life and death, and you're on about money!"

"He got drunk and poked his nose into the cupboard!" cried Dashenka, angrily slamming the door. "Oh, you men are monsters, tormentors! I am a sufferer, an unfortunate woman, and have no peace either by day or night! Basilisk vipers, cursed Herods – you should have to live like me in the next world! I'm moving out tomorrow! I'm a maid and won't allow you to stand in front of me in just your underwear. Don't you dare to look at me when I'm not dressed!"

And she went on and on… Knowing that an angry Dashenka cannot be pacified either with entreaties, oaths or even by the firing of cannons, Strizhin waved his hand, dressed and decided to find a doctor. But it's easy to find a doctor only when you don't need one. After running through three streets and ringing five times at Doctor Chepkharyantz's and seven times at Doctor Bultykhin's, Strizhin ran to the chemist's: perhaps the chemist could help. Here, after a long wait, there came out a little, dark-complexioned, curly-haired pharmacist, looking sleepy in a dressing gown, with such a serious and intelligent face that he was frightening to behold.

"How can I help you?" he asked in a voice reserved only for very intelligent and confident pharmacists of the Jewish faith.

"For God's sake… I beg you!" said Strizhin breathlessly. "Give me something… I have just now accidentally drunk paraffin! I'm dying!"

"Please don't get agitated, but just answer the questions I put to you. I won't be able to understand you if you're agitated. You drank paraffin? Is that right?"

"Yes, paraffin! Save me, please!"

The pharmacist coolly and with a serious look went to the counter, opened a book and became absorbed in reading. After reading two pages, he shrugged one shoulder, then the other, gave a scornful look and, after a little thought, went into the adjoining room. The clock struck four. When it showed ten past four the pharmacist returned with another book and again became absorbed in reading.

"Hm!" he said, as if perplexed. "By the very fact that you feel unwell, you need to see not a chemist, but a doctor."

"But I've already been to the doctor's! I rang, but no one answered!"

"Hm… You don't consider us, pharmacists, to be human beings, and disturb us even at four o'clock in the morning, at a time when every dog, every cat is enjoying peace… You don't want to understand anything, and feel that we are not human beings but have nerves like string."

Strizhin heard out the pharmacist, sighed and went home.

"It must be my fate to die!" he thought.

In his mouth there was a burning sensation and smell of paraffin, in his stomach a sharp pain and in his ears a pounding: boom, boom, boom! With every minute it seemed to him that his end was near, that his heart was no longer beating…

Arriving home, he hastened to write "I beg that no one be held responsible for my death", then said his prayers, lay down and covered his head. For the rest of the night he did not sleep, but awaited death, imagining his grave covered with fresh foliage, with birds twittering over it.

But in the morning he was sitting on the bed and, smiling, was talking to Dashenka:

"Whoever leads a correct and regular life will not be affected by poison. Take me, for example. I was about to perish, die, suffer, but now I'm all right. Just a burning in the mouth and a sore throat, but the rest of the body is healthy, thank God… And why? Because of a regular life."

"No, it means the paraffin was not strong enough!" sighed Dashenka, thinking about the expense and staring at one spot. "It means the shopkeeper didn't give me the best, but the one that's one and a half copecks a bottle. I am a sufferer, an unfortunate woman. A monster and tormentor like you should have to live like me in the next world, cursed Herod…"

And she went on and on…

Conversation of a Drunk
with a Sober Devil

A FORMER OFFICIAL of the commissariat authority, retired Collegiate Secretary Lakhmatov, was sitting at his table and, drinking his sixteenth glass of vodka, was reflecting on brotherhood, equality and freedom. Suddenly, from behind the lamp, a devil looked at him... But don't be frightened, reader. Do you know what a devil is? It's a young man of pleasing appearance with a face black like a boot and with red expressive eyes. On his head, though he is not married, are horns...* His hair is styled in the popular French manner. His body is covered with green fur, and smells of dog. Behind his back hangs a tail, tipped with an arrow... Instead of fingers he has claws; instead of feet, horses' hooves. Lakhmatov, seeing the devil, was rather confused, but then, remembering that green devils have a stupid habit of appearing in general to all tipsy people, he quickly calmed down.

"With whom do I have the honour of speaking?" he asked, turning to the uninvited guest.

The devil felt embarrassed and lowered his eyes.

"Don't be shy," continued Lakhmatov. "Come closer... I am an unprejudiced man and you can talk candidly to me... from the heart... Who are you?"

The devil hesitatingly approached Lakhmatov and, tucking his tail under himself, courteously bowed.

"I am a devil, or an evil spirit..." he introduced himself. "I am a special-assignments officer, attached to His Excellency the director of the diabolical clerical office of the Lord Satan."

"I see, I see... Very pleased to meet you. Sit down! Would you like some vodka? Very glad to see you... What do you do?"

The devil was yet more embarrassed...

"Strictly speaking, I have no particular jobs," he replied, coughing in confusion and blowing his nose in a sheet of *Rebus*.* "Indeed, we used to have things to do... We tempted people... We led them astray from the path of virtue to the way of evil... Now, though, this occupation is, just between us, worthless... The path of virtue no longer exists, so there is nothing to lead people astray from. And besides, they have become more cunning than us. Just try to tempt a person who has studied all the sciences at university: he knows it all! How can I teach you to steal a rouble if, without my help, you have already embezzled thousands?"

"That's true... But, all the same, surely you do something else?"

"Yes... Our previous job has now all but lapsed, but we still have work... We tempt lady teachers to encourage youths to write verses, and we compel drunken merchants to break mirrors...* As for politics, literature and science, we for a long time now have not meddled in them... We don't have a clue about those things... Many of us, contributing to *Rebus*, are those who have abandoned hell and have gone to join the people... Those retired devils who went to the people got married to rich merchants' daughters and now live excellently well. Some of them practise law, others publish newspapers; in general they are very business-like and respected!"

"Excuse the indiscreet question: how much are you paid?"

"Our circumstances are as they were, sir..." replied the devil. "The position has not changed... As before, the flat, lighting and heating are at public expense... They do not give us a salary as such, because we are all considered supernumeraries and because a devil holds an honorary position... In general, speaking frankly, life is hard, and we might have to go begging... Thanks to people, we learnt how to take bribes, otherwise we all would have perished... We only live on what we can get... You provide goods to sinners, and... well, you steal a bit. Satan grew old, kept going to look at Zucchi;* he doesn't feel like bookkeeping now.

Lakhmatov poured the devil a glass of vodka. The guest drank and warmed to his theme. He related all the secrets of hell, poured out his heart, shed a few tears; Lakhmatov was so pleased that he even asked the visitor to spend the night. The devil slept on the stove and raved all night. By morning he had disappeared.

To Paris!

THE SECRETARY of the regional administration Gryaznov and the district schoolteacher Lampadkin one day towards evening were returning from the name-day celebration of police inspector Vonyuchkin. Walking arm in arm together, they looked very much like the letter Ю.* Gryaznov, thin, tall and wiry, was dressed in a close-fitting outfit and resembled a stick, while Lampadkin, stout, fleshy and dressed in oversized clothes, resembled the letter O. Both were tipsy and swaying slightly.

"Grot's new grammar* has been recommended," muttered Lampadkin, making a squelching sound with his galoshes in the mud. "Grot presents this theory that masculine adjectives in the genitive singular should end not in *avo*, but *ovo**... What do you think of that? Yesterday Perkhotkin went without dinner for putting *ovo* in a word, but tomorrow I shall have to avert my eyes in front of him. Shame! Shame!"

But Gryaznov was not listening to the learned talk of the pedagogue. All his attention was directed at the muddy bridge in front of Shiryayev's tavern, where at this time a little fracas was occurring. Some two dozen local dogs, which had formed a chain around a black, rough-coated mongrel bitch, were filling the air with prolonged, triumphant barking. The mongrel was turning around as if on needles, baring her teeth at the enemies and trying as far as possible to tuck her plucked tail under her belly. The incident was not important, but the secretary was among those impressionable, easily roused people who cannot watch indifferently while others argue or fight. Drawing up alongside the pack of dogs, he could not refrain from meddling.

"Tear into her! Bite the devil! Fff-weet!" He began to whistle and snarl, stepping closer to the circle of dogs. "R-rrr... Let her have it! Give her a grilling!"

And in order to stir up the dogs even more, he bent down and pulled the mongrel by the hind leg. She yelped, and before Gryaznov could pull away his hand, bit his finger. Immediately, as if frightened by her own audacity, she jumped over the circle of dogs and, in passing, bit Lampadkin on the calf and ran off along the street. The pack ran after her...

"Oh, you devil!" Gryaznov cried after her, brandishing his finger. "Damn you, you devil's offspring! Catch her! Beat her!"

"Catch her!" voices were heard, mixing with the whistles. "Chase her! Beat her! My friends, she's rabid! Look how she holds her tail between her legs and her snout down! She really is rabid! Shoo!"

The friends waited until the dogs had disappeared from view, took each other by the arm and walked on. By the time they arrived home (for seven roubles a month the pedagogue lived and had meals at the secretary's), they had already forgotten the incident with the mongrel... After taking off their muddy trousers and hanging them on the doors to dry, they settled down to tea. Both were in an excellent mood, good-humouredly philosophical. But an hour and a half later, when they were sitting at the table and playing fofan* with an aunt, a sister-in-law and Gryaznov's four sisters, the district doctor Katashkin suddenly and unexpectedly arrived, somewhat disturbing their peace.

"It's all right, it's all right... I'm not a lady!" began the new arrival when he saw how the secretary and pedagogue tried to conceal under the table their long johns and bare feet. "I've been sent to you, gentlemen! They say that a dog bit both of you!"

"That's right, that's right... a dog bit us," said Gryaznov with a wide grin. "Pleased to see you! Sit down, Mitri Fomich! Haven't seen you for ages, God help me... Do you want tea? Glasha, bring some vodka! What will you snack on, radishes or sausage?"

"They say the dog was rabid!" continued the doctor, looking anxiously at the friends. "Whether it was rabid or not, the matter can't be dismissed so carelessly. You never know what might happen. Will you show me where you were bitten?"

"Oh, it doesn't matter!" The secretary waved his hand. "She gave me a little bite... on the finger... You won't go mad from that... Perhaps you'll have some beer? Glashka, run to the Jewish woman and tell her to give you two bottles of beer on the slate!"

Katashkin sat down and, with as much strength as he had to outshout the drunks, began to frighten them with rabies... They at first protested and defied him, but then grew fearful and showed him the bitten places. The doctor examined the wounds, cauterized them with silver nitrate and left. After this the friends went to bed and for a long time argued about what silver nitrate is made of.

The next morning Gryaznov was sitting at the top of a tall poplar tree, attaching a nesting box. Lampadkin was standing beneath the tree holding a hammer and string. The secretary's garden was still covered in snow, but each little branch and the wet bark of the trees were already smelling of spring.

"Grot also has another theory..." muttered the pedagogue, "that 'gate' is not neuter, but masculine. Hm... That would mean changing the ending of 'red', if you wrote 'red gate'... Well, let him drool over it! I would sooner tender my resignation than change my belief about gates."

The pedagogue had just opened his mouth, and was majestically raising the hammer in order to smash learned academics, when at that moment the garden gate creaked and there entered quite unexpectedly, like the Devil from a hatch, the council leader Pozvonochnikov. Seeing him, Lampadkin went pale with amazement and dropped the hammer.

"Hello, my friend!" the official said to him. "Well, how are you? They say that yesterday a rabid dog bit you and Gryaznov."

"Maybe it wasn't rabid at all," muttered Gryaznov from the top of the poplar. "It's just women's talk!"

"Maybe... but maybe it was rabid, after all," said the official. "So it's not really possible to argue about it... In any case, it's necessary to take measures."

"What kind of measures, sir?" quietly asked the pedagogue. "We were cauterized yesterday, sir."

"So the doctor has just been telling me – but it's not enough. Something more drastic is needed. You would have to go to Paris, I suppose. You would probably have to do just that: go to Paris!"

The pedagogue dropped the string and froze, while the secretary nearly fell out of the tree with astonishment...

"To Pa—ris?" he drawled. "And what would we do there?"

"You will go to see Pasteur...* Of course it will be expensive – but what can be done? It's dear, but life is dearer... You would be reassured, and so would we... I was just now speaking to the chairman Ivan Alexeich. He thinks that the council will give you some money for the trip... For her part, my wife will make a donation to you of two hundred roubles... What more do you need? Get ready! I shall quickly get passports for you..."

"They've gone mad, the fools!" grinned Gryaznov when the official had left. "To Paris! Oh, how awful, God save us! Well, if it were Moscow or Kiev... but just think!... to Paris! And why? Well, had it been a pedigree dog... but since it's a mongrel... tfoo! Good Lord, does he think we're a couple of aristocrats? To Paris! I'm damned if I'll go!"

For a long time the pedagogue looked thoughtfully at the ground, then gaily burst out laughing and said in an inspired voice:

"Do you know what, Vasya? Let's go! God punish me, let's go! After all, Paris is abroad... Europe!"

"What is there that I haven't seen? Enough talk of that!"

"Civilization!" continued the enraptured Lampadkin. "Lord, what civilization! Those sights, various Vesuviuses... the scenery! Wherever you go, there's scenery! Truly, let's go."

"You've gone mad, Ilyushka! What would we do there with those Germans?"

"They're not Germans there, but French!"

"Same thing! What would I do with them? Looking at them, I would die of laughter! With my character I would beat them all up! You go if you want, but you won't be happy... They'll rob you and you'll go hungry... And moreover, instead of Paris, you'll find yourself in such a filthy country that you'll keep spitting for five years..."

Gryaznov flatly refused to go, but nevertheless on the evening of that very day the friends were walking arm in arm through the town telling those they met about the forthcoming trip. The secretary was sullen, angry, uneasy, while the pedagogue was enthusiastically gesticulating, seeking those with whom he could share his happiness...

"Everything would be all right if only we were not going to Paris!" Gryaznov consoled himself aloud. "It wouldn't be life, but paradise! Everyone looks at you sympathetically, and everywhere, wherever you go, there's *zakuski* and drinks, and everybody gives you money, but... Paris! Going to Paris? It's a joke! Goodbye, friends!" He stopped those he met. "We are going to Paris! Remember us kindly! Perhaps we shall not meet again."

Five days later, at the local station, there was a ceremonial send-off for the secretary and pedagogue. All the notable residents, from the council leader to the weak-sighted stepson of police inspector Vonyuchkin, gathered to see them off. The council leader's wife provided the travellers with two letters of recommendation, and the magistrate's wife gave them a hundred roubles with a request to buy some samples of fabric... There was no end to the good wishes, sighs and groans. Gryaznov's aunt, sister-in-law and four sisters cried their eyes out. The pedagogue seemed to want to appear brave and not upset, but the secretary, who had been drinking and was deeply moved, kept drawing deep breaths so as not to burst out crying... When the second bell rang, he could stand it no longer and began to howl...

"I'm not going!" He rushed from the carriage. "I'd rather go mad than go to a pastor! To hell with him!"

But they persuaded him, consoled him and settled him in the carriage. The train set off.

If one is to hold strictly to chronological order, not more than four days after the send-off, Gryaznov's sisters, sitting by the window and feeling sad, saw Lampadkin walking home. The pedagogue was red-faced, soiled with mud and continually dropping his suitcase. At first the girls thought it was a revenant, but then, when the gate banged and the familiar quiet puffing was heard from the entrance hall, the apparition lost its ghostly character. The sisters froze with astonishment, and instead of asking questions turned their pale, fallen faces to the arrival. The pedagogue blinked his eyes and waved his arm, then he began to cry and once more waved his arm.

"We arrived in Kursk," he began, wheezily crying, "and Vasya said to me: 'At the station,' he said, 'it's expensive to dine, so let's go,' he said, 'there's a tavern near the station here. We shall have dinner there.' We took our suitcases with us and left." The pedagogue sobbed. "At the tavern Vasya drank one glass after another, one after another... 'You,' he cried, 'are leading me to ruin!' He began to make a scene... And when after the vodka he began to drink sherry, a complaint was made. Then it went from bad to worse, and... we were down to the last copeck. Hardly enough remained for the journey..."

"So where is Vasya?" The sisters were alarmed.

"In Ku... Kursk... He asked that you quickly send him money for the trip..."

The pedagogue shook his head, wiped his face and added:

"But Kursk is a fine town! Very fine! I spent a day there with pleasure..."*

The Playwright

A N UNIMPRESSIVE PERSON with a dull look and a catarrhal face enters the doctor's office. Judging by the size of his nose and the darkly melancholic expression on his face, the person is not a stranger to alcoholic beverages, chronic colds and philosophy.

The person sits down in an armchair and complains about shortness of breath, indigestion, heartburn, melancholy and a nasty taste in the mouth.

"What do you do for a living?" asks the doctor.

"I am a playwright!" declares the person, not without pride.

The doctor is momentarily inspired with respect for the patient, and deferentially smiles.

"Ah, it's such an unusual occupation..." he mutters. "It involves such a lot of sheer brain work and nervous energy!"

"I sup-pose so..."

"Writers are so special... their lives don't resemble those of ordinary people... and so I would ask you to describe to me your way of life, your activities, habits, environment... in short, how your occupation affects your everyday life..."

"Certainly, sir..." acquiesces the dramatist. "I rise, my good sir, at about twelve o'clock, and sometimes even earlier... After getting up, I immediately smoke a cigarette and drink two glasses of vodka, and sometimes even three... Sometimes, however, even four, depending on how much I drank the day before... But then, sir... If I don't drink, I see blinding lights and get a headache."

"In general, you probably drink a lot?"

"N-o-o, not a lot at all. If I drink on an empty stomach, I suppose it's because of my nerves... Then, after dressing, I go to the Livorno or to Savrasenkov's* for breakfast... In general, my appetite is bad... I eat a very small amount for breakfast: a little cutlet or half a portion of sturgeon with horseradish. I'll deliberately drink three or four glasses of vodka, but still have no appetite... After breakfast I'll drink beer or wine, depending on finances..."

"Well, and then?"

"Then I go to a pub somewhere, and from the pub again to the Livorno to play billiards... I spend an hour like that till six o'clock, then go to dinner... I dine without appetite... Believe me, sometimes I'll drink six or seven glasses of vodka, but as for appetite – I have none at all! I sometimes envy other people when I see them: they all drink soup, but I can't even look at soup, and instead of that drink beer... After dinner I go to the theatre..."

"Hm... The theatre, probably, excites you?"

"Terribly! I get excited and irritated, but my friends keep saying: let's drink, let's drink! With one I drink vodka, with another red wine, with a third beer, and suddenly by the third act I can barely stand on my feet. The Devil take them, these nerves... After the theatre I go to the *Salon de Varieté** or to Rrrodon's masquerade.* As you know, it's not so easy to tear yourself away from the *Salon* or the masquerade... If I wake up at home in the morning, then I'm thankful for it. Sometimes I don't sleep at home for whole weeks at a time..."

"Hm... Are you observing life?"

"Well, yes... Once my nerves were so upset that I didn't live at home for a whole month and even forgot my address... I had to enquire at the address bureau. So you see, almost every day is like that!"

"Well, then when do you write your plays?"

"My plays? How can I say?" The dramatist shrugged. "It all depends on circumstances..."

"Be so good as to describe to me the process of your work..."

"First of all, my dear sir, ideas come to me by chance, or through friends. I myself have no time to follow literary trends. They come to me from some French or German source. If they're suitable, I take them to my sister, or give a student five roubles... They translate them and then I, you understand, adapt them to Russian taste: instead of foreign surnames I give Russian ones, and so on... That's all... But it's hard work! Oh, it's hard!"

The dull person rolls his eyes and sighs... The doctor starts to tap his chest, listen to his heart and press his abdomen...

The Wastrel

I T WAS NOT LATER than six o'clock in the evening when Lieutenant Strekachov, who was wandering through the town, went past a big three-storeyed house and by chance cast a glance at the pink curtains on the first floor.

"This is where Madame Dudu lives," he recollected. "I haven't been at her place for a long time. Shall I call in?"

But before deciding this question, Strekachov took a purse from his pocket and looked timidly in it. He saw there one crumpled rouble which smelt of paraffin, a button, two copecks and... nothing else.

"It's not enough... Well, it doesn't matter," he decided. "I'll call in anyway, stay for a while."

A minute later Strekachov was standing in the entrance hall and taking in deep breaths of the scents of perfume and glycerine soap. It smelt also of something else impossible to describe, but that can be smelt in any single woman's flat: a mixture of a woman's cheap scent and a man's cigar. On a stand hung several women's fur coats, waterproofs and a man's shiny top hat. Entering the hall, the lieutenant saw the same things he had seen the year before: an upright piano with slightly torn sheet music, a little vase with fading flowers, a stain on the floor from spilt liqueur... One door led into the sitting room, another into a small room where Mme Dudu slept or played piquet with the dancing master, Vrondi, an elderly man who looked very much like Offenbach.* If one looked in the sitting room, one could see straight ahead a door, through which could be glimpsed the edge of a bed with a pink muslin bed skirt. There lived the "wards" of Mme Dudu: Barb and Blanche.

No one was in the hall. The lieutenant made for the sitting room, and there saw a human being. Behind a round table, sprawling on a divan, sat a young man with bristly hair and dark-blue, lacklustre eyes, with a cold sweat on his forehead, looking as if he had just climbed out of a deep pit that was dark and frightening. He was dressed foppishly in a new tricot suit which bore traces of ironing; on his chest hung a charm; on his red-stockinged feet were patent-leather shoes with buckles. The young man was resting his plump cheeks on his fists and looking dully at a small bottle of seltzer water that was standing in front of him. On another table were several bottles and a plate of oranges.

Having glanced at the lieutenant, who had entered, the dandy goggled and gaped. The surprised Strekachov took a step back… In the dandy he recognized with difficulty the clerk Filyenkov, whom he had only that morning told off in the clerical office for an illiterately written document, in which the word "cabbage" had been spelt "cubbidge".

Filyenkov rose slowly and leant with his hands on the table. For a minute he did not lower his eyes from the lieutenant, and even turned blue from the internal strain.

"So how did you get here?" Strekachov asked him severely.

"I, Your Honour," the clerk began to babble with downcast eyes, "for the birthday, sir… With universary militarial servation*, when all are equal, who…"

"I am asking you, how did you get here?" The lieutenant raised his voice. "And what sort of uniform is this?"

"I, Your Honour, know I am at fault, but… if you consider, that in a time of universary militarial… military universal, everyone is equal – and, furthermore, as I am nevertheless an educated man – I cannot appear on the birthday of mamzelle Barb in the uniform of a low-ranking person, so I put on the above-mentioned costume to accord with my position in life as I am, you see, an hereditary honourable citizen."

Seeing that the lieutenant's eyes were becoming more and more angry, Filyenkov fell silent and lowered his head, as if expecting now to have the back of it slapped. The lieutenant opened his mouth in order to say "Go away!", but at that moment there entered into the sitting room a blonde woman with raised eyebrows, wearing a bright-yellow house coat. Recognizing the lieutenant, she shrieked and rushed to him.

"Vasya! Officer!"

Seeing that Barb (this was one of Mme Dudu's wards) was acquainted with the lieutenant, the clerk recovered his composure and brightened up. Spreading wide his fingers, he leapt up from behind the table and started to wave his arms.

"Your Honour!" he began in a voice choked with emotion. "I have the honour to congratulate the loved one on her birthday! You would not find such a woman in Paris! I mean it, sir! She is full of life! I did not regret the three hundred roubles I paid to have this house coat made on the occasion of the birthday of the loved one! Your Honour, champagne! For the birthday girl!"

"But where is Blanche?" asked the lieutenant.

"She'll be out shortly, Your Honour!" replied the clerk, though the question was not addressed to him, but to Barb. "In a moment! The girl *la comprené a revoir consommé!** The other day a merchant from Kostroma arrived, forked out five hundred... That's quite something, five hundred. I would give a thousand, only first respect my character. Do I make myself clear? Your Honour, have a glass, sir!"

The clerk gave the lieutenant and Barb a glass of champagne each, and himself drank a small glass of vodka. The lieutenant drank, but immediately came to his senses.

"I see you are taking the most uncalled-for liberty," he said. "Leave this place now, and tell Demyanov to confine you for twenty-four hours."

"Your Honour, perhaps you think I'm some sort of swine? Is that what you think? Good Lord! You know, my father was an hereditary honourable citizen, the holder of orders! If you wish to know, a general was my godfather. And you think that if I'm a clerk, I must be a swine? Have another little glass of... bubbly... Barb, toss it back! Don't be shy, we can pay for everything. With modern education all are made equal. The son of a general or a merchant has to do military service the same as a peasant.

I, Your Honour, have been to high school, and technical college and business school… I was expelled from them all! Barb, toss it back! Take a hundred roubles, send for a dozen bottles! Your Honour, have a little glass!"

Mme Dudu – a tall, stout lady with a hawk-like face – entered the room. After her minced Vrondi, the man who looked like Offenbach. A little later also entered Blanche, a diminutive brunette of about nineteen, with a severe face and a Greek nose, evidently Jewish. The clerk pulled out one more hundred-rouble banknote.

"Spend it all! Blow it! Let me smash this vase. From feeling!"

Mme Dudu began to say that nowadays any honest girl could make a decent match for herself, and that it's improper for girls to drink, but if she does allow her girls to drink it's only because she hopes that men are decent – and if men were otherwise, she would not allow them to visit.

From the wine and the company of Blanche, the lieutenant's head began to spin, and he forgot about the clerk.

"Music!" cried the desperate voice of the clerk. "Let's have some music! Based on order number one hundred and twenty, I suggest to you that we dance! Qui-et!" The clerk continued to shout in full voice, thinking that it was not he himself who was shouting, but someone else. "Qui-et! I would like us all to dance! You must respect my nature! Cachucha! Cachucha!"*

Barb and Blanche consulted Mme Dudu; old man Vrondi sat down at the piano. The dance began. Filyenkov, stamping in time with his feet, kept up with the motion of the four legs of the women and neighed with pleasure.

"Go on! Good! Feel it! Keep moving!"

A little later all the company drove in carriages to the Arcadia.* Filyenkov drove with Barb, the lieutenant with Blanche, Vrondi with Mme Dudu. At the Arcadia they occupied a table and ordered supper. Here Filyenkov drank to the point where he became hoarse and lost the ability to wave his arms. He sat gloomily and, blinking his eyes and looking as if preparing to burst into tears, said:

"Who am I? Am I really a man? I'm a wastrel! Hereditary honorary citizen…" He began to mimic himself. "You are a wastrel, and not a citi… citizen."

The lieutenant, his vision clouded by wine, almost failed to notice him. Only once, seeing his drunken physiognomy through a mist, did he knit his brows and say:

"You, I see, are taking a great liberty…"

But immediately he lost the ability to think, and clinked glasses with him.

From the Arcadia they went to the Krestovsky Garden.* Here Mme Dudu bid farewell to the young people, saying that she fully trusted the decency of the men, and left with Vrondi. Then, for refreshment, they ordered coffee with brandy and liqueurs, followed by kvass, vodka and caviar. The clerk smeared his face with caviar and said:

"I am now like an Arab, or like the Devil."

The next morning the lieutenant, feeling as if he had lead in his head, and with his mouth hot and dry, set off to his office. Filyenkov was sitting at his place in his clerk's uniform and with shaking hands was putting together some documents. His face was gloomy, like a cobblestone, not sleek; his bristly hair stuck out in all directions, his eyes were half closed… Seeing the lieutenant, he rose heavily, sighed and stood to attention. The lieutenant, angry and not having had a hair of the dog that bit him, turned away and occupied himself with his work. Ten minutes passed in silence, and then his eyes met the lacklustre eyes of the clerk, and in those eyes he read everything: red curtains, the wild dance, the Arcadia, Blanche's profile…

"With universary militarial servation…" muttered Filyenkov, "when even… professors are taken for service… when everyone is equal… and there is even free speech…"

The lieutenant wanted to tell him off, to send him to Demyanov, but waved his hand and said quietly:

"Oh, to the Devil with you!"

And he left the office.

The Heroic Lady

L IDIA YEGOROVNA came out on the terrace to drink her morning coffee. The time was already approaching a hot and stuffy midday, but this did not prevent my heroine from wearing a black silk dress, buttoned up to the chin and tightly laced at the waist. She knew that the black colour went with her golden ringlets and strong profile, and dispensed with it only at night. As she took the first sip from her delicate china cup, the postman came up to the terrace and handed her a letter. The letter was from her husband: "Your uncle did not give a penny, and your estate has been sold. Nothing could be done…" Lidia Yegorovna went pale, tottered to a chair and continued reading: "I am going to Odessa for about two months on important business. I kiss you."

"We are ruined! In Odessa for two months…" groaned Lidia Yegorovna. "It means he's gone to *her*… My God!"

She rolled her eyes, swayed, grasped the railing with her hand and was about to fall when voices were heard from below. Up to the terrace was climbing her cousin from the neighbouring dacha, retired General Zazubrin, as old as an oft-repeated anecdote and as weak as a newborn kitten. He was stepping with great care, feeling the steps with his stick, as if fearing for their stability. Behind him minced a little clean-shaven old man, retired Professor Pavel Ivanovich Knopka, in a big, ancient top hat with wide elevated brims. The general, as usual, was all covered in bits of fluff and crumbs, but the professor stood out by the whiteness of his attire and the smoothness of his chin. Both were beaming.

"We have come to see you, *charmanochka*," tinkled the general, pleased with himself for having refashioned the word *charmante*.* "*Feya pyot kofeya!*"*

The general was being stupidly witty, but Knopka and Lidia Yegorovna burst out laughing. My heroine withdrew her hand from the railing, stood erect and with a fixed smile stretched out her hands to the visitors. They kissed her hands and sat down.

"You, cousin, are eternally cheerful!" said Lidia Yegorovna, starting a polite conversation with the guests. "You have a happy disposition!"

"What was it I said? Oh, yes! *Feya pyot kofeya!...* Ha-ha-ha. Herr Professor and I have already bathed, breakfasted and are making calls... This professor brings me trouble! I want to complain to you, Fairy! Trouble! I intend to prosecute him! He-he-he... He's a liberal! Another Voltaire,* you might say!"

"What do you mean?" Lidia Yegorovna smiled and thought: "To Odessa for two months... To that..."

"I tell you honestly! Such ideas he spreads... such ideas! He's a socialist, completely red. Do you know my friend Pavel Ivanovich, who likes red?* Do you know who? Heee... Try and answer! There's a riddle for you liberals!"

"What a man that general is!" Knopka burst out laughing, twisting his scholarly chin. "And we, Your Excellency, can invent a saying for you conservatives: only bulls fear red! Ha-ha-ha... There you are!"

"Good Heavens! What do I see? Your oleanders are blooming!" A woman's voice was heard from below the terrace, and a minute later Princess Dromaderova, the resident of the neighbouring dacha, appeared. "Ah! You have men, and I am dressed so scruffily! Please excuse me! What are you talking about? Go on, general, I won't interfere..."

"We were talking about red," continued Zazubrin, "and just now, incidentally, about bulls... You are right, Pavel Ivanovich, about bulls. Once, in Georgia, where I commanded a battalion, a bull saw my red lining,* got frightened and charged me... came straight at me with its horns... I had to draw my sabre. Word of honour! Thank goodness a Kazakh was nearby and chased away the scoundrel with a lance... Why are you laughing? Don't you believe me? It's true, he chased it away..."

Lidia Yegorovna was amazed. She made an exclamation and thought: "He's in Odessa now... the cheat!"

Knopka began to talk about bulls and buffaloes. Princess Dromaderova declared that it was all very boring. They began to talk about red linings...

"Concerning this lining, I recall an incident," said Zazubrin, sucking a dry rusk. "I had a colonel in the battalion, a certain Konvertov, Pyotr Petrovich... Such a nice old man... I remember him fondly... a simple soul, a story-teller... From private soldier he rose to the highest ranks, for special services... He was battle-hardened. I loved him, God rest his soul. He was seventy years old when he was promoted to the rank of colonel, but he could no longer ride a horse and was completely racked by gout. On manoeuvres he would pull his sabre out of the scabbard, but could no longer put it back; his orderly had to put it back... He could unfasten himself – I beg your pardon – but could no longer do himself up... And this weak man's dream was to be a general. He was old, weak, preparing to die, but dreamt... That was his nature, so to speak... He was a fighter! And he didn't want to retire, because of his dream to be a general... He served five years as a colonel, was recommended for promotion... But what do you think? Well? Here's fate! He had a stroke at the very time his promotion came through... The poor man's left cheek and right arm were paralysed, and his legs became very weak... He was forced to retire, and the ambitious man didn't have the chance to wear the metal shoulder straps! He retired and went with his old woman to Tiflis* to rest. He drove around, cried and laughed when his coachman called him 'Your Excellency'. One cheek cried and laughed, while the other stayed motionless, like a monument. Only one consolation remained to him: the red lining. He walked around Tiflis with his coat spread wide like a wing, showing the public its red colour. Look, he seemed to say, whom you see! He wandered around town all day, showing off the lining... That, my friend, was his only joy. He went to the bath house and put his coat on the bench with the lining up. He found consolation, took comfort from it, like a small child, but in old age he even became blind. He hired a man to lead him through the town and show the lining... This blind, grey-haired old man barely managed to stagger along, stumbling against the air, but pride was written on his face. The winter was fiercely cold, but his coat was unbuttoned... Strange man! Soon after that, his old woman died. He buried her, wailed, begged to join her in the grave, but at the same time showed the priest the lining. Another person, a widow, was engaged to look after him. But the widow, needless to say, thought she knew her duty better than the wife. She was a hoarder... She hid the sugar, the tea, the loose change... She fleeced him in front of his own eyes. She robbed him and robbed him, stole this thing and that, the despicable woman, and finally reached the limit. The bitch went and ripped off his red lining to make herself a jacket, and in place of the red lining sewed in a cheap, grey calico. My Pyotr Petrovich goes for a walk, turns his coat inside out before the public, but being blind does not see that, instead of a general's lining, he has a printed calico with spots!..."

Princess Dromaderova found all this very boring, and began to talk about her son, a lieutenant. Before dinner neighbours arrived – the Klyanchin girls with their mother. They sat down at the piano and sang Zazubrin's favourite song. Then they sat down to dine.

"Excellent radishes!" remarked the professor. "Where can you buy them?"

"He is now in Odessa... with that woman!" replied Lidia Yegorovna.

"What did you say?"

"Oh... My mind was wandering! I don't know where the cook gets them... What's the matter with me?"

And Lidia Yegorovna, throwing back her head, laughed heartily over her absent-mindedness... After dinner the professor's fat wife arrived with their children. They sat down to play cards. In the evening guests arrived from town...

Only at night, after seeing off the last of the guests and standing motionless until she ceased to hear their footsteps, was Lidia Yegorovna able to grasp with her hand the same railing, sway and begin to sob.

"It's not enough that he should spend all the money! That's not enough for him! He now also betrays me!"

Hot tears now burst from her eyes, and her pale face was distorted with despair. There was no longer the need to keep up appearances, and she was able to sob.

The devil knows to what extent strength can sometimes stretch!

The Drunks

A FACTORY OWNER, Frolov – a handsome, dark-haired man with a little round beard and a soft, velvety expression in his eyes – and his legal adviser, the lawyer Almyer, an elderly man with a big, coarse head, were carousing in one of the public rooms of a suburban restaurant. They had both come to the restaurant straight from a ball, and that is why they were in tails and white ties. Apart from them and the waiters at the door, there was not a soul in the room: on the instructions of Frolov, no one was admitted.

They began by drinking a big glass of vodka each and eating oyster *zakuski*.

"It's good!" said Almyer. "It is I, my friend, who started the fashion of serving oyster *zakuski*. Vodka burns and gives you a sore throat, but when you swallow an oyster it's soothing. Isn't that so?"

A dignified waiter with a clean-shaven upper lip and grey sideboards put a gravy boat on the table.

"What's this you're serving?" asked Frolov.

"*Sauce provençale* for the herring, sir…"

"What? Do you really serve it like that?" cried the factory owner without looking at the gravy boat. "Is this really the sauce? You don't know how to serve it, blockhead!"

Frolov's velvety eyes flared up. He wound a corner of the tablecloth around his finger, pulled deftly, and the *zakuski*, candlesticks and bottles… all fell to the floor with a ring and a crash.

The waiters, who had long been used to tavern-like accidents, ran up to the table and seriously, coolly, like surgeons during an operation, began to clear up the debris.

"How well you know how to deal with these incidents," Almyer said, and burst out laughing. "But… move away a little from the table, or you'll tread in the caviar."

"Call the engineer here!" cried Frolov.

The "engineer" referred to a decrepit, sour-faced old man who had indeed formerly been an engineer and a rich man; he had squandered his fortune, and towards the end of his life found himself in a restaurant, where he was in charge of the waiters and singers, and fulfilled various other roles in connection with the fair sex. Appearing at the summons, he inclined his head respectfully to one side.

"Listen, my dear man," said Frolov, turning to him. "What is this incompetence? How do they serve at your place? Do you really not know that I'm dissatisfied? The devil take you, I shall stop coming to you!"

"I beg you to be magnanimous and excuse us, Alexei Semyonych," said the engineer, pressing his hand to his heart. "I shall immediately take steps to see that your smallest wishes will be fulfilled in the very best and most efficient manner."

"Well, all right, go away…"

The engineer bowed, moved backwards still in a bent position and disappeared behind the door, the imitation diamonds on his shirt and fingers glinting one last time.

The table of *zakuski* was laid again. Almyer drank red wine, ate with gusto some bird with truffles and then ordered boiled fish in a piquant sauce, and sterlet that had been cooked in white wine and presented in a ring. Frolov drank only vodka and nibbled bread. He rubbed his face with his palms, frowned, panted and evidently was not in good spirits. Both were silent. It was quiet. Two electric lights* flickered in a frosted lampshade and sparked, as if angry. On the other side of the door, quietly singing in unison, walked some Gypsy women.

"I drink and don't feel cheerful," said Frolov. "The more I guzzle, the more I become sober. Others grow jolly from vodka, but I get angry, have nasty thoughts, insomnia. Why is it, my friend, that people can't imagine any pleasure other than drunkenness and dissipation? It's really disgusting!"

"You should call in the Gypsies."

"Why don't I!"

In the doorway from the corridor appeared the head of an old Gypsy woman.

"Alexei Semyonych, the Gypsies are asking for tea and brandy," said the old woman. "Can it be arranged?"

"It can!" replied Frolov. "You know, of course, that they take from the owner of the restaurant a percentage of whatever refreshment they demand from the guests. Nowadays it's not possible to believe someone who even asks just for vodka. Everyone is base, despicable, spoilt. Take even these waiters here. They look like professors, are grey-haired, earn two hundred roubles a month, live in their own houses, their daughters go to the high school – but you can swear at them and make them do whatever you like. The engineer for one rouble will eat a jar of mustard and crow like a cockerel. I give you my honest word, if even one of them took offence, I would give him a thousand roubles!"

"What's the matter with you?" asked Almyer, looking at him with astonishment. "Why this melancholy? You are red in the face, look very fierce... What's the matter with you?"

"I feel bad. A single thought lies in my head. It's stuck there like a nail, and nothing will pluck it out."

Into the room came a short, round, bloated-looking old man, entirely bald and shabbily dressed in a too-tight jacket and lilac-coloured waistcoat, carrying a guitar. He made an idiotic face and stood to attention after saluting like a soldier.

"Ah, the parasite!" said Frolov. "Let me introduce you. He made his fortune by grunting like a pig. Come here, my friend!"

The factory owner poured vodka, wine and brandy into a glass, sprinkled in salt and pepper, stirred the mixture and gave it to the parasite. The latter downed it at a gulp and grunted like a seasoned drinker.

"He's used to drinking slops, so pure wine makes him sick," said Frolov. "Well, parasite, sit down and sing."

The parasite sat down, touched the strings with his plump fingers and began to sing:

Neetka-neetka, Margaritka…

Having had too much champagne, Frolov was drunk. He banged his fist on the table and said:

"Yes, a single thought lies in my head! It doesn't give me a minute's peace!"

"So what's the matter?"

"I can't say. It's a secret. It's a secret I can reveal only in my prayers. However, if you wish, in the spirit of friendship, between us… only, be careful, to no one… no one whatsoever… I shall tell you; it will make me feel better, but you… for God's sake, hear me out and then forget all about it…"

Frolov leant towards Almyer, and for half a minute breathed into his ear.

"I hate my wife!" he said.

The lawyer looked at him in amazement.

"Yes, yes, my wife, Marya Mikhailovna," muttered Frolov, reddening. "I hate her, and that's all there is to it."

"But why?"

"I don't even know myself! I've been married for only two years. It was a love match, as you yourself know, but now I already hate her, like a detestable enemy, like this very – forgive me – parasite. And there is no reason at all, no reason whatever! When she sits near me, eats, or if she says something, then I seethe inwardly and I can barely restrain myself from being rude to her. It's a thing I can't even talk about. It's impossible to leave her or tell her the truth, because of the scandal, but for me, living with her is worse than hell. I can't stay at home! So, during the day, I'm always at work or in restaurants, and at night I frequent low dives. Well, how do you explain this hatred? After all, she's not just any woman, but beautiful, clever, gentle."

The parasite stamped his feet and began to sing:

I walked out with an officer
And told him all my secrets…

"To confess, I always thought that you and Marya Mikhailovna were not at all suited to each other," Almyer said after a silence, and sighed.

"Do you mean she's educated? Listen… I myself finished business school with a gold medal, have been to Paris three times. I'm not cleverer than you, of course, but not stupider than my wife. No, my friend, education is not the barrier! Listen to how this whole matter began. It began when I suddenly started to realize that she married me not for love, but for my money. This belief got lodged in my head. I've tried to dislodge it one way or another, but it just sits there, the cursed thing! And then my wife became a spendthrift. She used to be poor, and when she struck gold she began to throw money around right and left. She went off her head, forgot herself to such an extent that each month she squandered twenty thousand. But I am a suspicious man: I trust no one, I suspect everyone, and the kinder someone is to me, the more excruciating it is to me. I keep thinking that people flatter me because of my money. I trust no one! I'm a difficult man, my friend, very difficult!"

Frolov drained his glass of wine at a gulp and continued:

"However, that is all nonsense," he said. "These things should never be spoken of. It's stupid. I drunkenly shot my mouth off, and now you look at me with your lawyer's eyes – pleased that you've discovered someone else's secret. Well, well… let's leave this conversation. Let's drink! Listen," he said, turning to the waiter, "is Mustafa here? Call him over!"

After a while, a little Tatar boy of about twelve came into the room wearing a tailcoat and white gloves.

"Come here!" Frolov said to him. "Explain to us the following puzzle. There was a time when you Tatars dominated us and took tribute from us, but now you serve as waiters to the Russians and sell dressing gowns. How do you explain such a change?"

Mustafa raised his eyebrows and said in a refined sing-song voice:

"Vicissitudes of fate!"

Almyer looked at his serious face and rocked with laughter.

"Well, give him a rouble," said Frolov. "By the 'vicissitudes of fate' he makes money. Only because of those three words is he retained here. Drink, Mustafa! You'll turn out to be a b-i-i-g scoundrel! I mean, it's terrible how many of your people are parasites, hanging around rich men. How many of you submissive thieves and robbers are bred – it's impossible to say! Shouldn't we call the Gypsies in now? Well? Bring the Gypsies here!"

The Gypsies, who had long been waiting patiently in the corridors, burst into the room with a whoop, and wild revelry began.

"Drink!" Frolov cried to them. "Drink, tribe of the Pharaohs!* Sing! E-e-e!"

In winter time... E-e-e! Sleighs were winging...

The Gypsies sang, whistled, danced... In the frenzy that sometimes seizes the very rich who are gifted with a "generous nature", Frolov began to make a fool of himself. He called for supper and champagne to be given to the Gypsies, smashed the frosted glass of the lamp, flung bottles at the pictures and the mirrors, and did all this evidently without any pleasure, frowning and shouting angrily with contempt at everyone, an expression of hatred in his eyes and in his manner. He forced the engineer to sing a solo, gave the basses a mixture of wine, vodka and oil to drink...

At six o'clock he was presented with the bill.

"Nine hundred and twenty-five roubles and forty copecks," said Almyer, shrugging his shoulders. "What is it for? No, wait, we have to check it!"

"Leave it!" muttered Frolov, pulling out his wallet. "Well... let them rob me... That's why I'm rich, so they can rob me... Without parasites... you can't live... You are my attorney... You get six thousand a year, but... but for what? However, forgive me... I myself don't know what I'm saying."

Returning home with Almyer, Frolov muttered:

"To go home, for me... is terrible! I have no one to whom I can open my soul... All are robbers... traitors... Well, why did I tell you my secret? Wh... why? Tell me: why?"

At the entrance to his house he leant towards Almyer and, tottering, kissed him full on the lips, according to the old Moscow tradition of kissing indiscriminately, at any opportunity.

"Goodbye... I'm a difficult, nasty man," he said. "I lead a drunken, dissolute, shameless life. You are a clever, educated man and only carouse and drink with me, I... I get no help at all from any of you... But you would, if you were my friend, if you were an honourable man, and genuinely so, you would have to say: 'Eh, you are a despicable, nasty man! You are a louse!'"

"Well, well..." muttered Almyer. "Go to bed."

"There is no help at all from you. The only hope is that in summer, when I'm in the country, I shall go out to the field, a storm will arise, thunder will roar and flatten me on the spot... Good... goodbye..."

Frolov kissed Almyer once again and, muttering and nearly dozing off as he walked, supported by two footmen, started to climb the stairs.

The Happy Man

A PASSENGER TRAIN sets off from Bologoye Station on the Nikolayevsk Railway.* In one of the second-class smoking carriages, shrouded in the dim light of the coach, doze five male passengers. They have only just eaten, and now, having curled up against the backs of their seats, are trying to sleep. It is quiet.

The door opens, and into the carriage enters a tall, stick-like figure wearing a red hat and a foppish coat strongly reminiscent of characters in operettas or of the newspaper correspondents in Jules Verne novels.*

The figure stops in the middle of the carriage and, breathing heavily through his nose, screws up his eyes and peers for a long time at the seats.

"No, this is the wrong one too," he mutters. "The devil knows which one it is! It's just maddening. No, it's the wrong one!"

One of the passengers peers at the figure and emits a joyful cry:

"Ivan Alexeyevich! What brings you here? Is it you?"

The stick-like Ivan Alexeyevich quivers, looks vacantly at the passengers and, recognizing the speaker, throws out his hands in delight.

"Ha! Pyotr Petrovich!" he says. "How many years has it been! And I didn't even know you were on this train!"

"Are you well?"

"Not so bad – only, my dear man, I forgot which carriage I'm in, and can't seem to find it now. I'm such an idiot! I deserve a good thrashing!"

The stick-like Ivan Alexeyevich sways slightly and giggles.

"Such things do happen!" he goes on. "I went out for brandy after the second bell. I had one, of course. Then I thought, as the next station is still a long way off, why not have another? While I was thinking and drinking, the third bell went... I ran like a madman and leapt into the first carriage I could. Well, am I not an idiot? Am I not a bit of a lad?"

"But I see you're in good spirits," says Pyotr Petrovich. "Why not take a seat? Do join me!"

"No-no... I must go and find my carriage! Goodbye!"

"In the dark – who knows? – you may fall between the carriages. Sit down, and when we get to the next station, then you can find your carriage. Sit down!"

Ivan Alexeyevich sighs and reluctantly sits down opposite Pyotr Petrovich. He is evidently unsettled and fidgets as if on needles.

"Where are you going?" asks Pyotr Petrovich.

"I? To the wide open space. My head is in such turmoil that even I myself don't know where I'm going. So I'm going where fate takes me. Ha-ha... My dear man, have you ever seen a happy fool? No? Well, look at one now! Before you stands the happiest of mortals! Yes, sir! Do you notice nothing in my face?"

"I notice that... you, ah... are a little bit—"

"You must mean that I now have a terribly stupid face! Oh, it's a shame there's no mirror. I could look at my stupid mug! I feel, my dear man, that I'm turning into an idiot. Word of honour! Ha-ha... Believe it or not, I'm going on my honeymoon. Well, am I not a bit of a lad?"

"You? Have you really got married?"

"Today, my dear man! I got married and hopped straight on the train."

Congratulations and the usual questions follow.

"Well, how about that..." laughs Pyotr Petrovich. "That's why you're dressed like such a dandy."

"Yes, indeed... For full effect I've even sprayed on scent. I am giving myself up to vanity! I have no cares or thoughts, only a sensation of something like... the devil knows what to call it... serenity, maybe? Never yet in my life have I felt so good!"

Ivan Alexeyevich closes his eyes and rotates his head.

"Outrageously happy!" he says. "But judge for yourself. I shall now go to my carriage. There, on the seat near the window, is sitting the creature who is committed to me with all her being. This blonde with the little nose... with the little fingers... My darling! Angel of mine! What a little mite she is! My little aphid! And her little foot! Lord! A little foot not at all like our huge plates, but a miniature, magical thing... allegorical! I could go and just eat that little foot! Oh, but you don't understand! Because you're a materialist, you immediately analyse everything, this way and that! You are a withered-up bachelor, and nothing more! But when you're married, then you'll remember! And you'll say, 'Where are you now, Ivan Alexeyevich?' Yes, sir, I'll go now to my carriage. There, I am awaited with impatience... My arrival is eagerly anticipated. I shall be met with a smile. I shall sit down and chuck her under the chin with two fingers..."

Ivan Alexeyevich turns his head and goes off into fits of laughter.

"Then I shall put my head on her little shoulder and my arm around her waist. All around, don't you know, will be silence... poetic twilight. I could embrace the whole world at such a moment. Pyotr Petrovich, let me embrace you!"

"By all means."

To the delighted laughter of the other passengers, the friends embrace, and the happy newly-wed continues:

"And to make things even sillier – or, as they say in novels, to create a greater sense of illusion – I go to the buffet and knock back two or three glasses. Then, something starts to happen in my head and chest, something that you will not read about even in fairy tales. I am a little, insignificant man, but it seems to me that I have no limit... I could embrace the whole world!"

The passengers, looking at the drunken, happy married man, are infected by his gaiety and no longer feel drowsy. Instead of one listener, near Ivan Alexeyevich, there soon appear five. He fidgets as if sitting on needles, sprays saliva, waves his hands and jabbers incessantly. He laughs raucously, and they all do the same.

"The main thing, gentlemen, is to think less! To the devil with all this analysis... If you want to drink, then drink, but it's no good philosophizing about whether it's harmful or healthy. To the devil with all this philosophy and psychology!"

The conductor passes through the carriage.

"My good man," says the newly-wed, turning to him. "When you pass through carriage two hundred and nine and see there a lady in a grey hat with a white feather, tell her I'm here."

"Yes, sir. Only in this train there is no carriage two hundred and nine. It is two hundred and nineteen."

"Well, two hundred and nineteen. It's all the same! Even so, tell this lady that her husband is safe and sound!"

Ivan Alexeyevich suddenly clutches his head and groans:

"Husband... Lady... Is it so long ago? Husband... Ha-ha... I have to pinch myself, but here I am – a husband! Ah, idiot! But she! Yesterday she was just a girl... a little mite... It's just unbelievable!"

"Nowadays it's even somewhat strange to see a happy man," says one of the passengers. "You'll sooner see a white elephant."

"Yes, and whose fault is that?" says Ivan Alexeyevich, stretching his long legs and very pointed shoes. "If you are not happy, then it's your own fault! What do you think? Man is the author of his own happiness. You can be happy, if you want, but you don't really want to be. You stubbornly avoid happiness!"

"Well, who would have thought it! In what way?"

"Very simple!... Nature decreed that Man at a certain time of life should love. When this time comes, well, you have to love for all it's worth – but you really don't obey nature, keep waiting for something. Moreover... The law says that the normal person has to marry... Without marriage there's no happiness. When the time is right, get married, there's no point delaying... But you see, if you don't marry, you keep waiting for something! Then it's said in the Holy Scripture that wine maketh glad the heart of man...* If you feel good and want to feel even better, then go to the buffet and have a drink. The main thing is: don't philosophize – get into a routine! Routine is a great thing!"

"You say that man is the author of his own happiness. How the devil is he the author of it if a toothache or nasty mother-in-law is enough to make his happiness fly out the window? It all depends on luck. If we now had another accident like the one at Kukuevo,* you would sing another song."

"Nonsense!" protests the newly-wed. "Accidents happen only once a year. I fear no such accidents, because they happen for a reason. They are rare occurrences! The devil take them! I don't even want to talk about them! But it seems we are approaching a station."

"Where are you going now?" asks Pyotr Petrovich. "To Moscow or somewhere further south?"

"Good Lord! How can I be going somewhere further south if I'm travelling north?"

"But surely Moscow is not to the north of us."

"I know, but surely we are going now to St Petersburg!" says Ivan Alexeyevich.

"We are going to Moscow, I have to tell you!"

"What do you mean, 'to Moscow'?" says the newly-wed in astonishment.

"It's strange... Where did you get a ticket to?"

"To St Petersburg."

"In that case, congratulations. You got on the wrong train."

There is a half-minute's silence. The newly-wed rises and looks dully at his companion.

"Yes, yes," insists Pyotr Petrovich. "You got on the wrong train at Bologoye... After your brandy you must have boarded the oncoming train."

Ivan Alexeyevich goes pale, clutches his head and starts to pace briskly back and forth in the carriage.

"Oh, I'm an idiot!" he says indignantly. "I'm a fool, the devil take me! Well, what shall I do now? You see, my wife is on the other train! She is there alone, waiting, pining! Oh, I'll be a laughing stock!"

The newly-wed falls on the seat, cringing as if someone has trodden on his corn.

"I'm so unhappy!" he groans. "What on earth shall I do? What?"

"Come, come..." the passengers console him. "It's nothing... You send your wife a telegram and yourself try to get on the next fast train. That way you'll overtake her."

"The fast train!" cries the newly-wed, the "author of his own happiness". "But where shall I get the money for the fast train? My wife has all my money!"

After whispering among themselves, the laughing passengers pass round the hat and collect enough money for the happy man.

Typhus

A YOUNG LIEUTENANT, Klimov, was travelling from St Petersburg to Moscow in the smoking carriage of the mail train. Opposite him was sitting an elderly man with the clean-shaven face of a ship's captain, to all appearances a prosperous Finn or Swede, who during the whole journey was sucking a pipe and talking on one and the same theme:

"Ha, you are an officer! My brother is also an officer, but he's only a sailor... He's a sailor and serves in Kronstadt. Why are you going to Moscow?"

"I serve there."

"Ha! And do you have a family?"

"No, I live with an aunt and a sister."

"My brother is also an officer, a sailor, but he's a family man, has a wife and three children. Ha!"

The Finn was pleased about something, gave a wide, idiotic smile when he exclaimed "Ha", and continually puffed at his stinking pipe. Klimov, who was feeling unwell and was replying with difficulty to the questions, detested him with all his soul. He dreamt that it would be good to snatch the sizzling pipe out of his hands and fling it under the seat, and banish the Finn himself to another carriage.

"Horrible people, these Finns and... Greeks," he thought. "Quite unwanted, good for nothing, horrible people. They just take up space on the earth. What good are they?"

And the thought about Finns and Greeks induced something like nausea in his whole body. By way of comparison, he wanted to think about the French and Italians, but the memory of those people for some reason aroused in him only visions of organ grinders, naked women and the foreign oleographs which hung over the chest of drawers at his aunt's house.

In general the officer felt strange. Somehow he could not find room on the seat for his arms and legs, though he had the seat to himself; his mouth felt dry and sticky; his head seemed filled with a thick fog; it seemed as though thoughts were swirling not just in his head, but outside his skull, among the seats and people, shrouded in the darkness of the night. Through the murk in his head, as if in a dream, he heard the muttering of voices, the clattering of wheels, the banging of doors. The bells, the whistles of the conductor and the bustle of the public on the platform seemed louder than usual. Time was flying quickly, imperceptibly, and for that reason it seemed the train was stopping every minute at a station. From outside, he kept hearing harsh voices:

"Is the mail ready to go?"

"It's ready!"

It seemed that the stoker came in too often to look at the thermometer, and that the noise of an oncoming train, and the clattering of the wheels on a bridge, was continually heard. The noise, the whistles, the Finn, the tobacco smoke – all these things, mixing with the threats and flashing of obscure images, the form and nature of which cannot be recalled by a healthy person, oppressed Klimov like an unbearable nightmare. In great misery he raised his heavy head, looked at the lantern, in the rays of which danced shadows and dim spots, and wanted to ask for water, but his dry tongue hardly moved, and he had barely enough strength to reply to the Finn's questions. He tried to lie down more comfortably and go to sleep, but did not succeed; the Finn several times fell asleep, woke up and began to smoke his pipe, turned to him with his "Ha!" and again fell asleep – but the lieutenant's legs still found no room on the seat, and the threatening images kept appearing before his eyes.

At Spirovo he went out to the station for a drink of water. He saw people sitting at a table and hurriedly eating.

"How they can eat!" he thought, trying not to sniff the air, which smelt of fried meat, and not looking at the chewing mouths – both disgusted him to the point of nausea.

A beautiful lady was talking loudly to a soldier in a red forage cap, and showing wonderful white teeth when she smiled – and the smile and the teeth and the lady herself created in Klimov an impression as disgusting as the ham and fried cutlets. He could not understand how the soldier in the red forage cap could bear to sit next to her and look at her healthy, smiling face.

When Klimov returned to the carriage after a drink of water, the Finn was sitting and smoking. His pipe was giving off a low hissing sound and gurgling like a leaky galosh in wet weather.

"Ha!" he said in surprise. "What station is this?"

"I don't know," replied Klimov, lying down and covering his mouth so as not to breathe the acrid tobacco smoke.

"When will we be in Tver?"

"I don't know. Excuse me, I... I can't reply. I'm unwell, caught a cold today."

The Finn knocked his pipe against the window frame and began to talk about his brother the sailor. Klimov was no longer listening to him, and was sadly recalling his soft, comfortable bed, the decanter of cold water and his sister Katya, who would know how to put him to bed, calm him, give him water. He even smiled when there flashed through his mind a vision of his batman Pavel taking off his tight, heavy boots and putting water on the table. It seemed to him that he had only to go to bed and drink some water, and the nightmare would yield to sound, healthy sleep.

"Is the mail ready to go?" A muffled voice reached him from a distance.

"It's ready!" replied a bass voice right by the window.

This was already the second or third station from Spirovo.

Time was flying quickly, by leaps, and it seemed there would be no end to the bells, whistles and stops. Klimov buried his face despairingly in the corner of the seat, put his arms around his head and again began to think about his sister Katya and batman Pavel, but his sister and the batman got mixed up with foggy images, began to whirl and disappeared. His hot breath, rebounding from the back of the sofa, stung his face; his legs lay uncomfortably;

there was a draught on his back from the window; but, however agonizing it was, he no longer wanted to change position... A heavy, nightmarish lassitude seized him little by little and welded together his limbs.

When he decided to raise his head, it was already light in the carriage. The passengers were putting on their fur coats and moving about. The train stopped. Porters in white aprons and with badges jostled around the passengers and grabbed their suitcases. Klimov put on his greatcoat and left the carriage absent-mindedly after the others – and it seemed to him that it was not he himself who was walking, but someone else, a stranger, and he felt that along with him had come out of the carriage his fever, thirst and those threatening images which all night had given him no sleep. He collected his baggage unthinkingly and engaged a cab. The cabman asked for a rouble and twenty-five copecks to go to Povarskaya Street;* Klimov did not haggle, but unquestioningly, obediently, got into the sleigh. He could still distinguish numbers, but money no longer had any value to him.

At home Klimov was met by his aunt and sister Katya, a girl of eighteen. When Katya greeted him, she had an exercise book and pencil in her hands, and he remembered that she was preparing for her teacher's exam. Without replying to questions and greetings, but only panting from the fever, he walked aimlessly through all the rooms and, reaching his bed, collapsed on the pillow. The Finn, the red forage cap, the lady with the white teeth, the smell of the fried meat, the flashing spots – all filled his consciousness, and he no longer knew where he was, nor could he hear the anxious voices around him.

When he regained consciousness, he found himself in his bed, undressed; he saw the decanter of water and Pavel, but these things made the bed neither cooler, nor softer nor more comfortable for him. As before, his legs and arms could not settle, his tongue stuck to his palate and he could hear the gurgling of the Finn's pipe... Near the bed, brushing with his broad back against Pavel, a thick-set, black-bearded doctor was bustling around.

"It's all right, it's all right, young man!" he muttered. "Excellent, excellent... Zo, zo..."

The doctor called Klimov a young man, and instead of "so" said "zo", instead of "yes", "yah"...

"Yah, yah, yah," he gushed. "Zo, zo... Excellent, young man... No reason to be upset!"

The rapid, offhand talk of the doctor, his well-fed face and condescending "young man" irritated Klimov.

"Why do you call me 'young man'?" he groaned. "Why such familiarity? To the devil with you!"

And his voice frightened him. This voice was so dry, weak and melodious that he could not recognize it.

"Excellent, excellent," the doctor muttered, not in the least offended. "You needn't be angry... Yah, yah, yah..."

At home time flew as startlingly fast as in the carriage... The light of day in the bedroom was constantly yielding to the darkness of night. The doctor seemed not to leave the bedside, and his "yah, yah, yah" was heard every minute. A row of faces continually stretched across the bedroom. These were: Pavel, the Finn, Staff-Captain Yaroshevich, Sergeant-Major Maksimenko, the red forage cap, the lady with the white teeth, the doctor. They were all talking, waving their arms, smoking, eating. Once, in the light of day, Klimov even saw his regimental priest, Father Alexander, who in his vestments and with a prayer book in his hands was standing by the bed; he was muttering something, and his face appeared more serious than Klimov had ever known it to be. The lieutenant remembered that, in a friendly spirit, Father Alexander used to call all Catholic officers "Poles", and, wishing to make him laugh, shouted:

"Father, Yaroshevich the Pole has run to the Pole!"

Father Alexander, though a fun-loving, jolly man, was not laughing, but with a serious face was making the sign of the cross over Klimov. Time and again during the night two shadows noiselessly entered and left. These were his aunt and sister. His sister's shadow knelt and prayed: she bowed to the icon, and her grey shadow bowed to the wall, so that two figures seemed to be praying. All the time there was the smell of fried meat and the Finn's pipe, but once Klimov also noticed the strong smell of incense. He began to move around from nausea and began to shout:

"Incense! Take away the incense!"

There was no reply. All that could be heard was the quiet chanting of the priest somewhere and someone running on the staircase.

When Klimov regained consciousness, there was not a soul in the bedroom. The morning sun was shining through the half-closed curtain of the window and a shimmering ray, thin and graceful, like a blade, was playing on the decanter. He heard the clatter of wheels – it meant there was no longer snow on the street. The lieutenant looked at the ray, at the familiar furniture, at the door, and his first impulse was to laugh. His chest and stomach began to shake with sweet, happy, tickling laughter. His whole being, from head to foot, was seized with the sensation of boundless happiness and the joy of life, such as the first man must have felt when he was created and saw the world for the first time. Klimov wanted terribly to move about, see people, talk. He lay motionless on his back, moving only his hands, but he was hardly aware of this: all his attention was focused on trifles. He was delighted by his breathing, his laughter – delighted by the existence of the decanter, the ceiling, the rays of light, the lace on the curtain. God's world, even in such a confined space as the bedroom, seemed to him beautiful, diverse, grand. When the doctor appeared, the lieutenant was thinking about what a wonderful thing medicine was, how kind and likeable the doctor was, and in general how fine and interesting people were.

"Yah, yah, yah…" gushed the doctor. "Excellent, excellent… Now we really have recovered… Zo, zo."

The lieutenant listened and laughed joyfully. He recalled the Finn, the lady with the white teeth, the ham, and he wanted to smoke, to eat.

"Doctor," he said, "Tell them to give me a crust of rye bread with salt and… and sardines."

The doctor refused. Pavel did not obey the order, and did not go for bread. The lieutenant could not bear this, and burst into tears, like a capricious child.

"Little baby!" laughed the doctor. "Mama, bah-ha-ha!"

Klimov also began to laugh, and when the doctor left, he fell soundly asleep. He awoke with the same feeling of joy and the same sensation of happiness. His aunt was sitting near the bed.

"Ah, Auntie!" he rejoiced. "What was it I had?"

"Spotted typhus."

"So that was it. But now I'm well, very well! Where is Katya?"

"Not at home. She probably called in somewhere coming from her exam."

The old woman said this and bent down to her stocking; her lips began to tremble; she turned away and suddenly began to sob. In despair, having forgotten the instructions of the doctor, she said:

"Ah, Katya, Katya! Our angel is no more! No more!"

She dropped her stocking and bent down for it, and at that moment her cap fell off her head. Looking at her grey head and understanding nothing, Klimov grew frightened for Katya and asked:

"So where is she? Auntie!"

The old woman, who had already forgotten about Klimov and remembered only her grief, said:

"She caught typhus from you and... and died. She was buried the day before yesterday."

This terrible, unexpected news penetrated deeply into Klimov's consciousness, but however terrible and overpowering it was, it could not overcome the deep-seated joy that filled the recovering lieutenant. He cried, laughed and was soon telling them off for not giving him anything to eat.

Only a week later, when he, in a worn dressing gown, supported by Pavel, went to the window, looked at the overcast spring sky and listened to the unpleasant clatter of some old rails that were being carried past, did his heart tighten with pain; he burst into tears and pressed his forehead to the window frame.

"How unhappy I am!" he sobbed, "God, how unhappy I am!"

And joy yielded place to the grind of everyday life and the feeling of irrecoverable loss.

The Kind Acquaintance

THE BOOTS OF THE MEN AND THE WOMEN – the men's roughshod and the women's fur-lined – are slipping on the smooth ice. So many feet are sliding that even in China there would not be enough bamboo sticks to support them. The sun is shining especially brightly; the air is especially clear; cheeks are glowing more radiantly than usual, and the eyes of the girls promise more than they should. In short: live, man, and enjoy life! However...

"Not on your life!" says Fate in the guise of my... kind acquaintance.

I sit far from the skating rink on a bench under a bare tree and converse with "her". I feel as though I could eat her, together with her hat, fur coat and little feet, on which a pair of skates shine – she is so beautiful! I am suffering, but at the same time feeling happy! Oh, love! But... not on your life...

Past us walks our departmental "doorman", our Argus and Mercury,* pastry-cook and messenger, Spyevsip Makarov. In his hands he is carrying some galoshes, men's and women's, probably those of important people. Spyevsip salutes me and, regarding me with tenderness and affection, stops by the bench.

"It's cold, Your Hon... Honour..." He coughs and clears his throat. "Do you have a little something for a cup of tea... sir?"

I give him a twenty-copeck piece. This kindness touches him deeply. He repeatedly blinks, looks around and says in a whisper:

"I feel very sorry for you. It's a shame, Your Honour!... I pity you greatly! It's as if you were my son... You are such a good man! A dear soul! So kind! Such a modest person! When, the other day, *he* – that is to say, His Excellency, tore into you – I was very upset! God above! I thought: 'Why is he going for the young man?' 'You are a lazybones,' he said, 'and an ignorant youth, and I shall get rid of you' – and so on and so on... For what? When you left his presence, you were beside yourself. Dear God... I was looking on, and pitied you... Oh, I have always had a soft spot for you young clerks!"

And, turning to my companion, Spyevsip adds:

"They behaved so badly about those papers. They shouldn't concern themselves with highfalutin documents... They should have had a career in commerce... or the Church. Dear God! Not a single paper of theirs made sense... They were all useless! But he got the blame... The boss completely put him down... Wanted to get rid of him. But I pitied him. His Honour is a kind man..."

She looks me in the eye with puzzled concern.

"Leave us," I say angrily to Spyevsip. I am fuming with rage.

I feel that even my galoshes are growing red. He shamed me, the scoundrel! To one side, behind bare bushes, sits her father, listening and staring at us. Now I cannot dare even to think about becoming a titular councillor. On the other side, behind other bushes, strolls her mother, observing "her". I sense these four eyes on me... and feel I could die...

Difficult People

Y EVGRAF IVANOVICH SHIRYAEV, a small landholder and
the son of a priest (his deceased father, Father Ioann, had
received 102 *desyatins** of land as a gift from the wife of General
Kuvshinnikov), was standing in the corner before a copper wash-
stand, washing his hands. As usual, he appeared anxious and
gloomy, and his beard was uncombed.

"Well, this is some weather!" he was saying. "It's not weather,
but the scourge of God. It's raining again!"

He was muttering, and his family was sitting at the table waiting for him to finish washing his hands so they could start dinner.
His wife Fedosya Semyonovna, son Pyotr, a student, the eldest
daughter Varvara and three small children had already long since
been sitting at the table and waiting. The children – Kolka, Vanka
and Arkhipka, snub-nosed and unwashed, with chubby faces and
wiry hair that had not been cut for a long time, were impatiently
fidgeting on their chairs, while the grown-ups were sitting motionless; evidently for them it made no difference whether they ate
or waited...

As if trying their patience, Shiryaev slowly wiped his hands,
slowly said his prayers and unhurriedly sat down at the table.
Shchi was immediately served. From the yard came the sound
of carpenters' axes (the Shiryaevs were having a new barn built)
and the laughter of the farmhand Fomka, who was teasing a turkeycock. A fine but steady rain was driving against the window.

The student Pyotr, round-shouldered and wearing glasses, was
eating and exchanging glances with his mother. Several times he
put down his spoon and coughed, as if wishing to say something,
but, after looking intently at his father, again resumed eating.
Finally, when the *kasha** had been served, he coughed resolutely
and said:

"I would like to leave today on the evening train. It's high time, because even as it is, I've missed two weeks. Lectures begin on the first of September."

"Well, go," agreed Shiryaev. "What are you waiting for? Up and go with God."

A minute passed in silence.

"He needs money for the journey, Yevgraf Ivanich," his mother said quietly.

"Money? Good Lord! You can't leave without money. If you need it, take it now, if you like. You should have taken it long ago!"

The student sighed lightly and exchanged a look of relief with his mother. Shiryaev unhurriedly took a wallet out of his side pocket and put on his glasses.

"How much do you want?" he asked.

"The trip to Moscow actually costs eleven roubles forty-two..."

"Oh, money, money!" sighed his father (he always sighed when he saw money, even when receiving it). "Here is twelve for you. So, my boy, there will be change, which you may find useful on the trip."

"Thank you."

A little later the student said:

"Last year I didn't immediately find work tutoring. I don't know what it will be like this year – it will probably be a while before I can start earning. I would ask you to give me fifteen roubles for room and board."

Shiryaev thought for a moment and sighed.

"You can have ten more," he said. "Here, take it!"

The student thanked him. He should have asked for more – for clothes, for the fee for attendance at lectures, for books – but after looking intently at his father he decided not to pester him further. His mother, though, who like all mothers lacked diplomacy and common sense, could not remain silent and said:

"You should give him another six roubles for boots, Yevgraf Ivanich. Well, look, how can he go to Moscow in such tattered footwear?"

"Let him take my old ones. They're still quite good."

"At least give him money for trousers. It's shameful to look at him…"

After this, a stormy scene immediately blew up, in the face of which the whole family trembled: Shiryaev's short, plump neck suddenly turned red, like dyed calico. The colour slowly rose to his ears, and went from his ears to his temples, until little by little it covered his whole face. Yevgraf Ivanich began to squirm on his chair, and undid his shirt collar so as not to be suffocated. Evidently he was wrestling with the feelings that were taking hold of him. A deathly silence set in. The children held their breath. Fedosya Semyonovna herself, as if not understanding what was happening to her husband, continued:

"He's no longer a little boy, you know. It's shameful for him to go around badly dressed."

Shiryaev suddenly leapt up, and with all his strength threw his fat wallet down in the middle of the table, so that a chunk of bread fell off a plate. A terrifying expression of rage, resentment, greed – all of these things – flared up on his face.

"Take everything!" he cried in a voice not his own. "Rob me! Take everything! Finish me off!"

He leapt up from the table, clutched his head and, stumbling, began to run around the room.

"Fleece me!" he screamed in a shrill voice. "Squeeze out the last drop! Rob me! Grab me by the throat!"

The student reddened and lowered his eyes. He could no longer eat. Fedosya Semyonovna, who even after twenty-five years had not become accustomed to her husband's difficult character, shrank back and began to babble something in her defence. In her exhausted, bird-like face, always dull and frightened, appeared an expression of amazement and blind fear. The children and eldest daughter Varvara, an adolescent with a pale, plain face, put down their spoons and froze.

Shiryaev, growing more and more savage, uttering words each more terrible than the others, ran to the table and began to throw money out of the wallet.

"Take it!" he rasped, trembling all over. "You've eaten and drunk your fill, so there's money for you too! I don't need anything! Have new boots and full-dress uniforms made for yourself."

The student went pale and rose.

"Listen, Papa," he began, breathing heavily. "I… I beg you to stop, because—"

"Be quiet!" his father shouted at him, so loudly that his glasses fell off his nose. "Be quiet!"

"Before now, I… I was able to put up with such outbursts, but… I won't tolerate them. Understand? I won't tolerate them!"

"Be quiet!" cried his father, stamping his feet. "You have to listen to what I say! I say what I want, and you… be quiet! At your age I was earning money, but you, you scoundrel, do you know how much you cost me? I shall drive you out! Parasite!"

"Yevgraf Ivanich," muttered Fedosya Semyonovna, nervously moving her fingers. "Surely he… surely Petya…"

"Be quiet!" Shiryaev shouted at her, tears of rage in his eyes. "It's you who spoilt them! You! You are to blame for everything! He doesn't respect us, doesn't pray to God, doesn't earn money! There are ten of you, but I'm alone! I shall drive you out of the house!"

The daughter Varvara looked for a long time at her mother open-mouthed, then shifted her vacant look to the window, went pale and, giving a loud cry, leant back in her chair. The father waved his hand, swore and ran out to the yard.

The Shiryaev family scenes usually ended like this. But now, unfortunately, student Pyotr was suddenly seized by an irresistible fury. He was just as hot-tempered and difficult as his father and his grandfather the archpriest, who used to beat his parishioners on the head with a stick. Pale, with clenched fists, he went up to his mother and shouted in a high-pitched voice such as only he was able to summon:

"These reproaches are vile and disgusting to me! I don't need anything from you! Nothing! I would sooner die of hunger than eat even one more crumb of yours! Take back your despicable money! Take it!"

His mother pressed herself to the wall and began to wave her hands, as if it were not her son standing before her, but an apparition.

"How am I to blame?" She began to sob. "How?"

The son, just like his father, waved his hand and ran out to the yard. The Shiryaevs' house stood on its own by a gulch, which cut through the steppe like a furrow for five versts. Its edge was overgrown with young oaks and alders, and at the bottom ran a stream. On one side the house faced the gulch, on the other, a field. There was no fence or barrier. Instead, there were all kinds of farm buildings pressed closely one to another, enclosing in front of the house a small area. This was the yard, where hens, ducks and pigs wandered.

Going outside, the student walked along the muddy road to the field. Autumn was in the air, and there was a piercing dampness. The road was muddy, with puddles gleaming here and there, and on the yellow field the grass looked autumnal, cheerless, damp, dark. On the right-hand side of the road was a vegetable garden, all dark and dug up; in places, sunflowers were still standing, with downcast heads that had already turned black.

Pyotr thought it would not be a bad idea to go to Moscow on foot, to go as he was, without a hat, in tattered boots and without a copeck of money. After a hundred versts, his dishevelled and frightened father would overtake him and beg him to return or take money, but Pyotr would not even look at him, just keep walking and walking... The bare forests would give way to cheerless fields, the fields... to forests; soon the earth would turn white from the first snow, and the rivers would be covered in ice... Somewhere near Kursk or Serpukhov he, weak and dying of hunger, would collapse and die. They would find his dead body, and all the newspapers would report that somewhere such and such a student had died of hunger...

A muddy-tailed white dog, which had been wandering through the vegetable garden looking for something, stared at him and came plodding after him...

He walked along the road and thought about death, about the grief of his family, about the moral torments of his father, and right away imagined all kinds of adventures on the road, each more fantastical than the others: picturesque places, terrible nights, unexpected encounters. He imagined a file of pilgrims, a hut in the forest with one little window shining brightly through the darkness; he would stand before the window, ask to spend the night… They would let him in and… suddenly he would see that they were robbers. Or, even better, he would come across a big manor house where, after realizing who he was, they would give him things to eat and drink, play the piano for him and listen to his woes – and the beautiful daughter of the house would fall in love with him.

Occupied with his grief and similar thoughts, young Shiryaev kept walking and walking… Before him, far, far in the grey, cloudy distance, a dark coaching inn was visible. Still farther away, on the very horizon, a little bump could be seen; this was the railway station. This bump reminded him of the link that existed between the place where he was now standing and Moscow, where lights shone, carriages rattled along, lectures were given. And he almost burst into tears from melancholy and impatience. The solemnity of nature, with its order and beauty, the deathly hush around him, he found repulsive to the point of making him feel despair, disgust.

"Watch out!" He heard a loud voice behind him.

An old lady, a landowner well known to him, drove past the student in a light, elegant landau. He bowed to her and gave a wide smile. And at once he was taken aback by this smile, which did not accord at all with his sombre mood. Where did it come from, if his soul was full of vexation and melancholy?

And he thought that nature herself probably gave man this ability to put on a good face, so that even in difficult times of mental strain he was able to preserve the secrets of his home, as the fox or wild duck preserves them. Every family has its joys and its miseries, but however great they are, it is hard for other eyes to see them: they are secrets. For example, the father of the lady who had just driven by had for some offence suffered for half a lifetime the wrath of Tsar Nicholas; her husband had been a gambler; and of their four sons, not one had turned out well. One could imagine how many terrible scenes took place in their family, how many tears flowed. And yet, the old lady seemed happy, contented, and responded to his smile with one of her own. The student remembered his friends, who spoke reluctantly about their families – he remembered his mother, who almost always lied when she talked about her husband and children...

Pyotr walked far from home along the roads till dusk, abandoning himself to gloomy thoughts. When it began to drizzle, he made for home. As he walked back, he decided that, come what may, he would talk to his father, to make him realize once and for all that it was difficult and terrible to live with him.

He found the house quiet. His sister Varvara was lying behind the partition and gently moaning with a headache. His mother, with a surprised, guilty look, was sitting next to her on the trunk and mending Arkhipka's trousers. Yevgraf Ivanich was pacing from window to window and frowning at the weather. By his walk, by his cough and even by the back of his head, it was evident that he felt himself to be at fault.

"So you changed your mind about going today?" he asked.

The student felt a welling up of pity for him, but, mastering this feeling at once, he said:

"Listen... I have to talk seriously to you... Yes, seriously... I have always respected you and... and never wanted to talk to you in such a tone, but your behaviour... is the last straw..."

His father looked out of the window and was silent. The student, as if marshalling his words, rubbed his forehead and continued with strong emotion:

"Dinner and tea never finish without your causing an uproar. Your bread sticks in everyone's throat... There is nothing more insulting, more humiliating than reproaches about earning one's living... Though you are our father, no one, neither God nor nature, has given you the right to be so deeply offensive, to humiliate, to vent your nasty feelings on the weak. You torment mother, treat her like a slave; my sister is hopelessly downtrodden, while I—"

"It's not your business to teach me," said his father.

"Yes, it is my business! You can mock me as much as you like, but leave Mother in peace! I shall not let you torment Mother!" continued the student, his eyes flashing. "You are spoilt because no one has yet brought themselves to oppose you. They tremble before you, grow dumb, but now it's finished! Coarse, ill-mannered man! You are coarse… understand? You are coarse, difficult, callous! And the peasants can't stand you!"

By now the student had lost the thread and was no longer speaking, but just blurting out isolated words. Yevgraf Ivanich listened in silence, as if stunned, but suddenly his neck reddened, the colour spread to his face, and he began to stir.

"Silence!" he shouted.

"Very well!" His son did not calm down. "You don't like to hear the truth? Excellent! Good! Start shouting! Excellent!"

"Be quiet, I tell you!" roared Yevgraf Ivanich.

Fedosya Semyonovna appeared in the doorway with an astonished face, very pale; she wanted to say something, but was unable, just moved her fingers.

"You're the one to blame!" Shiryaev shouted at her. "You brought him up like this!"

"I don't want to live in this house any longer!" shouted the student, crying and looking angrily at his mother. "I don't want to live with you!"

The daughter Varvara cried out from behind the screen and began to sob loudly. Shiryaev waved his hand and ran out of the house.

The student went to his room and quietly lay down. Until midnight he lay motionless, without opening his eyes. He felt neither anger nor shame, but some vague mental anguish. He did not blame his father, did not pity his mother, did not torment himself with regret; it was clear to him that everyone in the house was now feeling the same anguish – but who was at fault, who was suffering more, who less, God alone knew.

At midnight he awoke the farmhand, told him to prepare the horses to go to the station at five o'clock in the morning, undressed and pulled the cover over himself – but he could not sleep. Until morning he heard how his father, who also could not sleep, was quietly pacing from window to window and sighing. No one slept; no one said more than a few words, and then only in whispers. Twice his mother came to him from behind the screen. Always with the same dazed, vacant expression, she for a long time made the sign of the cross over him and nervously shuddered.

At five o'clock in the morning the student affectionately said goodbye to everyone, and even cried. Going past his father's room, he looked through the doorway. Yevgraf Ivanich, who had not gone to bed and was still dressed, was standing at the window, drumming on the panes.

"Goodbye, I'm going," his son said.

"Goodbye… Money is on the round table…" replied his father without turning around.

A nasty, cold rain was falling as the farmhand took him to the station. The heads of the sunflowers were bending even lower, and the grass seemed darker.

Oh, Women, Women!

S ERGEI KUZMICH POCHITAYEV, editor of the provincial
newspaper *Odds and Ends*, returned home from the office
tired and worn out, and collapsed on the sofa.

"Thank God! I'm home at last... I shall rest my weary soul
here... on the domestic hearth, near my wife... my Masha...
the only person who can understand me, who will sincerely
sympathize..."

"Why are you so pale today?" asked his wife, Marya Denisovna.

"Well, I'm sad at heart... That's why I'm glad to come to you:
to rest my weary soul."

"So what happened?"

"Things are hard generally, but today in particular. Petrov
doesn't want to give paper on credit anymore. The secretary
has started to drink heavily again... Now, all this is trivial,
and will be resolved somehow... But here's where the trouble
lies, Manyechka... I am sitting in the office today and reading
the proofs of my leading article. Suddenly the door opens and
there enters Prince Prochukhantsyev, my long-time comrade
and friend, the one who in amateur theatricals always plays the
leading lovers, and who for a single kiss once gave the actress
Zryakina his white horse. 'Why the devil has he come?' I think.
'It must be for a good reason... He's come,' I think, 'to get
publicity for Zryakina'... We got into conversation... About
this and that, one thing and another... It turned out that he
had not come for publicity. He had brought some of his verses
for publication...

"'I feel,' he says, 'a fiery flame in my heart and... a flaming fire.
I want to taste the sweetness of authorship...'

"He takes from his pocket a pink sheet of paper drenched in
perfume and hands it to me...

"'Verses,' he says... 'They are,' he says, 'somewhat subjective, but after all... Even Nekrasov* was subjective...'

"I take these same subjective verses and read them... Most insufferable rubbish! You read them and feel that your eyes are stinging, and you have a sinking feeling in the pit of your stomach, as if you'd swallowed a millstone... He dedicated the verses to Zryakina. If he had dedicated the verses to me, I would have taken him to court. In one poem the word 'headlong' occurs five times! And the rhyming! There is 'lily of the vall-EE' instead of 'lily of the VALL-ee'! He rhymes 'horse' with 'house'.

"'No,' I say, 'you are my friend and mate, but I can't find a place for your verses...'

"'But why?'

"'Because... For editorial reasons beyond my control... They don't fit into the newspaper's programme...'

"I went red in the face, and my eyes began to itch. I lied that I had a headache... How could I tell him that his verses were no good at all? He noticed my embarrassment and puffed himself up like a turkeycock.

"'You,' he says, 'are angry with Zryakina, and that's why you don't want to publish my verses. I understand... I understa-a-a-nd, dear sir!'

"He accused me of being prejudiced, called me a philistine, a penpusher and something else... He lectured me for a good two hours. In the end he vowed to start a campaign against me... He left without saying goodbye... So that's what happened, my dear! The fourth of December is St Varvara's Day, Zryakina's name day – and the verses have to be published without fail... Even if I die doing it, I must get them in! But they are unprintable: the newspaper will be ridiculed throughout Russia. It's also impossible not to print them: Prochukhantsyev will scheme against me – all will be lost for no reason. Be so good now as to think of how I can get out of this ridiculous situation!"

"And the verses? What are they about?" asked Marya Denisovna.

"There is nothing to them. They are rubbish. Would you like me to read them? They start like this:

> Through the smoke of a dreamy cigar
> You drifted in my dreams,
> Bearing with you the blows of love
> With an ardent smile on your lips...

"And then straight on to:

> Forgive me, my snow-white angel,
> Friend of my days and my tender ideal,
> That, having forgotten love, I rush headlong,
> Where I surrender to death... Oh, I am terrified!

"And so on... it's rubbish."

"What do you mean? These verses are nice!" said Marya Denisovna, throwing up her hands. "Even very nice! Why aren't they good verses? You are just being over-critical, Sergei! 'Through the smoke... with an ardent smile'... You seem to understand nothing! You don't understand, Sergei!"

"It's you who don't understand, not I!"

"No, excuse me... Prose I don't understand, but poetry I understand very well! The prince writes superbly! Excellently! You hate him, and that is why you don't want to publish his verses!"

The editor sighed and drummed his fingers – first on the table, then on his forehead...

"Connoisseurs!" he muttered, smiling scornfully.

And, taking up his top hat, he shook his head bitterly and left the house...

"'I go to seek through the world, where the wounded can find refuge... Oh, women, women!'"* he thought, plodding to the London restaurant.

He needed a drink...

Fiancé and Father

Something Modern

A SCENE

"BUT YOU, I HEARD, are to be married!" an acquaintance said to Pyotr Petrovich Milkin at the dacha ball. "So when will the bachelor party be held?"

"Where did you get the idea that I'm going to be married?" Milkin flared up. "What fool told you that?"

"Everyone says so, and it's obvious to all... There's no need to be secretive, my friend. You think we know nothing, but we see through you and know! Heh-heh-heh... It's obvious to everyone... For days on end you sit at the Kondrashkins', dine there, sup, sing romances... You walk out only with Nastyenka Kondrashkina, you take flowers only to her... We see everything! The other day I met Kondrashkin, and he said that the whole matter is already settled, that the wedding will take place as soon as you move from the dacha to town... Isn't that so? God grant! I'm not as glad for you as for Kondrashkin himself... You see, the poor devil has seven daughters! Seven! It's not a joke! God knows it would be hard enough to fix up even one..."

"To the devil with him..." thought Milkin. "He's already the tenth person telling me about my marriage to Nastyenka. How did they get that idea, the devil take them all? They got it from the fact that every day I dine at the Kondrashkins', I walk out with Nastyenka... N-o-o, it's really time to stop these rumours – it's high time... otherwise, before you know it, they'll have me married off, curse them!... I'll go tomorrow and talk to that blockhead Kondrashkin, so that he doesn't entertain any hopes, and then – I'll be off!"

The next day, after the conversation just described, Milkin, feeling embarrassed and a little fearful, entered the dacha study of Court Councillor Kondrashkin.

"Pyotr Petrovich!" The host greeted him. "How are things with you? Have you missed her, dear boy? Heh-heh-heh… Nastyenka will be here shortly… She ran to the Gusyevs' for a minute…"

"I, as a matter of fact, did not come to see Nastasya Kirillovna," muttered Milkin, rubbing his eye in embarrassment, "but to see you… I have to talk to you about something… Something got into my eye…"

"So what is it you intend to talk to me about?" asked Kondrashkin with a wink. "Heh-heh-heh… Why are you so embarrassed, dear boy? Ah, men, men! The trouble there is with you young people! I know what it is you want to talk about! Heh-heh-heh… It's high time…"

"As a matter of fact, in a way, the point, do you see, is that I've come to say goodbye to you. I'm going away tomorrow…"

"What do you mean, 'you're going away'?" asked Kondrashkin, goggling with astonishment.

"It's very simple… I'm going away, that's all… I wish to thank you for your kind hospitality… Your daughters are so nice… I shall never forget the moments which—"

"Excuse me…" Kondrashkin went red. "I don't quite understand you. Of course, everyone has the right to go away… You may do anything you like, but, my dear sir, you… are being elusive… It's dishonourable!"

"I… I… I don't know… how is it that I'm being elusive?"

"You've been coming here all summer, eating, drinking, giving hope, chattering away with the young girls all day long, and suddenly, just like that, you say you're going away!"

"I… I was not giving hope."

"Of course, you didn't actually propose, but wasn't it quite clear what your behaviour was leading up to? Every day you dined, night after night walked arm in arm with Nastya… and was all this happening without intent? Only fiancés come to dine every day and, were you not a fiancé, would I really have been feeding you? Yes, sir! It's dishonourable! I don't wish to hear any more. Be so good as to propose, otherwise I... ah—"

"Nastasya Kirillovna is very nice... she's a good girl... I respect her and... one could not wish for a better wife, but... we don't agree on our beliefs and opinions."

"Is this really the reason?" smiled Kondrashkin. "Just that? My dear man, would it be at all possible to find such a wife, whose opinions were the same as her husband's? Ah, young man, young man! Inexperience, inexperience! How he launches a theory, so earnestly... heh-heh-heh... He's even starting to sweat... You don't agree now on your opinions, but live for a while and all these roughnesses will be smoothed over... You can't drive on a road when it's new, but after it's used a while you can really speed along!"

"That's all very well, but... I am unworthy of Nastasya Kirillovna..."

"You're worthy, worthy! That's nonsense! You are a fine young man!"

"You don't know of all my shortcomings... I am poor..."

"Nonsense! You receive a salary, and thank God—"

"I... am a drunkard..."

"Certainly not!... Not once have I seen you drunk!..." Kondrashkin waved his hands. "Youth has to drink... I myself was young, used to get carried away. It's impossible not to..."

"But you know, I drink like a fish. It's an hereditary vice."

"I don't believe you! Such a flower of manhood and suddenly... a drunkard! I don't believe you!"

"The devil won't be deceived!" thought Milkin. "How he wants to get rid of his daughters!"

"Not only do I suffer from drunkenness," he continued aloud, "but I also have other vices. I take bribes..."

"Dear boy, who on earth doesn't take them? Heh-heh-heh. Good Lord, I'm amazed!"

"And moreover, I'm not allowed to marry before I learn the decision about my fate... I have been keeping it from you, but now you must know all... I... I am awaiting trial for embezzlement..."

"Awaiting tri-al?" Kondrashkin was stupefied. "Y-yes... that's news... I did not know that. Indeed, you can't marry until you know your fate... But did you embezzle a lot?"

"A hundred and forty-four thousand."

"Y-yes, it's quite a sum! Yes indeed, the matter smells of Siberia... So a young girl can be ruined for no reason. In that case, nothing can be done, God save you..."

Milkin sighed with relief and reached for his hat...

"However," continued Kondrashkin after some thought, "if Nastyenka loves you, then she can follow you there. What sort of love is it if she fears sacrifices? And moreover, Tomsk Province is fertile. In Siberia, my friend, one can live better than here. I myself would go, if I had no family. You may propose to her!"

"What an intractable devil!" thought Milkin. "He would be prepared to marry his daughter to the Devil, if only to get her off his back."

"But that's not all," he continued aloud. "I shall be on trial not only for embezzlement, but for forgery."

"It's all the same. There will be one punishment!"

"Tfoo!"

"Why do you scoff so loudly?"

"This is why... Listen, I still have not revealed all to you... Don't force me to tell you the secret of my life... a terrible secret!"

"I don't wish to know your secrets! They're trivial!"

"They're not trivial, Kirill Trofimych! If you hear... learn who I am, you will recoil from me... I... I am an escaped convict!!"

Kondrashkin recoiled from Milkin as if stung, and seemed petrified. He stood silent and motionless for a minute, looking at Milkin with horror-filled eyes, then collapsed into an armchair and groaned:

"I did not expect this..." he mumbled. "Who have I harboured in my bosom! Go! For God's sake, leave! Let me never see you again! Oh!"

Milkin took his hat and, rejoicing in victory, made for the door...

"Wait!" Kondrashkin stopped him. "Why have they not captured you up to now?"

"I live under an assumed name... It's hard to capture me..."

"Perhaps you can live like that for the rest of your life, so that no one learns who you... Wait! Surely now you are an honourable man, who repented already long ago... God bless you, so be it, get married!"

Milkin broke out in a sweat... To lie further about being an escaped convict would get him nowhere, so only one course remained: to run away ignominiously, without justifying his escape... And he was about to scamper away to the door when a thought flashed through his mind...

"Listen, you still don't know everything!" he said. "I... I am a madman, and to the mad and insane marriage is forbidden..."

"I don't believe you! Madmen don't reason so logically..."

"You clearly don't understand, if you say that! Do you really not know that madmen act like madmen only at certain times, while in the intervals there is nothing to distinguish them from normal people?"

"I don't believe you. So don't talk!"

"In that case, I shall provide you with a certificate from the doctor!"

"I shall believe a certificate, but not you... A fine madman!"

"In half an hour I shall bring you a certificate. Meanwhile, goodbye."

Milkin grabbed his hat and hurriedly ran out. Five minutes later he was already with his friend Doctor Fityuyev, but, unfortunately, he happened to come at precisely the time when the doctor was tidying his hair after a little argument with his wife.

"My friend, I've come to you with a request!" he said to the doctor. "This is what it's about... They want to get me hitched at all costs... In order to escape this disaster I thought of acting like a madman... A kind of Hamlet-like trick... Madmen, you know, are forbidden to marry... Be a friend, give me a certificate to the effect that I'm mad!"

"You don't want to marry?" asked the doctor.

"Not for love or money!"

"In that case, I shall not give you a certificate," said the doctor, arranging his hair. "One who doesn't want to marry is not mad but, on the contrary, a wise man... But when you decide to marry, come to me for a certificate... Then it will be clear that you have taken leave of your senses..."

The Looking Glass

NEW YEAR'S EVE. Nellie, the young, pretty daughter of a landowning general, dreaming day and night about marriage, is sitting in her room and with tired, half-closed eyes is looking in the mirror. She is pale, tense and motionless, like the mirror.

A non-existent but very real vision, resembling a narrow, endless corridor, a row of innumerable candles, the reflection of her face, hands, the mirror frame – all this has already long been veiled with mist and blended into one boundless grey sea. The sea is swaying, twinkling, now and again blazing forth with a glow...

Looking at Nellie's fixed expression and open mouth, it is hard to know whether she is asleep or keeping vigil, but nonetheless she sees. At first she sees only a smile and the gentle expression, full of charm, of someone's eyes, but then in the swaying grey background gradually appear the contours of a head, face, eyebrows, beard. It is he, her intended, the object of long daydreams and hopes. Her intended is everything to Nellie: the meaning of life, personal happiness, a career, fate. Away from him, as in the grey background, is darkness, emptiness, meaninglessness. So it is no wonder that, seeing before her the attractive, gently smiling face, she feels delight, an inexpressibly sweet daydream which cannot be conveyed either in speech or writing. Moreover, she hears his voice, sees how she lives with him under one roof, how her life gradually blends with his. In the grey background months, years go by... and Nellie clearly, in every detail, sees her future.

Scene after scene flashes on the grey background. Now Nellie sees how on a cold winter's night she knocks on the door of the local doctor, Stepan Lukich. An old hound lazily and wheezily barks behind the gate. The doctor's windows are in darkness. Around is silence.

"For God's sake... for God's sake," whispers Nellie.

Now finally the gate creaks, and Nellie sees before her the doctor's cook.

"Is the doctor at home?"

"He's asleep, my dear…" whispers the cook in her sleeve, as if fearing to wake her master. "He has just returned from the epidemic. I was told not to wake him…"

But Nellie does not listen to the cook. Pushing her away, she runs like a madwoman to the doctor's apartments. After running through several dark and stuffy rooms and overturning on the way two or three chairs, she finally finds the doctor's bedroom. Stepan Lukich is lying dressed on his bed, but without his frock coat, and, having extended his lips, is breathing on his palm. Near him, a night lamp glows faintly. Without saying a word, Nellie sits down on a chair and starts to cry. She cries bitterly, her whole body shaking.

"My hus… husband is ill!" she says.

Stepan Lukich remains silent. He slowly rises, props his head up on his fist and looks at his guest with sleepy, motionless eyes.

"My husband is ill!" she repeats, restraining her sobbing. "For God's sake, let's go… Quickly… as quickly as possible!"

"What?" mumbles the doctor, blowing on his palm.

"Let's go! This very minute! Otherwise… otherwise… it will be terrible to say… For God's sake!"

And pale, exhausted Nellie, swallowing her tears and gasping for breath, starts to describe to the doctor the sudden illness of her husband and her inexpressible fear. Her suffering is capable of moving a stone, but the doctor looks at her, blows on his palm and… does not move.

"I'll come tomorrow…" he mutters.

"It's impossible!" says Nellie in fright. "I know, my husband has… typhus! Now… you have to come this minute!"

"I… ah… have only just returned," mutters the doctor. "Three times I was called out to the epidemic. I am exhausted, and ill myself… I absolutely cannot! Absolutely! I… I am myself infected… Look!"

The doctor shows the thermometer to Nellie.

"My temperature is nearly forty... I absolutely cannot! I... I can't even sit up. Excuse me, I'm lying down..."

The doctor lies down.

"But I'm begging you, doctor!" Nellie groans in despair. "I implore you! Help me, for God's sake. Summon all your strength and let's go... I shall pay you, doctor!"

"My God... Surely I've already told you! Ah!"

Nellie leaps up and paces nervously back and forth in the bedroom. She wants to explain to the doctor, to make him understand... It occurs to her that if he could know how dear to her is her husband and how unhappy she is, he would forget his tiredness and his illness. But how to find the eloquence?

"Go to the district doctor," she hears the voice of Stepan Lukich.

"It's impossible! He lives twenty-five versts from here, and time is precious. The horses will not make it: here from us is forty versts, and from here to the district doctor almost as many... No it's impossible! Let's go, Stepan Lukich! I beg you to be brave. Come on, do a brave deed! Take pity on me!"

"The devil take it... I have a fever... I cannot think straight, but she does not understand. I cannot! Leave me alone."

"But you are obliged to go! You cannot refuse to go! It's selfish of you! Man must sacrifice his life for others, yet you... you refuse to go! I shall bring an action against you!"

Nellie knows that she is making an offensive and undeserved threat, but to save her husband she is capable of forgetting even logic and tact, as well as consideration for others... In reply to her threat the doctor greedily drinks a glass of cold water. Like the very meanest beggar, Nellie begins again to entreat the doctor, to appeal to his compassion... At last the doctor yields. He rises slowly, gasps, groans and looks for his frock coat.

"Here it is, your coat!" Nellie helps him. "Allow me to put it on for you... There you are. Let's go. I shall pay you... I shall be grateful for the rest of my life..."

But what torture! After putting on his frock coat, the doctor lies down again. Nellie lifts him and drags him to the hall... In the hall there are prolonged, excruciating difficulties with the galoshes, the overcoat... The hat cannot be found... But then at last Nellie is sitting in the carriage. Next to her is the doctor. Now all that remains is to drive forty versts, and medical help will be with her husband. A mist hangs over the land: it is pitch dark... A cold winter wind is blowing. Beneath the wheels are frozen tussocks. The coachman continually stops and ponders over which road to take...

Nellie and the doctor are silent all the way. They are terribly shaken about, but feel neither the cold nor the shaking.

"Faster! Faster!" Nellie begs the coachman.

By five o'clock in the morning the exhausted horses are driving into the yard. Nellie sees the familiar gate, the well with its lifting device, the long row of stables and sheds. At last she is at home.

"Wait a moment, I'll be back directly..." she says to Stepan Lukich, putting him in the dining room on a divan. "Rest, and I shall go and see how he is."

Returning from her husband a minute later, Nellie finds the doctor lying down. He is lying on the divan, muttering something.

"Be so kind, doctor... Doctor!"

"What? Ask Domna..." mutters Stepan Lukich.

"What?"

"At the conference they said... Vlasov said... Who? What?"

To her great horror, Nellie sees that the doctor is delirious, like her husband. What should she do?

"I'll go to the district doctor," she decides.

Then again follows the dark, harsh, cold wind, the frozen tussocks. She suffers body and soul, but the trickster nature has not enough ways, not enough tricks to compensate her for these sufferings.

Further on, in the grey background, she sees how each spring her husband tries to find enough money to pay the interest to the bank on the mortgage for the estate. He does not sleep, she does not sleep, and both rack their brains to think of a way to escape a visit from the court bailiff.

She sees children. Here, there is perpetual fear about chest cold, scarlet fever, diphtheria, low marks at school, parting. Of five or six healthy children, one will certainly die.

The grey background is not free of death. That is understood. A husband and wife may not die at the same time: whatever happens, one of the two will have to witness the funeral of the other. And Nellie sees how her husband dies. This terrible misfortune appears to her in every detail. She sees the coffin, the candles, the sacristan and even the footprints that the undertaker has left in the hall.

"Why? What is it for?" she asks, looking dully at the face of her dead husband.

And all her previous life with her husband seems to her just a stupid, unnecessary prelude to this death.

Something falls from Nellie's hand and crashes on the floor. She shudders, jumps up and opens her eyes wide. One of the mirrors, she sees, is lying at her feet; the other is standing on the table as before. She looks at herself in the mirror and sees a pale, tearful face. The grey background has vanished.

"It seems I fell asleep…" she thinks, sighing lightly.

Strong Feelings

THIS INCIDENT OCCURRED not so long ago in the Moscow regional court. The jurors, who were being detained in court for the night, before going to sleep started a conversation about strong feelings. The idea occurred to them when they recalled the testimony of a witness who had developed a stammer and had gone grey, according to his account, because of some terrible experience. The jurors decided that, before going to sleep, they would each rummage in their memory and find something to tell. Human life is short, but nevertheless there is no man who can boast that he has not in the past had some terrible moments.

One juror told how he had almost drowned; another told how, one night, in a place where there was neither a doctor nor a chemist, he poisoned his own child by giving him in error zinc sulphate instead of soda. The child did not die, but the father nearly went out of his mind. The third, a not-yet-old but sickly man, described two of his attempts at suicide: once he shot himself; another time he threw himself under a train.

The fourth juror, a short, foppishly dressed fat man, spoke as follows:

"I was twenty-two or twenty-three years old, not more, when I fell head over heels in love with my present wife, and proposed to her... If I were young again now I would happily flog myself at the thought of marrying early, but then I did not know what would become of me if Natasha refused me. My love was the most sincere, such as is described in novels – mad, passionate and so on. I was breathless with happiness, and I did not know how to escape from it; I bored my father and friends and the servants, constantly telling them about how passionately I loved. Happy people are the most boring, most tiresome people. Even now I'm ashamed to think about how terribly boring I was...

"Among my friends then was a young lawyer. Now, this lawyer is famous throughout Russia, but then he was only just getting established, and was not yet so rich and famous as to have the right not to acknowledge old friends, or take off his hat when he met them. I used to visit him once or twice a week. I would arrive at his place and we would both lounge on divans and start to philosophize.

"Once I was lying on his divan and talking about how there was not a more thankless profession than the law. I wanted to prove how, when the interrogation of witnesses is finished, a court can easily manage without a public prosecutor or a defence lawyer, because neither are needed, and only hinder the proceedings. If an adult and mentally sound juror is convinced that the ceiling is white, or that Ivanov is guilty, then to challenge these beliefs and persuade him otherwise would be beyond the powers of a Demosthenes.* Who can convince me that I have a ginger moustache, if I know it's black? Listening to an orator, I, perhaps, would be deeply moved and would start to cry, but my fundamental belief, based largely on evidence and fact, would not at all change. But my lawyer argued that I was still young and stupid, and that I was talking childish nonsense. In his opinion, if responsible, knowledgeable people shed light for him on an obvious fact, it becomes more obvious – that is the first point; secondly, eloquence… it is elemental power, it is a whirlwind that allows an eloquent person to turn into dust even stones, let alone such trifles as the beliefs of the petty bourgeois and merchants of the second guild. Human frailty struggles hard against eloquence, as if looking unblinkingly at the sun or trying to stop the wind. A mere mortal by the strength of a word can turn thousands of convinced barbarians to Christianity; Odysseus was the most convinced man in the world, but was lured by the song of the sirens, and so on. All of history consists of similar examples, and they are met with at every step in life – and it has to be so, otherwise a clever and eloquent man would have no advantage over a fool and mediocre person.

"I stood my ground and continued to demonstrate that conviction is stronger than any eloquence – though, frankly speaking, I myself could not precisely define what exactly is conviction and what is eloquence. Probably, I only spoke in order to have something to say.

"'Take you, for example,' said the lawyer. 'You are convinced now that your fiancée is an angel and that there is no man in the whole town happier than you. But I say to you: ten or twenty minutes would be enough for me to get you to sit at this table and write a letter to break your engagement.'

"I laughed.

"'Don't you laugh – I speak seriously,' said my friend. 'If I were to try, then after twenty minutes you'd be happy at the thought that you don't have to marry. I'm not that eloquent, but surely even you are not that strong.'

"'Very well then, try!' I said.

"'No, why should I? It's just for the sake of talking. You're a good man, and it would be cruel to subject you to such a trial. Besides, I'm not in good form today.'

"We sat down to dine. The wine, and thoughts about Natasha and my love filled my whole being with a sense of youth and happiness. My happiness was so boundlessly great that the green-eyed lawyer who was sitting opposite me seemed to be unhappy – such a petty, dull creature…

"'Do try!' I pressed him. 'Come on, I'm asking you!'

"The lawyer shook his head and made a wry face. Evidently I had already begun to annoy him.

"'I know,' he said, 'that after my intervention you will thank me and call me your saviour, but surely you have to think about your fiancée. She loves you; if you were to break your engagement, she would suffer. And how lovely she is! I envy you.'

"The lawyer sighed, drank some wine and began to talk about how lovely my Natasha was. He had a rare gift to describe. He could talk a whole pile of words to you about women's eyelashes or little fingers. I listened to him with delight.

"'I've seen many women in my time,' he said, 'but I give you my honest word, speaking as a friend, that your Natalya Andreyevna is a pearl, a rare girl. Of course, she has shortcomings too – even many of them, if you wish – but all the same she is charming.'

"And the lawyer began to talk about the shortcomings of my fiancée. At first, I understood very well that he was speaking about women in general, about their weaknesses in general, but then he began to talk only about Natasha. He was delighted with her snub nose, with her shrill, piercing laughter, her affectation – namely with all those things I so disliked in her. All these things, in his opinion, were endlessly dear, graceful, feminine. Imperceptibly to me, his tone soon changed from one of rapture to one of paternal solicitude, then to one of lightness and disdain. The president of the court was not with us, so there was no one to stop the lawyer from getting worked up. I couldn't open my mouth, so what could I say? What my friend said was not new, but well known for already a long time, and all the poison was not in what he said, but in the way he said the damned things. That is to say, the devil knows in what way! Hearing him then, I was convinced that one and the same word has a thousand meanings and nuances, depending on how it is uttered, in what form, and how it is attached to a phrase. Of course, I cannot communicate to you either the tone or the form; I shall only say that, listening to my friend and pacing back and forth, I was indignant, outraged, felt the same contempt as he did. I even believed him when, with tears in his eyes, he declared that I was a great man, that I deserved a better fate, that I would accomplish something special in the future, something that would be hindered by marriage!

"'My friend,' he exclaimed, vigorously shaking my hand. 'I entreat you, I implore you: stop, before it's too late. Stop! Heaven save you from making this strange, cruel mistake! My friend, don't ruin your youth!'

"Believe it or not, in the end I sat down at the table and wrote a letter to break my engagement. I wrote, and rejoiced that there was still time to correct the mistake. After sealing the letter, I rushed from the house in order to drop it into the post box. The lawyer went with me.

"'Excellent! Well done!' He praised me when my letter to Natasha vanished into the void of the post box. 'I congratulate you with all my heart. I am pleased for your sake.'

"After walking some ten paces with me, the lawyer continued:

"'Of course, marriage does have its good side. I, for example, am among those who believe strongly in the married state.'

"By now he was describing his life, and there appeared before me all the ghastliness of the solitary, unmarried life.

"He spoke with delight about his future wife, about the joys of ordinary family life, and went into raptures so eloquently, so sweetly, that by the time we reached his door I was already in despair.

"'What are you doing to me, wretched man?' I said, gasping. 'You have destroyed me! Why did you force me to write that damn letter? I love her, I love her!'

"I swore that I loved her, and was horrified at my deed, which now seemed to me absurd and foolish. It is impossible to imagine any stronger feeling than that which I experienced then, gentlemen. Oh, what I experienced then, what I felt! Had I found a kind soul who at that moment would have handed me a revolver, I would with pleasure have put a bullet in my head.

"'Well, enough, enough...' said the lawyer, slapping me on the shoulder and laughing. 'Stop crying. The letter will not get to your fiancée. It was I, not you, who wrote the address on the envelope, and I so muddled it up that they'll never decipher it at the post office. All this will serve as a lesson to you: don't argue about what you don't understand.'

"Now, gentlemen, I suggest the next person speaks."

The fifth juror settled down more comfortably, and had already opened his mouth in order to begin his tale when the clock on the Spasskaya Tower* was heard striking.

"Twelve..." counted one of the jurors. "And what kind of feelings, gentlemen, are being experienced now by our defendant?

He, this murderer, spends the night in court under arrest, lies or sits, and of course does not sleep – and in the course of the whole sleepless night listens to that sound. What is he thinking about? What reveries visit him?"

And somehow all the jurors suddenly forgot about "strong feelings", so that what their fellow juror felt, having once written a letter to his Natasha, seemed unimportant, not even funny – and no one spoke any longer, but grew quiet, and silently lay down to sleep...

How I Was Married

A Little Story

ONCE THE PUNCH HAD BEEN DRUNK, our parents exchanged whispered comments and left us alone.

"Carry on!" my father whispered to me as he went out. "Go at it!"

"But how can I make a declaration of love to her," I whispered back, "if I don't love her?"

"That's not the point... You fool, you know nothing..."

Having said this, Papa gave me an angry look and left the summer house. An old woman's hand appeared in the half-open door and removed the candle from the table. We were left in darkness.

"Well, what must be must be," I thought, and, after clearing my throat, boldly said:

"The circumstances are favourable for me, Zoya Andreyevna. At last we are alone, and the darkness assists me, for it hides the embarrassment on my face... This embarrassment comes from the feeling that glows in my heart..."

But here I stopped. I heard how Zoya Zhelvakova's heart was beating and how her teeth were chattering. A trembling that was audible and could be felt through the shaking of the bench arose in her whole body. The poor girl did not love me. She hated me, like a dog hates a stick, and despised me, if only it can be admitted that the stupid are capable of despising the clever. Now I resemble a little orang-utan – ugly, though honoured with decorations and orders – but then I was like all immature youths: fat-faced, pimply, with a stubbly beard... My nose was red and swollen from a constant head cold and heavy drinking. Even bears could not envy my dexterity. And as to my mental qualities, there is nothing to say. From her, though, from Zoya, when she was

173

not yet my fiancée, I exacted an unfair bribe. I stopped, because I began to pity her.

"Let's walk in the garden," I said. "It's stuffy here..."

We went out and walked along the tree-lined path. My parents, who were eavesdropping behind the door, darted away into the bushes at our appearance. Moonlight was illuminating Zoina's face. I was stupid then, but managed to read on her face all the sweetness of vulnerability. I sighed and continued:

"The nightingale is singing, and amusing his little wife... But who can I, a bachelor, amuse?"

Zoya reddened and lowered her eyes. She had been trained to act in this way. We sat down on the bench, facing the stream. Behind the stream, the white church could be seen, and behind the church rose the landowner Count Kuldarov's house, where lived the clerk Bolnitzyn, the man Zoya loved. As Zoya sat down on the bench, she fixed her gaze on this house... My heart shrivelled, and I knitted my brow out of pity. My God, my God! All honour to our parents, but... if only they would spend a week in hell!

"All my happiness depends on one person," I continued. "I nourish feelings for this person... I feel she is the right one... I love her, and if she does not love me, then I, well, shall perish... shall die... This person is you. Can you love me? Well? Do you love me?"

"I love you," she whispered.

I, to confess, grew numb from these words of hers. Earlier, I had thought she would prove obstinate and refuse me, as she was deeply in love with another. I had hoped passionately for that, but it ended up differently... She had not the strength to swim against the tide.

"I love you," she repeated, and burst into tears.

"That can't be so!" I began, not knowing myself what I was saying, and shaking all over. "Is it really possible? Zoya Andreyevna, my dear, don't deceive yourself! Really and truly, don't deceive yourself! I don't love you! And you don't love me! Damn me three times if I love you! And you don't love me! All this is just nonsense..."

I jumped up and began to run around the bench.

"Please don't! All this is just a farce! They'll force us to marry, Zoya Andreyevna, for the sake of property interests. What sort of love is that? It would be better for a millstone to be hung around my neck than for me to take you as my own – that's all! Why the devil are they forcing us? What right do they have? What are we to them? Serfs? Dogs? We won't marry! Out of spite! They're such swine! We have already indulged them enough! I shall go now and say that I don't want to marry you – that's all!"

Zoya's face was no longer tearful, and in an instant her eyes were dry.

"I shall go and tell them!" I continued. "And you tell them too. You tell them that you don't love me at all, but that you love Bolnitzyn. And I shall shake Bolnitzyn's hand... I know very well how much you love him!"

Zoya laughed happily and began to walk beside me.

"But surely you too love someone else," she said, rubbing her hands. "You love Mademoiselle Debé."

"Yes," I said. "Mademoiselle Debé. Though she is not Orthodox and is not rich, I love her for her mind and noble qualities... Let them curse me, but I shall marry her. I love her, perhaps, more than I love life! I cannot live without her! If I don't marry her, I won't want to live! I shall go now... Let's go and tell those fools... Thank you, my dear... How you've relieved me!"

I felt a rush of happiness, and I started to thank Zoya, and Zoya me. And we both, happy and grateful, began to kiss each other's hands and call each other noble souls... I was kissing her hands, and she was kissing me on the head, on my bristly beard. I think I even embraced her, having forgotten etiquette. And, I can tell you, this declaration of non-love was more satisfying than any declaration of love. We went home joyfully, glowing and trembling, prepared to tell our parents. We walked, cheering each other up.

"Let them scold us," I said, "beat us, even drive us away, but at least we'll be happy!"

We entered the house, and there by the door our parents were standing and waiting. They looked at us, saw that we were happy and waved suddenly to the footman. The footman arrived with champagne. I started to protest, wave my hands, shout... Zoya cried, also shouted... The noise rose, uproar ensued, and it was impossible to drink the champagne.

But, all the same, we were married.

Today we celebrate our silver anniversary. We've lived together for a quarter of a century! At first we had a terrible time. I scolded her, cursed her, but ended up loving her out of grief. We had children out of grief... Later on... It was all right... We got a little used to each other... At the moment she, Zoyechka, is standing behind my back and, having put her hands on my shoulders, is kissing my bald patch.

The Cobbler and the Devil

IT WAS CHRISTMAS EVE. Marya had already long been snoring on the stove, and all the paraffin in the lamp had burnt out, but Fyodor Nilov was still sitting and working. He would have abandoned his work long ago and gone out, but a customer on Kolokolny Lane,* who two weeks before had asked him to make a pair of boots, had the previous day sworn at him and ordered him to finish the job now, before matins.

"A life of drudgery!" muttered Fyodor as he worked. "Some people have long been asleep, others are enjoying themselves, but I sit here like some Cain, sewing for the devil knows whom…"

So as not to fall asleep accidentally, he now and again got a bottle from under the table and drank straight from it, and after each swallow he rotated his head and said loudly:

"Be so good as to tell me why customers make merry while I am obliged to stitch for them. Is it because they have money, and I am a pauper instead?"

He hated all customers, especially the one who lived on Kolokolny Lane. He was a gentleman of gloomy appearance, long-haired, yellow-faced, who wore big blue spectacles and spoke with a husky voice. He had some unpronounceable German surname. What his rank was, and what he did for a living, was impossible to know. When, two weeks before, Fyodor had gone to take his measurements, he, the customer, was sitting on the floor and pounding something in a mortar. Before Fyodor could greet him, the contents of the mortar suddenly flared up and began to burn with a bright-red flame; there was a stink of sulphur and burnt feathers, and the room filled with thick pink smoke, making Fyodor sneeze five times. On returning home after this, he thought: "God-fearing people do not occupy themselves in such ways."

When the bottle was empty, Fyodor put the boots on the table and fell to thinking. He supported a heavy head on his fist and began thinking about his poverty, about his difficult, hopeless life; then about rich men, about their big houses, carriages, about their hundred-rouble banknotes... How good it would be if the homes of these rich people – the devil take them – collapsed, their horses died, their fur coats and sable hats moulted! How good it would be if rich people little by little turned into paupers, who had nothing, while he, the poor cobbler, became a rich man and himself bullied another poverty-stricken cobbler on Christmas Eve!

Dreaming thus, Fyodor suddenly remembered his work and opened his eyes.

"What a to-do!" he thought, looking at the boots. "These boots were ready long ago, but I'm still sitting here. I have to take them to the customer!"

He wrapped his work in a red handkerchief, dressed and went out to the street. A fine hard snow was falling, pricking his face like needles. It was cold, slippery, dark; the gas lamps were burning dimly, and for some reason there was a smell of paraffin on the street, causing Fyodor to clear his throat and cough. Rich people were driving back and forth along the road, and each rich person had in his hands a piece of ham and a *chetvert** of vodka. From the carriages and sleighs rich young ladies looked at Fyodor, stuck out their tongues and shrieked with laughter:

"Pauper! Pauper!"

Students, officers, merchants and generals were walking behind Fyodor and mocking him:

"Drunkard! Drunkard! Cobbler-Dobbler, soul of a boot top! Pauper!"

All this was hurtful, but Fyodor remained silent and just spat. But when fellow cobbler Kuzma Lebyedkin, a master craftsman from Warsaw, met him and said "I married a rich woman, have apprentices working at my place, but you are a pauper, you have nothing", Fyodor could not bear it and ran after him. He pursued him until he came to Kolokolny Lane. His client lived in the fourth house from the corner, in a flat on the top floor. He had to go through a long dark courtyard and then climb a very steep, slippery staircase, which wobbled under his feet. When Fyodor entered the flat, the man, as on the previous occasion two weeks before, was sitting on the floor and pounding something in a mortar.

"Your Honour, I have brought the boots!" Fyodor said sullenly.

The customer rose and silently began to try on the boots. Wishing to help him, Fyodor went down on one knee and pulled one old boot off his foot, but immediately leapt up and backed towards the door in terror. The client had not a foot, but a hoof like a horse.

"Good God!" thought Fyodor. "What's this?" The first thing he should have done was to make the sign of the cross, then abandon everything and run downstairs, but he immediately realized that he was meeting the Devil for the first and probably the last time in his life, and that it would be stupid not to profit by what the creature had to offer. He controlled himself and decided to try his luck. Putting his hands behind his back so as to keep from crossing himself, he coughed respectfully and began:

"They say there is nothing fouler and worse in the world than an evil spirit, but I believe, Your Honour, that an evil spirit is the most educated. The Devil has, excuse me, hooves and a tail behind, but then he also has greater intelligence than some students."

"I love to hear such words," said the flattered customer. "Thank you, cobbler! What would you like?"

And the cobbler, without wasting time, began to complain about his fate. He started by saying that from his very childhood he had envied the rich. To him it was offensive that not all people alike lived in big houses and rode on good horses. The question was: why was he poor? In what way was he worse than Kuzma Lebyedkin from Warsaw, who had his own house and whose wife went about in a hat? He had the same nose, the same hands, feet, head, back as a rich man, so why on earth was he obliged to work, when others were enjoying themselves? Why was he married to Marya, and not to a perfumed lady? In the houses of rich clients he often happened to see beautiful young women, but they paid no attention to him, and sometimes only laughed and whispered to one another: "What a red nose that cobbler has!" True, Marya was a good, kind, hard-working woman, but really she was uneducated, her hand was heavy and she could give a painful smack – and when he happened to talk to her about politics or something intelligent, she would change the subject and talk terrible nonsense.

"So what do you want?" the customer interrupted him.

"Well, I ask, Your Honour, Devil Ivanych, if Your Worship would make me rich!"

"Delighted. Only, for that you must give me your soul! Before the cocks have crowed, go and sign this paper saying you will give me your soul."

"Your Honour!" said Fyodor politely. "When you ordered the boots from me, I did not take money from you beforehand. The order must first be fulfilled, and only then money demanded."

"Well, all right," agreed the customer.

A bright flame suddenly blazed up in the mortar, and thick pink smoke began to pour out, and there was a stink of burnt feathers and sulphur. When the smoke cleared, Fyodor rubbed his eyes and saw that he was no longer Fyodor, nor a cobbler, but some other man, in a waistcoat with a watch-chain, in new trousers, and that he was sitting in an armchair at a big table. Two footmen were giving him food, bowing low and saying:

"Have as much as you like, Your Honour!"

What riches there were! The footmen gave him a big piece of roast mutton and a bowl of cucumbers, then brought roast goose on a frying pan, and a little later... boiled pork with horseradish. And how refined it all was – how discreet! Fyodor ate, and before each dish drank a big glass of excellent vodka, like some general or count. After the pork they gave him *kasha* with goose fat, then a fried egg with pork fat and fried liver, and he kept eating and was transported with delight. And what else? They also gave him a *pirog* with onion, and steamed turnip with kvass. "How gentlemen don't burst from such food!" he thought. To wrap things up, they gave him a big pot of honey. After dinner the Devil appeared in blue spectacles and, bowing low, asked:

"Were you satisfied with the dinner, Fyodor Pantelyeich?"

But Fyodor was unable to utter a single word, so replete was he after eating. He felt unpleasantly full, heavy, and in order to divert himself he began to examine the boot on his left foot.

"For such boots I would not have charged less than seven roubles fifty. Who was the cobbler who made them?" he asked.

"Kuzma Lebyedkin," replied the footman.

"Send for him, the fool."

Kuzma Lebyedkin from Warsaw soon appeared. He stopped deferentially by the door and asked:

"What may I do for you, Your Honour?"

"Silence!" shouted Fyodor, stamping his foot. "Don't you dare to speak, but remember your cobbler's rank, what sort of man you are! Blockhead! You don't know how to make boots! I shall punch you in the face! Why have you come?"

"For money, sir."

"What money is there for you? Get out! Come on Saturday. My good man, give him a cuff on the neck!"

But immediately he remembered how he himself had been treated by customers, and began to feel guilty; to divert himself, he pulled from his pocket a fat wallet and began to count his money. There was a lot of money, but Fyodor wanted still more. The Devil in the blue spectacles brought him another wallet, fatter, but he wanted yet more – and the more he counted, the more dissatisfied he became.

In the evening the Devil brought him a tall, full-bosomed lady in a red dress and said that this was his new wife. Until night came, he kept kissing her and eating spice cakes. And at night he lay on a soft, down-filled feather bed, tossing and turning, and in no way was he able to fall asleep. He was terrified.

"There's a lot of money," he said to his wife. "We have to be on our guard: thieves might break in. You should take a candle and go and have a look!"

He did not sleep at all that night, and continually rose to check whether the trunk was secure. Early in the morning he went to church for matins. In church all were equal, rich and poor. When Fyodor was poor, he used to pray in church like this: "Lord, forgive me, I'm a sinner!" Even now, having become rich, he said the same. So what was the difference? After death, they will bury the rich Fyodor not in gold, not in diamonds, but in the same black earth as the meanest pauper. Fyodor will burn in the same fire as will cobblers. All this seemed a pity to Fyodor, and now, with the heaviness of dinner still inside him, instead of prayers there lay in his head various thoughts about the trunk with the money, about thieves, and about his ruined, forfeited soul.

He came out of church angry. In order to dispel his unpleasant thoughts, he, as so often in the past, broke into a full-throated song. But he had only just begun when a policeman ran up to him and, saluting, said:

"*Barin*, it's forbidden for gentlemen to sing in the street! You are not a cobbler!"

Fyodor leant against a fence and began to think how could he amuse himself.

"*Barin*!" cried a caretaker. "It's not good to lean against the fence. You'll soil your fur coat!"

Fyodor went to a shop and bought himself the very best harmonica, then walked along the street playing. All the passers-by pointed at him and laughed.

"He's quite some *barin*!" the cabmen mocked him. "He behaves like a cobbler…"

"Is it right for a gentleman to make a nuisance of himself?" the policeman said to him. "You should go to a tavern!"

"*Barin*, give alms, for Christ's sake!" wailed beggars, surrounding Fyodor on all sides. "Give alms!"

Before, when he was a cobbler, beggars paid him no attention, but now they gave him no respite.

At home he was met by his new wife, the fine lady, dressed in a green jacket and red skirt. He wanted to show affection, and had already raised his arm to give her a slap on the back, but she said angrily:

"Peasant! Lout! You don't know how to treat a lady! If you love me, then kiss my hand, but I won't tolerate being beaten."

"Oh, what a damned life," thought Fyodor. "The way some people live! You can't sing a song, or play a harmonica or have a slap and tickle with a woman... Tfoo!"

He had only just sat down to have tea with the lady when the Devil appeared in his blue spectacles and said:

"Well, Fyodor Pantelyeich, I kept strictly to our agreement, now you sign the paper and grant me my request. Now you know what it's like to live like a rich man. That's what your life would be like!"

And he dragged Fyodor to hell, straight to the fiery furnace. Devils flew in from all directions, crying:

"Fool! Blockhead! Ass!"

In hell it stank horribly of paraffin, so that one could choke.

But suddenly everything vanished. Fyodor opened his eyes and saw his table, the boots and the tin lamp. The glass of the lamp was black, and from a little flame on the wick poured stinking smoke, as from a chimney. Next to him stood the customer in the blue spectacles, angrily shouting:

"Fool! Blockhead! Ass! I'll teach you, you crook! You took my order two weeks ago, and even now the boots are not ready! Do you think I have time to come and see you about the boots five times a day? Swine! Bastard!"

Fyodor was confused, and straight away got down to the boots. The customer for a long time kept swearing and threatening. When he finally calmed down, Fyodor sullenly asked:

"And what is your occupation, *Barin*?"

"I make sparklers and rockets. I am a pyrotechnician."

The church bells began to ring for matins. Fyodor handed over the boots, received payment and went to church.

Back and forth along the street dashed carriages and sleighs with rich clients under bearskin rugs. Along the pavement, together with ordinary people, walked merchants, *barins*, officers... But

Fyodor no longer envied them, and did not grumble about his fate. It seemed to him now that rich and poor ended alike. Some had the chance to ride in a carriage, and others to sing songs in full voice and to play a harmonica, but on the whole the same end awaited everyone: only the grave, and there was nothing in life for which it was worth giving the Devil even a small part of one's soul.

Patronage

A WRINKLED LITTLE OLD MAN with a decoration around his neck was walking along Nevsky Prospekt. Skipping behind him followed a short young man with a purple nose and a cockade in his hat. The old man was scowling and concentrated; the young man was blinking anxiously and seemed about to cry. The two were going to see Yevlampy Stepanovich.

"I am not guilty, Uncle!" the young man was saying, trying hard to keep up with the old man. "I was wrongly dismissed. Dryankovsky drinks more than I do, but he wasn't let go! He came to the office drunk every day, but I wasn't drunk every day. It's so unfair of His Excellency that I can't even tell you!"

"Shut up... you swine!"

"Hm... Well, I may be a swine, but even I have my pride. I was not dismissed for drunkenness, but because of the picture. The office presented him with an album of our photos. Everyone was photographed, and I was photographed too, but my photo didn't turn out well, Uncle. I looked goggle-eyed, and my arms were spread wide apart. My nose was never so long as came out in that photo. I was ashamed to put my picture in the album. You know, ladies often visit His Excellency, and I didn't want to compromise myself with the ladies. I am not handsome, just attractive, but in the picture I came out looking like a fool. Yevlampy Stepanych was offended that my photo was missing. He thought I was too proud, or that I was a freethinker. But how am I a freethinker? I go to church, and fast during Lent, and don't put on airs like Dryankovsky. Stand up for me, Uncle! I shall pray for you for the rest of my life! It's better to lie in the grave than loaf about without a position."

The old man and his companion turned the corner, went along three more streets and finally pulled the bell at Yevlampy Stepanych's door.

"You stay here," said the old man, entering the hall with his nephew, "and I shall go in to him. Because of you, there is nothing but trouble. Blockhead... Stand and wait here... Good-for-nothing boy..."

The old man blew his nose, straightened the decoration around his neck and entered the study. The young man stayed in the hall, his heart pounding.

"What are they talking about?" he thought, growing cold and shifting anxiously from one foot to the other. From the study there reached him the muttering of two old men's voices. "Is he listening to Uncle?"

Being unable to bear the uncertainty, he went up to the door and pressed a big ear to it.

"I cannot, sir!" He heard the voice of Yevlampy Stepanych. "God knows I cannot, sir! I respect you, I am a friend of yours, Prokhor Mikhailych, and am prepared to do anything for you, but... I cannot, sir! Don't even ask!"

"I agree with you, Your Excellency. He is a spoilt boy. I cannot deny it, and even admit to you, as my friend and benefactor, that he is also a drunkard. Nor is that all, sir. He is a scoundrel! He'll steal anything in sight; he is a master at deception and will inform on anyone. He's completely without principles; I can't even begin to tell you. Do him a favour today, and tomorrow he'll inform against you. He's scum... I don't feel at all sorry for him. If it had been up to me, I would have banished him long ago to some godforsaken place... But for my sake, Your Excellency, take pity on his mother. I ask only for his mother. He robbed his mother, the villain, and drank it all away..."

The young man turned away from the door and paced back and forth in the hall. Five minutes later he again went to the door and pressed his ear to it.

"Do this for an old woman, Your Excellency," said his uncle. "She is dying from grief that her son has no job."

"Very well, then, so be it. But only on this condition: the moment he sets a foot wrong, he will be out immediately!"

"Drive him away immediately, the scoundrel, if he does anything."

The young man turned away from the door and began to pace the hall.

"Good man, Uncle!" he whispered, rubbing his hands in delight. "Movingly presented! He's an uneducated man, but how cleverly it all came out…"

His uncle came out of the study.

"He'll take you," he said sullenly. "Useless boy… Let's go."

"Thank you, dear Uncle!" sighed the young man, blinking his eyes, full of gratitude, and kissing his uncle's hand. "Without your patronage, I long ago would have been lost…"

They went out to the street together and strode home. The old man was frowning and concentrated in thought; the young man was radiant with delight.

A Doctor's Visit

T HE PROFESSOR received a telegram from the Lyalikovs' factory: they asked him to come as quickly as possible. The daughter of a certain Mrs Lyalikova, evidently the owner of the factory, was ill, and no further information could be gleaned from the long, incoherently written telegram. The professor himself did not go, but instead sent his registrar Korolyov.

Korolyov had to travel two stations from Moscow, and then about four versts by horse. A troika was sent to the station for him; the coachman wore a hat with a peacock feather, and to all questions replied loudly, in military fashion: "No, sir!" – "Yes, sir!" It was Saturday evening; the sun was setting. Crowds of workers were walking from the factory to the station and bowing to the horses conveying Korolyov. He was charmed by the evening, the estates, the dachas along the way, the birch trees and the peaceful mood around: it seemed that now, on the eve of a holiday, the field and forest and sun were preparing to rest along with the workers – who will rest and, perhaps, will pray…

He was born and raised in Moscow, did not know the country, had never been interested in factories and had never been to one. But he had read about factories, had been a guest at manufacturers' homes and had talked to them – and when he saw a certain factory in the distance or nearby, he thought each time about how on the outside all was peaceful and quiet, but inside there was probably rank ignorance and the insufferable arrogance of the owner, the boring, unhealthy labour of the workers, squabbles, vodka, insect infestations. And now, as the workers respectfully and timidly made way for the carriage, he guessed at their uncleanliness, drunkenness, irritability and bewilderment by the look on their faces, their peaked caps and the way they walked. He drove in through the factory gate.

Along both sides could be seen the little houses of the workers, women's faces, linen and blankets on the porches. "Watch out!" cried the coachman, not restraining the horses. There was a wide courtyard without grass, five huge factory buildings with chimneys set at some distance one from another, warehouses, huts and some grey deposit lying on everything, like dust. Here and there, like oases in the desert, were wretched little gardens and the green or red roofs of the houses where the bosses lived. The coachman suddenly reined in the horses, and the carriage stopped by a house newly painted in grey; there was a small front garden with a lilac bush covered in dust, and a strong smell of paint on the yellow porch.

"This way please, doctor, sir." Women's voices were speaking in the vestibule and entrance hall, and these were accompanied by sighs and whisperings. "This way please, we've been waiting for a long time... it's sheer misery. Come this way, please."

Mrs Lyalikova – a stout, elderly lady in a black silk dress with fashionable sleeves but, judging by her face, simple and uneducated – looked anxiously at the doctor and decided not to offer him her hand, did not dare to. Next to her stood a woman with short hair and pince-nez, in a motley-coloured blouse, gaunt and no longer young. The maid called her Khristina Dmitrievna, and Korolyov guessed she was the governess. As the most educated one in the house, she had probably been charged with meeting and receiving the doctor, because she immediately, hurriedly, began stating the causes of the illness, with trivial, unnecessary details, without saying who was sick and what was the matter.

The doctor and governess sat and talked, while the mistress stood motionless by the door, waiting. From what the governess said, Korolyov understood that the patient was Liza, a twenty-year-old girl, the only daughter of Mrs Lyalikova, and the heiress; she had already been ill for a long time, and had been treated by various doctors, but the previous night, from the evening till the morning, she had had such palpitations that no one in the house had slept; they feared she would die.

"We can tell you that she has been sick from childhood," Khristina Dmitrievna was saying in a melodious voice, continually wiping her lips with her hand. "The doctors say it's nerves, but when she was small she showed signs of latent tuberculosis, so I think, perhaps, it may be due to that."

They went to the patient. She was already quite grown up, big and tall, but ugly, like her mother, with the same small eyes and with a broad, heavy jaw. With uncombed hair, and body covered to the chin, she in the first minute created an impression on Korolyov of an unhappy, pathetic creature who out of pity was being sheltered and protected here; it was hard to believe she was the heiress of the five huge buildings.

"I've come to visit you," began Korolyov. "I've come to help you. Hello."

He gave his name and shook her hand, a big, cold, unattractive hand. She sat up, and being evidently long accustomed to doctors, and unconcerned about baring her shoulders and chest, presented herself for his attention.

"I have palpitations," she said. "All night it was so terrible... I almost died of fright! Give me something."

"I will, I will! Don't worry."

Korolyov examined her and shrugged his shoulders.

"Your heart is all right," he said. "All is well, everything is in order. Your nerves must be a little frayed, but this is not unusual. I suppose the attack is already over. Try and go to sleep."

Just then a lamp was brought into the bedroom. The patient screwed up her eyes at the light and suddenly, clutching her head in her hands, burst into tears. The impression of a pathetic and unattractive being suddenly vanished, and Korolyov no longer noticed either the little eyes or the heavy jaw; he saw a gentle, suffering expression that was so intelligent and touching, a being so well proportioned, feminine and simple, that he wanted to calm her not with medicines, not with advice, but with simple, tender words. Her mother put her arms around the girl's head and hugged her. How much despair, how much grief there was on the face of the old woman! She, the mother, raised, brought up her daughter begrudging nothing, devoted all her life to having her daughter taught the French language, dancing, music; engaged a dozen teachers for her, consulted the best doctors, kept a governess, and now could not understand why there were tears, why so much suffering; she did not understand, and felt lost; she wore a guilty, anxious, desperate expression, as if she had missed something very important, as if there was something she had not yet done, someone she had not yet engaged – but who, she did not know.

"Lizanka, you again… you again," she said, hugging her daughter. "My own girl, darling, my child, tell me, what's wrong with you? Pity me, tell me."

Both were crying bitterly. Korolyov sat on the edge of the bed and took Liza's hand.

"Enough of that – is it worth crying over?" he said tenderly. "Surely there is nothing in the world worth such tears. Come, you shouldn't cry, it's not necessary."

But to himself he thought: "It's time she was married…"

"Our factory doctor gave her potassium bromide," said the governess, "but I notice it has only made her worse. In my opinion, if it is for her heart, then give her drops… I forget what they are called… Lily of the valley, perhaps."

And again she went into all the details. She interrupted the doctor, prevented him from speaking; her face wore an expression of determination, as if she supposed that, as the most educated woman in the house, she was obliged to carry on a continuous conversation with the doctor, and about medicine too.

Korolyov grew bored.

"I find nothing unusual," he said to her mother, leaving the bedroom. "If the factory doctor has been treating your daughter, let him continue to do so. The treatment until now has been correct, and I see no need to change doctors. Why change? The illness is so common, nothing serious…"

He spoke unhurriedly, putting on his gloves, while Mrs Lyalikova stood motionless, looking at him with tearful eyes.

"The ten o'clock train leaves in half an hour," he said. "I hope I won't be late."

"But can you not stay with us?" she asked, and again tears flowed down her cheeks. "I'm ashamed of troubling you, but be so kind... for God's sake," she continued in an undertone, looking at the door, "spend the night with us. She is my only... my only daughter... I was frightened last night, could not recover. Don't go, for God's sake..."

He wanted to tell her that he had much to do in Moscow, that his family was waiting for him at home, that it was hard to spend all evening and all night needlessly in a strange house, but he looked at her face, sighed and without a word began to take off his gloves.

All the lamps and candles were lit for him in the hall and sitting room. He sat at the piano and looked through a score, then examined the pictures and portraits on the wall. The pictures, oil paintings in golden frames, were views of the Crimea, a stormy sea with a small boat, a Catholic monk with a little wine glass, and all the faces were plain, bare and undistinguished... There was not a single attractive, interesting face in all the portraits: all had wide cheekbones, astonished eyes. Lyalikov, Liza's father, had a low forehead and self-satisfied face; his full-dress uniform hung like a bag on his big, common body; on his chest he had a medal and Red Cross badge. There was little sign of culture; the affluence seemed accidental, inappropriate, awkward, like the uniform; the floors irritated him with their shine, the chandelier irritated him, and for some reason he recalled the story about the merchant who was going to the steam bath with a medal around his neck...

The sound of a whisper reached him from the entrance hall; someone was quietly snoring. Suddenly, from outside, came sharp, abrupt, metallic sounds which Korolyov had never heard before and which now puzzled him; they resounded strangely and unpleasantly in his soul.

"I don't think I could live here for anything," he thought, and again turned his attention to the score.

"Doctor, please come and have something to eat," invited the governess in a quiet voice.

He went to have supper. The table was big, with an array of *zakuski* and wines, but only two of them were supping: he and Khristina Dmitrievna. She drank Madeira, ate quickly and, looking at him through her pince-nez, said:

"Our workers are very contented. Every winter we put on shows at the factory; the workers themselves perform, and there are readings with magic lanterns, a wonderful tea room and other things of that sort. They are very devoted to us, and when they discovered that Lizanka was worse, they organized a church service. They are uneducated, but also, you know, capable of feeling."

"You don't appear to have any men in the house," said Korolyov.

"Not a single one. Pyotr Nikanorych died a year and a half ago, and we are now alone. So there are just the three of us. In the summer we are here, and in winter we live in Moscow, on Polyanka Street. I've been with them for eleven years now. I am like one of the family."

Sterlet, chicken cutlets and steamed fruit were served for supper; the wine was expensive, French.

"Please, doctor, don't stand on ceremony," said Khristina Dmitrievna, eating and wiping her mouth with her fist; and it was clear that she fully enjoyed her life there. "Please, have some more."

After supper the doctor was taken to a room, where a bed had been made up for him. But he did not want to sleep; it was stuffy, and there was the smell of paint in the room. He put on his coat and went out.

It was cool outside; the last light of day was fading in the sky, but all five of the factory buildings with their tall chimneys, their huts and warehouses, were clearly visible in the damp air. As it was a holiday, they were not operating; the windows were dark, and in only one of the buildings was a stove still burning: two windows appeared crimson, and, along with smoke, fire was now and again coming from the chimney. Far away from the yard could be heard the croaking of frogs and the singing of nightingales.

Looking at the buildings and at the huts where the workers were sleeping, he again thought what he always thought when he saw factories. Even if there were shows for the workers, magic lanterns, factory doctors and various improvements, all the same there was nothing in the appearance of all those workers whom he had met today along the way from the station to distinguish them from the workers he had seen long ago in childhood, when there were not yet factory shows and improvements. He – as a medic, judging correctly about chronic diseases, the fundamental causes of which were incomprehensible and untreatable – he regarded factories as something baffling, the causes of which were also unclear and irremediable, and he did not consider improvements in the life of workers to be unnecessary, but likened them to the treatment of incurable diseases.

"Here is what is baffling, of course…" he thought, looking at the crimson windows. "Fifteen hundred or two thousand workers labour without rest, in an unhealthy environment, manufacturing cheap cotton goods; they half-starve and only occasionally find relief from this nightmare in a tavern; a hundred people oversee the work, and the whole life of these hundred is spent in imposing fines, in abuse and injustice – and only two or three so-called 'owners' enjoy the benefits, though they do no work at all, and despise cheap cotton. But how do they benefit? Lyalikova and her daughter are unhappy, it's pitiful to look at them; only Khristina Dmitrievna, the elderly, silly maiden in pince-nez, is completely contented. And it all comes down to this: that all those five buildings operate and sell bad cotton to eastern markets only so that Khristina Dmitrievna can eat sterlet and drink Madeira."

Suddenly Korolyov heard strange sounds, the same that he had heard before supper. Near one of the buildings someone was beating a sheet of metal, beating and at once silencing the sound, so that what was heard were short, sharp, unclear sounds, like "dyer… dyer… dyer…" Then half a minute of silence, and at another building were heard sounds just as abrupt and unpleasant, now deeper, in the bass register – "drin... drin... drin..." Eleven times. This was evidently the watchman sounding eleven o'clock.

From a third building was heard "zhak... zhak... zhak..." And thus from all the buildings, and then from the huts and behind the gates. And it was as if in the night's silence the sounds were being emitted by some monster with crimson eyes, the Devil himself, who controlled the owners and workers and deceived both them and others.

Korolyov walked out of the yard to a field.

"Who goes there?" A gruff voice hailed him by the gate.

"Just like in a prison..." he thought, and did not reply.

Here the nightingales and frogs were heard more clearly; the May night made itself felt. From the station could be heard the sound of a train; sleepy cockerels were crowing somewhere, but apart from that the night was silent, the world was sleeping peacefully. In a field not far from the factory was a shelter where construction material was piled. Korolyov sat on some boards and continued to think:

"The governess is the only one who feels good here, and the factory operates for her pleasure. But it only seems so: she is just a symbol here. The main thing for which everything is made here is... the Devil."

And he thought about the Devil, in which he did not believe, and looked back at the two windows in which fires were burning. It seemed to him that those crimson eyes that were looking at him were those of the Devil himself, that supernatural force that created conflict between the strong and the weak, that crude mistake that now cannot be set right. The strong must prevent the weak from living, such is the law of nature, but this is understood and easily conveyed only in newspaper articles and textbooks, in the chaos of everyday life, in the muddle of all trifles from which human relations are spun; this is no longer a law, but a logical incongruity, where the strong and the weak alike fall victim to their mutual relations, involuntarily submitting to some guiding force that is unknown, existing outside life, alien to man. Thus thought Korolyov, sitting on the boards, and little by little he was seized by the feeling that this unknown, mysterious force really was near and was watching. Meanwhile, the sky in the east was growing more and more pale, time was passing quickly. Five buildings and chimneys, on a grey background of darkness, when there was not a soul around and all was as if deserted, looked different from how they did during the day; it was easy to forget that inside there were steam engines, electricity, telephones, but somehow everything seemed like pile dwellings of the Stone Age, and gave the impression of crude, unconscious strength...

And again was heard:

"Dyer... dyer... dyer... dyer..."

Twelve times. Then there was silence, silence for half a minute – and then, from the other end of the yard was heard:

"Drin... drin... drin..."

"Terribly unpleasant!" thought Korolyov.

"Zhak... zhak..." was heard from the third place, abruptly, sharply, as if in vexation. "Zhak... zhak..."

And it took some four minutes to strike twelve o'clock. Then all fell silent, and again there was the impression that everything around was dead.

Korolyov sat a little longer, then returned to the house, but still did not go to bed for a long time. In the rooms next door were heard whispering and the shuffling of slippers and bare feet.

"Is she having another attack?" thought Korolyov.

He went out to look at the patient. There was some faint light in the rooms, and in the hall weak moonlight glimmered on the wall and the floor, penetrating inside through the early morning mist. The door to Liza's room was open, and she was sitting in an armchair near the bed, wearing a bonnet and wrapped in a shawl, her hair uncombed. The window blinds were drawn.

"How are you feeling?" asked Korolyov.

"I am better."

He felt her pulse, then arranged her hair, which had fallen on her forehead.

"You are not asleep," he said. "The weather outside is beautiful; it's spring, the nightingales are singing, but you're sitting in the dark and thinking about something."

She listened and looked into his face; her eyes were sad, intelligent, and she clearly wanted to say something to him.

"Are you often like this?" he asked.

She moved her lips and replied:

"Often. Almost every night is difficult for me."

Just then in the yard the watchmen began to beat two o'clock. The sound was heard – "dyer... dyer..." – and she winced.

"Do these sounds upset you?" he asked.

"I don't know. Everything here upsets me," she replied, and fell to thinking. "Everything upsets me. I sense concern in your voice; from the moment I first saw you, for some reason it seemed I could talk to you about everything."

"Please talk, I beg you."

"I want to give you my opinion. It seems to me that I'm not ill, but I'm upset and terrified because that's how it is and it cannot be otherwise. Even the healthiest person may be troubled if he sees, for example, a thief walking behind the window. They often get me treatment," she continued, looking at her knees and smiling shyly. "Of course I'm very grateful, and do not deny the benefit of medical treatment, but I would like to talk not with a doctor, but with someone close to me, with a friend, who would understand me, advise me as to whether or not I am right."

"Do you really not have friends?" asked Korolyov.

"I am lonely. I have my mother; I love her, but still I'm lonely. That's how it is... Lonely people read a lot, but talk little and hear little; their life is secretive, they are mystics, and often see the Devil where he is not. Lermontov's Tamara was lonely and saw the Devil."*

"So do you read a lot?"

"Yes, a lot. You see, I'm free all day, from morning till evening. During the day I read, but at night… my head is empty: instead of thoughts, it is filled with shadows."

"Do you see anything at night?" asked Korolyov.

"No, but I sense…"

Again she smiled, and raised her eyes to the doctor, and looked so sad, so intelligent – and it seemed to him that she trusted him, wanted to talk candidly to him, and that she thought the same as he did. But she was silent, perhaps waiting to see whether he would start talking.

And he knew what to say to her; it was clear to him that she should quickly renounce her claim to the five buildings and a million roubles, assuming she had that money, and abandon this devil that she saw at night; to him it was also clear that she thought the same, and was just waiting for someone she trusted to persuade her.

But he did not know how to say this. How? People are embarrassed to ask those who have been sentenced what they have been sentenced for; so it is likewise embarrassing to ask the very rich why they need so much money, why they manage their wealth so badly, why they don't get rid of it, even when they see in it their unhappiness – and if they start a conversation about it, the talk usually ends by being embarrassing, awkward and tiresome.

"How can I say it?" thought Korolyov. "And is it even necessary to speak?"

And he said what he wanted to say – not directly, but in a roundabout way.

"You, in the position of a factory owner and a rich, discontented heiress, do not believe in your entitlement, and so now you don't sleep; this of course is better than if you were contented, slept well and thought that all was well. You suffer from insomnia – that at any rate is a good sign. Indeed, such a conversation as we are having now would be unthinkable to our parents; at night they did not discuss anything, and slept well, but we, our generation, sleep badly, are tormented, talk a lot, and keep trying to decide whether or not we are right. But for our children and grandchildren this question – whether or not they are right – will already have been decided. To them it will be more evident than to us. Life will be good in about fifty years – it's just a pity we won't live till then. It would be interesting to see."

"So what will our children and grandchildren do?" asked Liza.

"I don't know... It could be that they will abandon everything and escape."

"Where will they escape to?"

"Where?... Well, wherever they like," said Korolyov, and burst out laughing. "There are all kinds of places a good, intelligent person can go."

He looked at his watch.

"However, it will soon be day," he said. "It's time you slept. Undress and have a good sleep. I'm very glad to have met you," he continued, shaking her hand. "You are a fine, interesting person. Goodnight!"

He went to his room and lay down to sleep.

The next morning, when the carriage was brought, they all came out on the porch to see him off. Liza was dressed as for a holiday, in a white dress, with a flower in her hair, pale, languid; she looked at him as she had the day before, with a sad and intelligent expression on her face; she was smiling, talking, and all with an air as if she wanted to tell him – but only him – something special, important. The singing of the larks and the ringing of the church bells could be heard. The windows in the factory buildings were gaily lit, and, driving through the yard and then along the road to the station, Korolyov no longer thought about the workers or the piled dwellings or the Devil, but thought about the time, perhaps already near, when life would be as radiant and joyful as a peaceful Sunday morning. And he thought about how pleasant it was on such a morning, in spring, to drive in a troika, in a good carriage, and warm oneself in the sunshine.

Notes

p. 3, "*O tempora, o mores!*": "O times, o customs!" (Latin).

p. 3, "*Salvete, boni futuri conjuges!*": "Long live the future fine married couple!" (Latin).

p. 5, *Be fruitful, multiply and replenish the earth*: God's words to Noah and his sons (see Genesis 9:1).

p. 6, *Malthus*: The English economist and cleric Thomas Robert Malthus (1766–1834), who warned against the dangers of overpopulation, claiming that the growth of population is exponential, whereas the growth of the food supply is linear.

p. 6, *Walter Scott*: The Scottish poet, historian and novelist Sir Walter Scott (1771–1832). His life, beset by illness and financial problems, was not particularly eventful, but the reference here is to the adventurous and at times rascally lives of some of the Romantic heroes he created.

p. 6, *Zola*: The French naturalist writer Émile Zola (1840–1902).

p. 11, *Jean*: Ivan is the Russian equivalent of John in English and Jean in French. The Russian upper classes often spoke French among themselves.

p. 11, '*Strelochka*': A popular song of the day.

p. 18, *Grey hair in the beard, but a demon in the belly*: A Russian saying.

p. 19, *We love to go sledging... carry the sledge*: A reference to the Russian proverb "If you like to go sledging, you have to carry the sledge".

p. 21, *barin's anger*: A *barin* is a landowner or gentleman, a man deserving of respect.

p. 24, *Turgenev-like... heroes*: Heroes like those found in the works of the Russian novelist Ivan Turgenev (1818–83).

p. 24, *forty thousand ridiculous brothers*: A reference to Hamlet's words in Shakespeare's play (Act v, Sc. 1. ll. 266–68):

"I lov'd Ophelia. Forty thousand brothers / Could not (with all their quantity of love) / Make up my sum."

p. 24, *Bismarck*: The Prusso-German statesman and diplomat Otto von Bismarck (1815–98).

p. 24, *Shchedrin*: The Russian satirist Mikhail Saltykov-Shchedrin (1826–89).

p. 25, *ma chère*: "My dear" (French).

p. 29, *artel*: In pre-revolutionary Russia, a cooperative association of craftsmen living and working together.

p. 31, *shchi*: Cabbage soup.

p. 34, *To those without birds... a nightingale*: Kuzma is probably thinking of the Russian proverb "To one who is hungry, even a crayfish provides a meal."

p. 35, *the Marshal's Widow*: Catherine the Great made the nobility or landed gentry into a self-governing corporation, with an elected marshal in each province and district.

p. 35, *panikhida*: A requiem mass.

p. 35, *kamilavka*: An Orthodox priest's headgear.

p. 35, *kutya*: A dish of mixed ingredients – usually wheat, peas and rice – served with honey at a funeral repast.

p. 37, *pirog*: A pie, usually of meat or cabbage.

p. 41, *Mütterchen*: "Mummy" (German).

p. 41, *mon petit*: "My dear" (French).

p. 41, *mon ange*: "My angel" (French).

p. 43, *jour fixe*: A reception, or "at home".

p. 47, *All grains are for the use of man*: A Russian proverb.

p. 55, *the goose*: A slang term for an important personage.

p. 56, *hunger is no friend*: A Russian saying.

p. 57, *Nana*: The title of an 1880 novel by Émile Zola (see third note to p. 6) about a Parisian courtesan.

p. 57, *krug*: A glade or clearing in the country set aside for dancing.

p. 57, *it was not stone against stone... kingdom against kingdom*: A muddled recollection of a biblical reference (Matthew 24:7): "For nation will rise against nation and kingdom against kingdom." (The prelude to the end of the world and the coming of the Messiah.)

p. 65, *zakuski*: Little snacks or appetizers (singular: *zakuska*).

p. 73, *St Sergius*: The Trinity Lavra of St Sergius (located around forty-five miles north-east of Moscow), the most important monastery of the Russian Orthodox Church, where all-night vigils were held.

p. 74, *was wollen Sie?*: "What do you want?" (German).

p. 74, *Was wollen Sie doch*: "What is it you want?" (German).

p. 74, *Was wollen Sie noch*: "What else do you want?" (German).

p. 75, *Ich will…*: "I want…" (German).

p. 75, *tsirlimanirli*: From the German *zierlich-manierlich*, a pejorative term for someone's affected mannerisms.

p. 77, *kalatch*: A bread roll baked in the form of a padlock.

p. 80, *one can't drink water from a face*: A Russian proverb.

p. 91, *On his head… are horns*: Cuckolds were fancifully said to wear horns on the brow.

p. 92, *Rebus*: A weekly St Petersburg magazine that came to be associated chiefly with spiritualism.

p. 92, *break mirrors*: Superstitiously considered to be bad luck.

p. 92, *Zucchi*: Virginia Zucchi (1849–1933), a popular Italian female ballet dancer who was living and performing in Russia at this time.

p. 95, *Ю*: A letter in the Russian alphabet, pronounced "you".

p. 95, *Grot's new grammar*: A reference to the Russian philologist of German extraction Yakov Grot (1812–93).

p. 95, *masculine adjectives… ovo*: Russian is an inflected language, with three genders declined into six cases.

p. 96, *fofan*: A popular card game of the time.

p. 98, *Pasteur*: The French microbiologist Louis Pasteur (1822–95).

p. 100, *But Kursk is a fine town!… with pleasure*: This indicates that the pedagogue probably did not see much of the town: in the nineteenth century Kursk had the reputation of being an ugly, stinking place.

p. 101, *Livorno... Savrasenkov's*: Moscow restaurants.

p. 102, *Salon de Varieté*: A notorious Moscow café chantant frequented by prostitutes.

p. 102, *Rrrodon's masquerade*: A reference to Victor Ivanovich Rodon (1846–92), a comedian and a star of the operetta theatre in Moscow.

p. 105, *Offenbach*: The German-born French composer Jacques Offenbach (1819–80).

p. 106, *universary militarial servation*: Filyenkov is referring to "universal military service" (that is, conscription), which was in force at the time.

p. 107, *la comprené a revoir consommé!*: A senseless attempt at French.

p. 108, *Cachucha*: An Andalusian solo dance accompanied by castanets.

p. 108, *the Arcadia*: A place of entertainment in a new part of St Petersburg.

p. 109, *Krestovsky Garden*: A place of entertainment with a theatre and restaurant on Krestovsky Island in St Petersburg.

p. 111, *charmante*: "Charming" (French).

p. 111, *Feya pyot kofeya!*: "The fairy is drinking coffee!" (Russian).

p. 112, *Voltaire*: The French philosopher and writer Voltaire (1694–1778), famous for his anticlericalism and for his liberal ideas on religion and society.

p. 112, *who likes red*: An allusion to the proverb "Any fool likes beauty", which could be interpreted as "Any fool likes red", because in colloquial speech the Russian words for "red" and "beauty" are the same.

p. 112, *Once, in Georgia... my red lining*: Generals wore a coat with a red lining.

p. 113, *Tiflis*: The name of Georgia's capital Tbilisi before 1936.

p. 118, *electric lights*: Electric lighting first appeared in St Petersburg in 1884.

p. 122, *Drink, tribe of the Pharaohs!*: Gypsies were thought to have originated in Egypt.

p. 125, *the Nikolayevsk Railway*: The line from Moscow to St Petersburg, opened in 1851.

p. 125, *Jules Verne novels*: The French novelist Jules Verne (1828–1905), author of many famous adventure stories.

p. 128, *wine maketh glad the heart of man*: Psalms 104:15.

p. 129, *another accident like the one at Kukuevo*: Site of a terrible train crash in June 1882, where a hundred people died or were injured.

p. 134, *Povorskaya Street*: A street in Moscow.

p. 139, *our Argus and Mercury*: In Greek mythology, Hermes (Mercury for the Romans) is the "messenger of the gods"; Argus is a hundred-eyed giant used as a watchman by Hera, Zeus's wife. Hermes and Argus are the protagonists of a famous story in Greek legend. When Zeus falls in love with Io, a priestess of Hera, to shield her from his wife's jealous wrath, he turns her into a beautiful heifer. Hera discovers the ploy and takes charge of the animal, entrusting it to Argus for safekeeping. Hermes charms Argus to sleep before slaying him. By killing the monster, Hermes restores Io to freedom.

p. 141, *desyatins*: The *desyatin* is an old Russian measure of land, equal to 2.7 acres.

p. 141, *kasha*: A form of gruel, like porridge, made from buckwheat.

p. 152, *Nekrasov*: The Russian poet Nikolai Nekrasov (1821–78).

p. 153, *I go to seek through the world... women!*: The first part is a quote from Griboyedov's play *Woe from Wit* (Act IV, Sc. 14); the second is an allusion to *Hamlet* (Act I, Sc. 2, l. 146): "Frailty, thy name is woman!"

p. 168, *Demosthenes*: An Athenian statesman famed for his eloquence.

p. 171, *Spasskaya Tower*: The main tower on the eastern wall of the Kremlin in Moscow.

p. 177, *Kolokolny Lane*: A street in St Petersburg.

p. 178, *chetvert*: A liquid measure of approximately 3 litres.

p. 198, *Lermontov's Tamara was lonely and saw the Devil*:
A reference to the heroine of 'The Demon', a poem by the
Russian novelist and poet Mikhail Lermontov (1814–41).

Extra Material

on

Anton Chekhov's

*The Looking Glass
and Other Stories*

Anton Chekhov's Life

Anton Pavlovich Chekhov was born in Taganrog, on the Sea *Birth and Background* of Azov in southern Russia, on 29th January 1860. He was the third child of Pavel Yegorovich Chekhov and his wife Yevgenia Yakovlevna. He had four brothers – Alexander (born in 1855), Nikolai (1858), Ivan (1861) and Mikhail (1865) – and one sister, Marya, who was born in 1863. Anton's father, the owner of a small shop, was a devout Christian who administered brutal floggings to his children almost on a daily basis. Anton remembered these with bitterness throughout his life, and possibly as a result was always sceptical of organized religion. The shop – a grocery and general-supplies store which sold such goods as lamp oil, tea, coffee, seeds, flour and sugar – was kept by the children during their father's absence. The father also required his children to go with him to church at least once a day. He set up a liturgical choir which practised in his shop, and demanded that his children – whether they had school work to do or not, or whether they had been in the shop all day – should join the rehearsals to provide the higher voice parts.

Chekhov described his home town as filthy and tedious, and *Education and Childhood* the people as drunk, idle, lazy and illiterate. At first, Pavel tried to provide his children with an education by enrolling the two he considered the brightest, Nikolai and Anton, in one of the schools for the descendants of the Greek merchants who had once settled in Taganrog. These provided a more "classical" education than their Russian equivalents, and their standard of teaching was held in high regard. However, the experience was not a successful one, since most of the other pupils spoke Greek among themselves, of which the Chekhovs did not know a single word. Eventually, in 1868, Anton was enrolled in one of the town's Russian high schools. The courses at the Russian school included Church Slavonic, Latin and Greek, and if the entire curriculum was successfully completed, entry to a university was guaranteed. Unfortunately, as the shop was making less and less money, the school fees were often unpaid and lessons were missed. The teaching was generally mediocre, but the religious education teacher, Father Pokrovsky, encouraged his pupils to read the Russian classics and such foreign authors as Shakespeare, Swift and Goethe. Pavel also paid for private French and music lessons for his children.

Every summer the family would travel through the steppe by cart some fifty miles to an estate where their paternal grandfather was chief steward. The impressions gathered on these journeys, and the people encountered, had a profound impact on the young Anton, and later provided material for one of his greatest stories, 'The Steppe'.

At the age of thirteen, Anton went to the theatre for the first time, to see Offenbach's operetta *La Belle Hélène* at the Taganrog theatre. He was enchanted by the spectacle, and went as often as time and money allowed, seeing not only the Russian classics, but also foreign pieces such as *Hamlet* in Russian translation. In his early teens, he even created his own theatrical company with his school friends to act out the Russian classics.

Adversity   In 1875 Anton was severely ill with peritonitis. The high-school doctor tended him with great care, and he resolved to join the medical profession one day. That same year, his brothers Alexander and Nikolai, fed up with the beatings they received at home, decided to move to Moscow to work and study, ignoring their father's admonitions and threats. Anton now bore the entire brunt of Pavel's brutality. To complicate things further, the family shop ran into severe financial difficulties, and was eventually declared bankrupt. The children were withdrawn from school, and Pavel fled to Moscow, leaving his wife and family to face the creditors. In the end, everybody abandoned the old residence, with the exception of Anton, who remained behind with the new owner.

Although he was now free of his father's bullying and the hardship of having to go to church and work in the shop, Anton had to find other employment in order to pay his rent and bills, and to resume his school studies. Accordingly, at the age of fifteen, he took up tutoring, continuing voraciously to read books of Russian and foreign literature, philosophy and science, in the town library.

In 1877, during a summer holiday, he undertook the seven-hundred-mile journey to Moscow to see his family, and found them all living in one room and sleeping on a single mattress on the floor. His father was not at all abashed by his failures: he continued to be dogmatically religious and to beat the younger children regularly. On his return to Taganrog, Anton attempted to earn a little additional income by sending sketches and anecdotes to several of Moscow's humorous magazines, but they were all turned down.

The young Chekhov unabatedly pursued his studies, and in June 1879 he passed the Taganrog High School exams with distinction, and in the autumn he moved to Moscow to study medicine. The family still lived in one room, and Alexander and Nikolai were well on the way to becoming alcoholics. Anton, instead of finding his own lodgings, decided to support not only himself, but his entire family, and try to re-educate them. After a hard day spent in lectures, tutorials and in the laboratories, he would write more sketches for humorous and satirical magazines, and an increasing number of these were now accepted: by the early 1880s, over a hundred had been printed. Anton used a series of pseudonyms (the most usual being "Antosha Chekhonte") for these productions, which he later called "rubbish". He also visited the Moscow theatres and concert halls on numerous occasions, and in 1880 sent the renowned Maly Theatre a play he had recently written. Only a rough draft of the piece – which was rejected by the Maly and published for the first time in 1920, under the title *Platonov* – has survived. Unless Chekhov had polished and pruned his lost final version considerably, the play would have lasted around seven hours. Despite its poor construction and verbosity, *Platonov* already shows some of the themes and characters present in Chekhov's mature works, such as rural boredom and weak-willed, supine intellectuals dreaming of a better future while not doing anything to bring it about.

As well as humorous sketches and stories, Chekhov wrote brief résumés of legal court proceedings and gossip from the artistic world for various Moscow journals. With the money made from these pieces he moved his family into a larger flat, and regularly invited friends to visit and talk and drink till late at night.

Studies in Moscow and Early Publications

In 1882, encouraged by his success with the Moscow papers, he started contributing to the journals of the capital St Petersburg, since payment there was better than in Moscow. He was eventually commissioned to contribute a regular column to the best-selling journal *Oskolki* ("Splinters"), providing a highly coloured picture of Moscow life with its court cases and bohemian atmosphere. He was now making over 150 roubles a month from his writing – about three times as much as his student stipend – although he managed to save very little because of the needs of his family. In 1884 Chekhov published, at his own expense, a booklet of six of his short stories, entitled *Tales of Melpomene*, which sold quite poorly.

Start of Medical Career   There was compensation for this relative literary failure: in June of that year Anton passed all his final exams in medicine and became a medical practitioner. That summer, he began to receive patients at a village outside Moscow, and even stepped in for the director of a local hospital when the latter went on his summer vacation. He was soon receiving thirty to forty patients a day, and was struck by the peasants' ill health, filth and drunkenness. He planned a major treatise entitled *A History of Medicine in Russia* but, after reading and annotating over a hundred works on the subject, he gave the subject up and returned to Moscow to set up his own medical practice.

First Signs of   Suddenly, in December 1884, when he was approaching the
Tuberculosis   achievement of all his ambitions, Chekhov developed a dry cough and began to spit blood. He tried to pretend that these were not early symptoms of tuberculosis but, as a doctor, he must have had an inkling of the truth. He made no attempt to cut down his commitments in the light of his illness, but kept up the same punishing schedule of activity. By this time, Chekhov had published over three hundred items, including some of his first recognized mature works, such as 'The Daughter of Albion' and 'The Death of an Official'. Most of the stories were already, in a very understated way, depicting life's "losers" – such as the idle gentry, shopkeepers striving unsuccessfully to make a living and ignorant peasants. Now that his income had increased, Chekhov rented a summer house a few miles outside Moscow. However, although he intended to use his holiday exclusively for writing, he was inundated all day with locals who had heard he was a doctor
212   and required medical attention.

Chekhov made a crucial step in his literary career, when in *Trip to St Petersburg and* December 1885 he visited the imperial capital St Petersburg *Meeting with Suvorin* for the first time, as a guest of the editor of the renowned *St Petersburg Journal*. His stories were beginning to gain him a reputation, and he was introduced at numerous soirées to famous members of the St Petersburg literary world. He was agreeably surprised to find they knew his work and valued it highly. Here for the first time he met Alexei Suvorin, the press mogul and editor of the most influential daily of the period, *Novoye Vremya (New Times)*. Suvorin asked Chekhov to contribute stories regularly to his paper at a far higher rate of pay than he had been receiving from other journals. Now Chekhov, while busy treating numerous patients in Moscow and helping to stem the constant typhus epidemics that broke out in the city, also began to churn out for Suvorin such embryonic masterpieces as 'The Requiem' and 'Grief' – although all were still published pseudonymously. Distinguished writers advised him to start publishing under his own name and, although his current collection *Motley Stories* had already gone to press under the Chekhonte pseudonym, Anton resolved from now on to shed his anonymity. The collection received tepid reviews, but Chekhov now had sufficient income to rent a whole house on Sadova-Kudrinskaya Street (now maintained as a museum of this early period of Chekhov's life), in an elegant district of Moscow.

Chekhov's reputation as a writer was further enhanced *Literary Recognition* when Suvorin published a collection of sixteen of Chekhov's short stories in 1887 – under the title *In the Twilight* – to great critical acclaim. However, Chekhov's health was deteriorating and his blood-spitting was growing worse by the day. Anton appears more and more by now to have come to regard life as a parade of "the vanity of human wishes". He channelled some of this ennui and his previous life experiences into a slightly melodramatic and overlong play, *Ivanov*, in which the eponymous hero – a typical "superfluous man" who indulges in pointless speculation while his estate goes to ruin and his capital dwindles – ends up shooting himself. *Ivanov* was premiered in November 1887 by the respected Korsh Private Theatre under Chekhov's real name – a sign of Anton's growing confidence as a writer – although it received very mixed reviews.

However, in the spring of 1888, Chekhov's story 'The Steppe' – an impressionistic, poetical recounting of the experiences

213

of a young boy travelling through the steppe on a cart – was published in *The Northern Herald*, again under his real name, enabling him to reach another milestone in his literary career, and prompting reviewers for the first time to talk of his genius. Although Chekhov began to travel to the Crimea for vacations, in the hope that the warm climate might aid his health, the symptoms of tuberculosis simply reappeared whenever he returned to Moscow. In October of the same year, Chekhov was awarded the prestigious Pushkin Prize for Literature for *In the Twilight*. He was now recognized as a major Russian writer, and began to state his belief to reporters that a writer's job is not to peddle any political or philosophical point of view, but to depict human life with its associated problems as objectively as possible.

Death of his Brother   A few months later, in January 1889, a revised version of *Ivanov* was staged at the Alexandrinsky Theatre in St Petersburg, arguably the most important drama theatre in Russia at the time. The new production was a huge success and received excellent reviews. However, around that time it also emerged that Anton's alcoholic brother, Nikolai, was suffering from advanced tuberculosis. When Nikolai died in June of that year, at the age of thirty, Anton must have seen this as a harbinger of his own early demise.

Chekhov was now working on a new play, *The Wood Demon*, in which, for the first time, psychological nuance replaced stage action, and the effect on the audience was achieved by atmosphere rather than by drama or the portrayal of events. However, precisely for these reasons, it was rejected by the Alexandrinsky Theatre in October of that year. Undeterred, Chekhov decided to revise it, and a new version of *The Wood Demon* was put on in Moscow in December 1889. Lambasted by the critics, it was swiftly withdrawn from the scene, to make its appearance again many years later, thoroughly rewritten, as *Uncle Vanya*.

Journey to   It was around this time that Anton Chekhov began con-
Sakhalin Island templating his journey to the prison island of Sakhalin. At the end of 1889, unexpectedly, and for no apparent reason, the twenty-nine-year-old author announced his intention to leave European Russia, and to travel across Siberia to Sakhalin, the large island separating Siberia and the Pacific Ocean, following which he would write a full-scale examination of the penal colony maintained there by the Tsarist authorities. Explanations put forward by commentators both then and since include a

search by the author for fresh material for his works, a desire to escape from the constant carping of his liberally minded colleagues on his lack of a political line; desire to escape from an unhappy love affair; and disappointment at the recent failure of *The Wood Demon*. A further explanation may well be that, as early as 1884, he had been spitting blood, and recently, just before his journey, several friends and relations had died of tuberculosis. Chekhov, as a doctor, must have been aware that he too was in the early stages of the disease, and that his lifespan would be considerably curtailed. Possibly he wished to distance himself for several months from everything he had known, and give himself time to think over his illness and mortality by immersing himself in a totally alien world. Chekhov hurled himself into a study of the geography, history, nature and ethnography of the island, as background material to his study of the penal settlement. The Trans-Siberian Railway had not yet been constructed, and the journey across Siberia, begun in April 1890, required two and a half months of travel in sledges and carriages on abominable roads in freezing temperatures and appalling weather. This certainly hastened the progress of his tuberculosis and almost certainly deprived him of a few extra years of life. He spent three months in frantic work on the island, conducting his census of the prison population, rummaging in archives, collecting material and organizing book collections for the children of exiles, before leaving in October 1890 and returning to Moscow, via Hong Kong, Ceylon and Odessa, in December of that year.

Travels in Europe The completion of his report on his trip to Sakhalin was to be hindered for almost five years by his phenomenally busy life, as he attempted, as before, to continue his medical practice and write at the same time. In early 1891 Chekhov, in the company of Suvorin, travelled for the first time to western Europe, visiting Vienna, Venice, Bologna, Florence, Rome, Naples and finally Monaco and Paris.

Move to Melikhovo Trying to cut down on the expenses he was paying out for his family in Moscow, he bought a small estate at Melikhovo, a few miles outside Moscow, and the entire family moved there. His father did some gardening, his mother cooked, while Anton planted hundreds of fruit trees, shrubs and flowers. Chekhov's concerns for nature have a surprisingly modern ecological ring: he once said that if he had not been a writer he would have become a gardener.

215

Although his brothers had their own lives in Moscow and only spent holidays at Melikhovo, Anton's sister Marya – who never married – lived there permanently, acting as his confidante and as his housekeeper when he had his friends and famous literary figures to stay, as he often did in large parties. Chekhov also continued to write, but was distracted, as before, by the scores of locals who came every day to receive medical treatment from him. There was no such thing as free medical assistance in those days and, if anybody seemed unable to pay, Chekhov often treated them for nothing. In 1892, there was a severe local outbreak of cholera, and Chekhov was placed in charge of relief operations. He supervised the building of emergency isolation wards in all the surrounding villages and travelled around the entire area directing the medical operations.

Ill Health   Chekhov's health was deteriorating more and more rapidly, and his relentless activity certainly did not help. He began to experience almost constant pain and, although still hosting gatherings, he gave the appearance of withdrawing increasingly into himself and growing easily tired. By the mid-1890s, his sleep was disturbed almost nightly by bouts of violent coughing. Besides continuing his medical activities, looking after his estate and writing, Chekhov undertook to supervise – often with large subsidies from his own pocket – the building of schools in the local villages, where there had been none before.

Controversy around   By late 1895, Chekhov was thinking of writing for the theatre
The Seagull   again. The result was *The Seagull*, which was premiered at the Alexandrinsky Theatre in October 1896. Unfortunately the acting was so bad that the premiere was met by jeering and laughter, and received vicious reviews. Chekhov himself commented that the director did not understand the play, the actors didn't know their lines and nobody could grasp the understated style. He fled from the theatre and roamed the streets of St Petersburg until two in the morning, resolving never to write for the theatre again. Despite this initial fiasco, subsequent performances went from strength to strength, with the actors called out on stage after every performance.

Olga Knipper   By this time, it seems that Chekhov had accepted the fact that he had a mortal illness. In 1897, he returned to Italy to see whether the warmer climate would not afford his condition some respite, but as soon as he came back to Russia the coughing and blood-spitting resumed as violently as before. It was around this time that the two founders of the

Moscow Arts Theatre, Vladimir Nemirovich-Danchenko and Konstantin Stanislavsky, asked Chekhov whether they could stage *The Seagull*. Their aims were to replace the stylized and unnatural devices of the classical theatre with more natural events and dialogue, and Chekhov's play seemed ideal for this purpose. He gave his permission, and in September 1898 went to Moscow to attend the preliminary rehearsals. It was there that he first met the twenty-eight-year-old actress Olga Knipper, who was going to take the leading role of Arkadina. However, the Russian winter was making him cough blood violently, and so he decided to follow the local doctor's advice and travel south to the Crimea, in order to spend the winter in a warmer climate. Accordingly, he rented a villa with a large garden in Yalta.

When his father died in October of the same year, Chekhov *Move to the Crimea* decided to put Melikhovo up for sale and move his mother and Marya to the Crimea. They temporarily stayed in a large villa near the Tatar village of Kuchukoy, but Chekhov had in the mean time bought a plot of land at Autka, some twenty minutes by carriage from Yalta, and he drew up a project to have a house built there. Construction began in December.

Also in December 1898, the first performance of *The Seagull* at the Moscow Arts Theatre took place. It was a resounding success, and there were now all-night queues for tickets. Despite his extremely poor health, Chekhov was still busy raising money for relief of the severe famine then scourging the Russian heartlands, overseeing the building of his new house and aiding the local branch of the Red Cross. In addition to this, local people and aspiring writers would turn up in droves at his villa in Yalta to receive medical treatment or advice on their manuscripts.

In early January 1899, Chekhov signed an agreement with *Collected Works Project* the publisher Adolf Marx to supervise the publication of a multi-volume edition of his collected works in return for a flat fee of 75,000 roubles and no royalties. This proved to be an error of judgement from a financial point of view, because by the time Chekhov had put some money towards building his new house, ensured all the members of his family were provided for and made various other donations, the advance had almost disappeared.

Chekhov finally moved to Autka – where he was to spend *Romance* the last few years of his life – in June 1899, and immediately *with Olga*   217 began to plant vegetables, flowers and fruit trees. During a short period spent in Moscow to facilitate his work for Adolf Marx, he re-established contact with the Moscow Arts Theatre and Olga Knipper. Chekhov invited the actress to Yalta on several occasions and, although her visits were brief and at first she stayed in a hotel, it was obvious that she and Chekhov were becoming very close. Apart from occasional short visits to Moscow, which cost him a great expenditure of energy and were extremely harmful to his medical condition, Chekhov now had to spend all of his time in the south. He forced himself to continue writing short stories and plays, but felt increasingly lonely and isolated and, aware that he had only a short time left to live, became even more withdrawn. It was around this time that he worked again at his early play *The Wood Demon*, reducing the dramatis personae to only nine characters, radically altering the most significant scenes and renaming it *Uncle Vanya*. This was premiered in October 1899, and it was another gigantic success. In July of the following year, Olga Knipper took time off from her busy schedule of rehearsals and performances in Moscow to visit Chekhov in Yalta. There was no longer any attempt at pretence: she stayed in his house and, although he was by now extremely ill, they became romantically involved, exchanging love letters almost every day.

By now Chekhov had drafted another new play, *Three Sisters*, and he travelled to Moscow to supervise the first few rehearsals. Olga came to his hotel every day bringing food and flowers. However, Anton felt that the play needed revision, so he returned to Yalta to work on a comprehensive rewrite. *Three Sisters* opened on 31st January 1901 and – though at first well received, especially by the critics – it gradually grew in the public's estimation, becoming another great success.

Wedding and But Chekhov was feeling lonely in Yalta without Olga, and
Honeymoon in May of that year proposed to her by letter. Olga accepted, and Chekhov immediately set off for Moscow, despite his doctor's advice to the contrary. He arranged a dinner for his friends and relatives and, while they were waiting there, he and Olga got married secretly in a small church on the outskirts of Moscow. As the participants at the dinner received a telegram with the news, the couple had already left for their honeymoon. Olga and Anton sailed down the Volga, up the Kama River and along the Belaya River to the village

EXTRA MATERIAL

of Aksyonovo, where they checked into a sanatorium. At this establishment Chekhov drank four large bottles of fermented mare's milk every day, put on weight, and his condition seemed to improve somewhat. However, on their return to Yalta, Chekhov's health deteriorated again. He made his will, leaving his house in Yalta to Marya, all income from his dramatic works to Olga and large sums to his mother and his surviving brothers, to the municipality of Taganrog and to the peasant body of Melikhovo.

After a while, Olga returned to her busy schedule of rehearsals and performances in Moscow, and the couple continued their relationship at a distance, as they had done before their marriage, with long and frequent love letters. Chekhov managed to visit her in Moscow occasionally, but by now he was so ill that he had to return to Yalta immediately, often remaining confined to bed for long periods. Olga was tortured as to whether she should give up her acting career and nurse Anton for the time left to him. Almost unable to write, Anton now embarked laboriously on his last dramatic masterpiece, *The Cherry Orchard*. Around that time, in the spring of 1902, Olga visited Anton in Yalta after suffering a spontaneous miscarriage during a Moscow Art Theatre tour, leaving her husband with the unpleasant suspicion that she might have been unfaithful to him. In the following months, Anton nursed his wife devotedly, travelling to Moscow whenever he could to be near her. Olga's flat was on the third floor, and there was no lift. It took Anton half an hour to get up the stairs, so he practically never went out. *Difficult Relationship*

When *The Cherry Orchard* was finally completed in October 1903, Chekhov once again travelled to Moscow to attend rehearsals, despite the advice of his doctors that it would be tantamount to suicide. The play was premiered on 17th January 1904, Chekhov's forty-fourth birthday, and at the end of the performance the author was dragged onstage. There was no chair for him, and he was forced to stand listening to the interminable speeches, trying not to cough and pretending to look interested. Although the performance was a success, press reviews, as usual, were mixed, and Chekhov thought that Nemirovich-Danchenko and Stanislavsky had misunderstood the play. *Final Play*

Chekhov returned to Yalta knowing he would not live long enough to write another work. His health deteriorated even *Death*

219

further, and the doctors put him on morphine, advising him to go to a sanatorium in Germany. Accordingly, in June 1904, he and Olga set off for Badenweiler, a spa in the Black Forest. The German specialists examined him and reported that they could do nothing. Soon oxygen had to be administered to him, and he became feverish and delirious. At 12.30 a.m. on 15th July 1904, he regained his mental clarity sufficiently to tell Olga to summon a doctor urgently. On the doctor's arrival, Chekhov told him, "*Ich sterbe*" ("I'm dying"). The doctor gave him a strong stimulant, and was on the point of sending for other medicines when Chekhov, knowing it was all pointless, simply asked for a bottle of champagne to be sent to the room. He poured everybody a glass, drank his off, commenting that he hadn't had champagne for ages, lay down, and died in the early hours of the morning.

Funeral   The coffin was transported back to Moscow in a filthy green carriage marked "FOR OYSTERS", and although it was met at the station by bands and a large ceremonial gathering, it turned out that this was for an eminent Russian General who had just been killed in action in Manchuria. Only a handful of people had assembled to greet Chekhov's coffin. However, as word got round Moscow that his body was being transported to the graveyard at the Novodevichy Monastery, people poured out of their homes and workplaces, forming a vast crowd both inside and outside the cemetery and causing a large amount of damage to buildings, pathways and other graves in the process. The entire tragicomic episode of Chekhov's death, transportation back to Moscow and burial could almost have featured in one of his own short stories. Chekhov was buried next to his father Pavel. His mother outlived him by fifteen years, and his sister Marya died in 1957 at the age of ninety-four. Olga Knipper survived two more years, dying in 1959 at the age of eighty-nine.

Anton Chekhov's Works

Early Writings   When Chekhov studied medicine in Moscow from 1879 to 1884, he financed his studies by writing reports of law-court proceedings for the newspapers and contributing, under a whole series of pseudonyms, hundreds of jokes, comic sketches and short stories to the numerous Russian humorous magazines and more serious journals of the time. From 1885, when he began to practise as a doctor, he concentrated far more on serious literary works, and between then and the end of his life he produced over 200 short stories, plus a score or so of dramatic pieces, ranging from monologues through one-act to full-length plays. In 1884 he also wrote his only novel, *The Hunting Party*, which was a rather wooden attempt at a detective novel.

A number of his stories between the mid-Eighties and his journey to Sakhalin were vitiated by his attempt to propagate the Tolstoyan moral principles he had espoused at the time. But even before his journey to the prison island he was realizing that laying down the law to his readers, and trying to dictate how they should read his stories, was not his job: it should be the goal of an artist to describe persons and events non-judgementally, and let the reader draw his or her own conclusions. This is attested by his letter to Suvorin in April 1890: "You reproach me for 'objectivity', calling it indifference to good and evil, and absence of ideals and ideas and so forth. You wish me, when depicting horse thieves, to state: stealing horses is bad. But surely people have known that for ages already, without me telling them so? Let them be judged by jurymen – my business is to show them as they really are. When I write, I rely totally on the reader, supposing that he himself will supply the subjective factors absent in the story." After Chekhov's return from Sakhalin, this objectivity dominated everything he wrote.

Invention of a New, "Objective" Style of Writing

A further feature of Chekhov's storytelling, which developed throughout his career, is that he does not so much describe events taking place, but rather depicts the way that characters react to those – frequently quite insignificant – events, and the way people's lives are often transformed for better or worse by them. His dramatic works from that time also showed a development from fully displayed events and action – sometimes, in the early plays, quite melodramatic – to, in the major plays written in the last decade or so of his life, depicting the effects on people's lives of offstage events, and the way the characters react to those events.

His style in all his later writing – especially from 1890 onwards – is lucid and economical, and there is a total absence of purple passages. The works of his final years display an increasing awareness of the need for conservation of the natural world in the face of the creeping industrialization of Russia. The breakdown of the old social order in the face of the new rising entrepreneurial class is also depicted non-judgementally; in Chekhov's last play, *The Cherry Orchard*, an old estate belonging to a long-established family of gentry is sold to a businessman, and the final scenes of the play give way to the offstage sounds of wood-chopping, as the old cherry orchard – one of the major beauties of the estate – is cut down by its new owner to be sold for timber.

Major Short Stories   It is generally accepted that Chekhov's mature story-writing may be said to date from the mid-1880s, when he began to contribute to the "thick journals". Descriptions of a small representative selection of some of the major short stories – giving an idea of Chekhov's predominant themes – can be found below.

On the Road   In 'On the Road' (1886), set in a seedy wayside inn on Christmas Eve, a man, apparently from the privileged classes, and his eight-year-old daughter are attempting to sleep in the "travellers' lounge", having been forced to take refuge from a violent storm. The little girl wakes up, and tells him how unhappy she is and that he is a wicked man. A noblewoman, also sheltering from the storm, enters and comforts the girl. The man and the woman both tell each other of the unhappiness of their lives: he is a widowed nobleman who has squandered all his money and is now on his way to a tedious job in the middle of nowhere; she is from a wealthy family, but her father and her brothers are wastrels, and she is the only one who takes care of the estate. They both part in the morning, on Christmas Day, profoundly unhappy, and without succeeding in establishing that deep inner contact with another human being which both of them obviously crave.

Enemies   Chekhov's 1887 tale 'Enemies' touches on similar themes of misery and incomprehension: a country doctor's six-year-old son has just died of diphtheria, leaving him and his wife devastated; at precisely this moment, a local landowner comes to his house to call him out to attend to his wife, who is apparently dangerously ill. Though sympathetic to the doctor's state, he is understandably full of anxiety for his wife, and insists that the doctor come. After an uncomfortable carriage journey, they arrive at the landowner's mansion to discover that the wife was never ill at all, but was simply getting rid of her husband so that she could run off with her lover. The landowner is now in a state of anger and despair, and the doctor unreasonably blames him for having dragged him out under false pretences. When the man offers him his fee, the doctor throws it in his face and storms out. The landowner also furiously drives off somewhere to assuage his anger. Neither man can even begin to penetrate the other's mental state because of their own problems. The doctor remains full of contempt and cynicism for the human race for the rest of his life.

In 1888, Chekhov's first indubitably great narrative, the *The Steppe* novella-length 'The Steppe', was published to rapturous reviews. There is almost no plot: in blazing midsummer, a nine-year-old boy sets out on a long wagon ride, lasting several days, from his home in a small provincial town through the steppe, to stay with relatives and attend high school in a large city. The entire story consists of his impressions of the journey – of his travelling companions, the people they meet en route, the inns at which they stay, the scenery and wildlife. He finally reaches his destination, bids farewell to his travelling companions, and the story ends with him full of tears of regret at his lost home life, and foreboding at what the future in this strange new world holds for him.

Another major short story by Chekhov, 'The Name-Day *The Name-Day Party* Party' (also translated as 'The Party'), was published in the same year as 'The Steppe'. The title refers to the fact that Russians celebrate not only their birthdays, but the day of the saint after whom they are named. It is the name day of a selfish lawyer and magistrate; his young wife, who is seven-months pregnant, has spent all day organizing a banquet in his honour and entertaining guests. Utterly exhausted, she occasionally asks him to help her, but he does very little. Finally, when all the guests have gone home, she, in extreme agony, gives birth prematurely to a stillborn baby. She slips in and out of consciousness, believes she too is dying, and, despite his behaviour, she feels sorry for her husband, who will be lost without her. However, when she regains consciousness he seems to blame her for the loss of the child, and not his own selfishness, leading to her utter exhaustion at such a time.

'A Dreary Story' (also known as 'A Tedious Story') is one *A Dreary Story* of Chekhov's longer stories, originally published in 1889. In a tour de force, the twenty-nine-year-old Chekhov penetrates into the mind of a famous sixty-two-year-old professor – his interior monologue constituting the entire tale. The professor is a world expert in his subject, fêted throughout Russia, yet has a terminal disease which means he will be dead in a few months. He has told nobody, not even his family. This professor muses over his life, and how his body is falling apart, and he wonders what the point of it all was. He would gladly give all his fame for just a few more years of warm, vibrant life. Chekhov wrote this story the year before he travelled to Sakhalin, when he was beginning to display the first symptoms of the tuberculosis which was to kill him at the age of forty-four.

The Duel In Chekhov's 1891 story 'The Duel', a bored young civil servant has lost interest in everything in life, including his lover. When the latter's husband dies, she expects him to marry her, but he decides to borrow money and leave the town permanently instead. However, the acquaintance from whom he tries to borrow the money refuses to advance him the sum for such purposes. After a heated exchange, the civil servant challenges the acquaintance to a duel – a challenge which is taken up by a friend of the person who has refused to lend the money, disgusted at the civil servant's selfish behaviour. Both miss their shot, and the civil servant, realizing how near he has been to death, regains interest in life, marries his mistress, and all are reconciled.

Ward Six In 'Ward Six' (1892), a well-meaning but apathetic and weak provincial hospital director has a ward for the mentally disturbed as one of his responsibilities. He knows that the thuggish peasant warden regularly beats the lunatics up, but makes all kinds of excuses not to get involved. He ends up being incarcerated in his own mental ward by the ruse of an ambitious rival, and is promptly beaten by the same warden who used to call him "Your Honour", and dies soon afterwards. This is perhaps Chekhov's most transparent attack on the supine intelligentsia of his own time, whom he saw as lacking determination in the fight against social evils.

Three Years In 1895, Chekhov published his famous story 'Three Years', in which Laptev, a young Muscovite, is nursing his seriously ill sister in a small provincial town, and feels restricted and bored. He falls in love with the daughter of her doctor and, perhaps from loneliness and the need for companionship, proposes marriage. Although she is not in love with him, she accepts, after a good deal of hesitation, because she is afraid this might be her only offer in this dull town. For the first three years this marriage – forged through a sense of isolation on one side and fear of spinsterhood on the other – is passionless and somewhat unhappy. However, after this period, they manage to achieve an equable and fulfilling relationship based on companionship.

In the 'The House with a Mezzanine' (1896), a talented but *The House with a* lazy young artist visits a rich landowning friend in the country. *Mezzanine* They go to visit the wealthy family at the title's "house with a mezzanine", which consists of a mother and two unmarried daughters. The artist falls in love with the younger daughter, but her tyrannical older sister sends both her and her mother abroad. The story ends some years later with the artist still wistfully wondering what has become of the younger sister.

In 'Peasants' (1897), Nikolai, who has lived and worked *Peasants* in Moscow since adolescence, and now works as a waiter at a prestigious Moscow hotel, is taken very ill and can no longer work, so he decides to return to the country village of his childhood, taking with him his wife and young daughter, who was born in Moscow. He has warm recollections of the village, but finds that memory has deceived him. The place is filthy and squalid, and the local inhabitants all seem to be permanently blind drunk. Since anybody with any intelligence – like Nikolai himself – is sent to the city as young as possible to work and send money back to the family, the level of ignorance and stupidity is appalling. Nikolai dies, and the story ends with his wife and daughter walking back to Moscow, begging as they go.

In 1898, Chekhov published 'The Man in a Case', in which *The Man in a Case* the narrator, a schoolmaster, recounts the life of a recently deceased colleague of his, Byelikov, who taught classical Greek. A figure of ridicule for his pupils and colleagues, Byelikov is described as being terrified of the modern world, walking around, even in the warmest weather, in high boots, a heavy overcoat, dark spectacles and a hat with a large brim concealing his face. The blinds are always drawn on all the windows in his house, and these are permanently shut. He threatens to report to the headmaster a young colleague who engages in the appallingly immoral and progressive activity of going for bicycle rides in the countryside. The young man pushes him, Byelikov falls down and, although not hurt, takes to his bed and dies, apparently of humiliation and oversensitivity.

The Lady with   'The Lady with the Little Dog' (1899) tells the story of a bored
the Little Dog and cynical bank official who, trapped in a tedious marriage in
Moscow, takes a holiday by himself in Yalta. There he meets
Anna, who is also unhappily married. They have an affair, then
go back to their respective homes. In love for possibly the first
time in his life, he travels to the provincial town where she lives,
and tracks her down. They meet in a theatre, and in a snatched
conversation she promises to visit him in Moscow. The story
ends with them both realizing that their problems are only just
beginning.

Sakhalin Island   As well as being a prolific writer of short fiction, Chekhov
also wrote countless articles as a journalist, and the volume-
length *Sakhalin Island* ranks as one of the most notable
examples of his investigative non-fiction. As mentioned above,
Chekhov's decision to travel to Sakhalin Island in easternmost
Siberia for three months in 1890 was motivated by several
factors, one of them being to write a comprehensive study of
the penal colonies on the island.

Chekhov toured round the entire island, visiting all the
prisons and most of the settlements, and generally spending up
to nineteen hours a day gathering material and writing up his
findings. Chekhov returned from Sakhalin at the end of 1890,
but it took him three years to write up and start publishing
the material he had collected. The first chapter was published
in the journal *Russian Thought* (*Russkaya Mysl*) in late 1893,
and subsequent material appeared regularly in this magazine
until July 1894, with no objection from the censor, until finally
the chapters from number twenty onwards were banned from
publication. Chekhov took the decision to "publish and be
damned" – accordingly the whole thing appeared in book
form, including the banned chapters, in May 1895.

The book caused enormous interest and discussion in
the press, and over the next decade a number of substantial
ameliorations were brought about in the criminals' lives.

Major Plays   Chekhov first made his name in the theatre with a series
of one-act farces, most notably *The Bear* and *Swan Song*
(both 1888). However, his first attempts at full-length plays,
Platonov (1880), *Ivanov* (1887) and *The Wood Demon* (1889),
were not entirely successful. The four plays which are now
considered to be Chekhov's masterpieces, and outstanding
works of world theatre, are *The Seagull* (1896), *Uncle Vanya*
(1899), *Three Sisters* (1901) and *The Cherry Orchard* (1904).

The central character in *The Seagull* is an unsuccessful *The Seagull*
playwright, Treplyov, who is in love with the actress Nina.
However, she falls in love with the far more successful writer
Trigorin. Out of spite and as an anti-idealist gesture, Treplyov
shoots a seagull and places it in front of her. Nina becomes
Trigorin's mistress. Unfortunately their baby dies, Nina's career
collapses and Trigorin leaves her. However, on Treplyov renewing
his overtures to Nina, she tells him that she still loves Trigorin.
The play ends with news being brought in that Treplyov has
committed suicide offstage.

The second of Chekhov's four dramatic masterpieces, *Uncle Vanya*
Uncle Vanya, a comprehensive reworking of the previously unsuccessful *Wood Demon*, centres on Vanya, who has for many
years tirelessly managed a professor's estate. However, the
professor finally retires back to his estate with his bored and idle
young wife, with whom Vanya falls in love. Vanya now realizes
that the professor is a thoroughly selfish and mediocre man
and becomes jealous and embittered at his own fate, believing
he has sacrificed his own brilliant future. When the professor
tells him that he is going to sell the estate, Vanya, incensed, fires
a pistol at him at point-blank range and misses – which only
serves to compound his sense of failure and frustration. The
professor and his wife agree not to sell up for the time being
and leave to live elsewhere. Vanya sinks back into his boring
loveless life, probably for ever.

In *Three Sisters*, Olga, Masha and Irina live a boring life *Three Sisters*
in their brother's house in a provincial town, remote from
Moscow and St Petersburg. All three remember their happy
childhood in Moscow and dream of one day returning. A
military unit arrives nearby, and Irina and Masha start up
relationships with officers, which might offer a way out of
their tedious lives. However, Irina's fiancé is killed in a duel,
Masha's relationship ends when the regiment moves on, and
Olga, a schoolteacher, is promoted to the post of headmistress
at her school, thus forcing her to give up any hope of leaving
the area. They all relapse into what they perceive to be their
meaningless lives.

The Cherry Orchard, Chekhov's final masterpiece for the *The Cherry*
theatre, is a lament for the passing of old traditional Russia *Orchard*
and the encroachment of the modern world. The Ranevsky
family estate, with its wonderful and famous cherry orchard,
is no longer a viable concern. Various suggestions are made to

stave off financial disaster, all of which involve cutting down the ancient orchard. Finally the estate is auctioned off, and in the final scene, the orchard is chopped down offstage. The old landowning family move out, and in a final tragicomic scene, they forget to take an ancient manservant with them, accidentally locking him in the house and leaving him feeling abandoned.

Select Bibliography

Biographies:

Hingley, Ronald, *A New Life of Anton Chekhov* (Oxford: Oxford University Press, 1976)

Pritchett, V.S., *Chekhov: A Spirit Set Free* (London: Hodder & Stoughton, 1988)

Rayfield, Donald, *Anton Chekhov* (London: HarperCollins, 1997)

Simmons, Ernest, *Chekhov: A Biography* (London: Jonathan Cape, 1963)

Troyat, Henri, *Chekhov*, tr. Michael Henry Heim (New York: Dutton, 1986)

Additional Recommended Background Material:

Hellman, Lillian, ed., *Selected Letters of Anton Chekhov* (New York: Farrar, Straus and Giroux, 1984)

Magarshack, David, *Chekhov the Dramatist*, 2nd ed. (London: Eyre Methuen, 1980)

Malcolm, Janet, *Reading Chekhov: A Critical Journey* (London: Granta, 2001)

Pennington, Michael, *Are You There, Crocodile?: Inventing Anton Chekhov* (London: Oberon, 2003)

EVERGREENS SERIES

Beautifully produced classics, affordably priced

Alma Classics is committed to making available a wide range of literature from around the globe. Most of the titles are enriched by an extensive critical apparatus, notes and extra reading material, as well as a selection of photographs. The texts are based on the most authoritative editions and edited using a fresh, accessible editorial approach. With an emphasis on production, editorial and typographical values, Alma Classics aspires to revitalize the whole experience of reading classics.

ALMA CLASSICS

ALMA CLASSICS aims to publish mainstream and lesser-known European classics in an innovative and striking way, while employing the highest editorial and production standards. By way of a unique approach the range offers much more, both visually and textually, than readers have come to expect from contemporary classics publishing.

LATEST TITLES PUBLISHED BY ALMA CLASSICS

www.almaclassics.com